THE PHARAOH'S STONE

The "Stone Collection" Book 8

NICK HAWKES

Hawkesflight Media

Titles in The Stone Collection:

The Pharaoh's Stone

First published in Australia in 2018
by "Rhiza Connect,"
an imprint of "Rhiza Press"

Reedited and re-released
in 2021 (*v.1.1*)
by Hawkesflight Media

The characters in this novel are purely fictional.
Any resemblance to people who have existed, or are existing, is coincidental.

ISBN 978-0-6487041-4-0

www.author-nick.com

Cover Design by Karri Klawiter

To Lily Mae

...to encourage you in your search for adventure and truth.

The Pharaoh's Stone

A novel

by
Nick Hawkes

Prologue

December 31st, 2001

Peter watched the explosions erupt from the froth on his beer.

The fireworks were actually being released from the top of Sydney Harbor Bridge. He lowered the glass he'd lifted in salute to his home country and continued to observe the display on the pub's TV from half a world away. New Year's Eve had been celebrated many hours ago in Australia, and was about to arrive in London... at the dingy pub where Peter was sitting with his beer.

The TV newsreader switched from reporting on the New Year and began covering other news. A terrorist had tried to blow up a plane with a bomb in his shoe. Peter blinked. *A shoe!*

The noise in the pub made listening difficult. Glass smashed on the floor, and a roar of laughter came from a group of young men in the corner.

Peter hiccuped and tried to concentrate on the TV. It was now showing pictures of the crowd that had gathered in Trafalgar Square, waiting for the New Year. Peter knew himself to be several beers on the wrong side of sobriety. He lowered his head, and forced himself to focus.

Someone turned up the music, and Kylie Minogue belted out 'Can't Get You Out Of My Head.'

"Come on, Peter, let's dance."

A hand grabbed his forearm. He looked at it. *Hands were amazing.* He hiccuped again. *And girl hands were so ridiculously feminine.* Peter ran a forefinger over it. *Velvet.*

The hand was insistent. It pulled again at his arm. "Come on, Peter."

He looked up and grinned, fishing desperately in his mind for her name.

Belinda.

He sighed with relief. *Belinda.* That was her name.

The TV presenter was now summing up the news. Sydney's fireworks again featured. Evidently, the worthy citizens of Sydney were pleased to have something to celebrate after having to fight the devastating bush-fires that had ringed their city.

"How far are those fires from your home?" Belinda asked.

He blinked. "Home?"

"Is your place near the fires?"

"It depends what you mean by 'home.'"

Belinda rolled her eyes. "The place where you were brought up, of course."

"I was brought up on the other side of Australia…in a house I very much wish was burning down."

"Why's that?"

"Because my father lives there."

She giggled. "You've got issues, young man," She put her hands above her head, and began to dance—gyrating seductively. "Come on. Dance."

Before he could lever himself from his stool, a young man pushed his way in front of Belinda. Peter recognized him from the group in the corner. The man began to dance with her, drunkenly. He tripped and grabbed at Belinda to stop himself from falling, burying his face in Belinda's cleavage.

The good fortune of the young man's predicament seemed to

register, because he moved a hand over one of her breasts and began to grope it. "Oooh. Lovely."

Belinda yelped in alarm.

His mates laughed and yelled encouragement.

It took a moment for Peter to realize what was going on. He gripped the empty beer bottle in front of him.

Glass shattered, and the man dropped to the floor. Peter looked down at the broken bottle in his hand.

The man's friends lunged toward him.

Peter swung round…and felt the jagged edge of the bottle slice across the neck of his nearest assailant.

Blood. A ridiculous amount of blood spurted from the man's neck. *Where had it all come from?*

He was still wondering, when the fists of the other men began to pound into him.

Chapter 1

February, 2004

"EF6834. Peter Jacobs. You have a visitor. Look lively!"

Peter wasn't sure he'd heard correctly. Apprehension washed over him as he rolled off his bed. *A visitor?*

"Jump about, lad," the prison officer barked.

Peter knew that the mention of his prison number was unnecessary theatrics. It was simply an attempt by Prison Officer Carter, to put Peter in his place. *Never rise to the bait.* Twenty-six months in Her Majesty's prison, Belmarsh, had taught him that. Keep your head down. Be invisible.

"Bleedin' hell! You've got one fan after all." This derisive comment came from Peter's cellmate, Jack Tanner, known as 'Hammer.' He was currently serving five years at Her Majesty's pleasure for undue vigor in carrying out his job as an 'enforcer' for his East End employers. Peter said nothing and joined Carter and the two other prisoners waiting on the landing.

One of them, Silky Gordon, whispered to Peter, "Joey—can you write my missus? I phoned last week. She ain't coping too good."

Peter kept his eyes down and murmured, "See me at association tonight."

Silky nodded his thanks.

"Move along," Carter ordered as he led them off. Each and every gate on the way to the visiting room played the same percussive tune as it was unlocked and relocked. *Click, clunk, squeak. Squeak, clunk, click.* Like everything in prison, it was a tedious business.

Peter had never been to the visiting room before, for the simple reason that since March, 2002—twenty-six months ago—he had never received a visitor. That fact had attracted the concern of the 'Listeners'—prisoners trained by the Samaritans to talk with inmates at risk of suicide.

"Are you coping?"

Coping...yeah.

They were well intentioned, but they didn't understand. Peter greatly preferred that no one contact him. Indeed, he had gone to some lengths to ensure it. He found the dense network of relationships in prison more than enough to occupy him. There were the hard men, the soft men, the 'wannabees,' those protesting innocence, the hot heads, the hop-heads, the comedians, the career villains, the short stay 'backpackers,' the broken, and the resigned.

So...who could possibly be visiting him?

Peter reflected back on the time his nightmare began—when prison guards had escorted him in handcuffs to the communal holding cell to be processed. With a sense of unreality, he had stood among other inmates, who appeared to hail from every corner of the world—each reacting to their situation in different ways. Some sobbed with their heads bowed. Others kicked at the cell bars whilst effing and blinding. Those aggrieved yelled out that they were innocent. A few, like Peter, stood silent, appalled at what they had done.

He had killed.

After sentencing, he'd been 'processed' and escorted to 'Beirut' HB2.

The door to cell 24 was unlocked, and Peter, hugging his prison-issue kit to his chest, entered a world of sweat, urine, and despair.

A bleak eye had opened and stared at him from the prostrate

form of a heavily muscled man lying on a bunk. The man had simply growled, "You don't fart, bawl, snore, or give me bovver," and gone back to sleep. It was his first introduction to Hammer.

Peter recalled having to endure the usual initiation rights of intimidation and attempted shake-downs. The former failed because of Peter's bland indifference to his well-being, and the latter due to the fact he had no money to extort.

Did he need any drugs? "Me name's Tesco. I'm open all hours."

"No thanks."

"Let me know if you change your mind. I'm the cheapest on the wing."

Peter had been incredulous. "How do drugs get in here?"

"They're squashed, swapped, or dropped." Tesco tapped the side of his nose, and didn't go into details.

In time, the rawness of his shame and despair was overtaken by the tedious routine of prison. Peter's response to the mind-numbing boredom of being confined to his cell for eighteen hours a day, was to read. He read voraciously.

Hammer was not impressed, but eventually curiosity got the better of him. "Watcha do all that reading for?"

Peter's explanation—to take his mind to another place—was met with mockery. Peter then retold the story he'd been reading. Hammer had wrinkled his nose. Nonetheless, he'd continued to ask Peter to tell him about the stories he was reading. Consequently, Hammer, who'd never learned to read well, became motivated to read himself. It had now been many months since he'd needed Peter's help. A consequence of this schooling was the development of a firm friendship.

The three prisoners were herded down a series of corridors. Apprehension doused any sense of novelty at being outside his cell. Would his visitor have links to the man he'd killed? Was he about to be told he was an 'old score' that would soon be settled?

Prison suddenly felt a lot safer. Right now, he couldn't imagine how he would cope with life outside. He pondered for a moment the absurdity of considering prison 'safe.' It was never safe. When prisoners were released from their cells at 5pm for 'association,' there was danger. It provided an opportunity for old scores to be settled and for rivals to clash. Peter usually used his time to write letters for those who could not write. He'd been staggered to learn that over a third of the prisoners at Belmarsh were illiterate. Writing gave him something to do and enabled him to keep his head down—literally. Making eye contact was risky.

He'd been rewarded for his passivity by being 'enhanced' to a level that made him eligible to use the gym twice a week. The gym was Hammer's kingdom. Hammer had a disciplined training regime, and was part of a coaching course organized by Charlton Athletic Football Club with whom the prison was in partnership.

"I fink I might have to go straight an' do this coaching stuff when I get outside," Hammer once confided.

Over time, Peter's gangling frame had bulked up and become strong under Hammer's supervision.

"Don't go overboard wiv' it. Gently, gently; little by little. A lot o' geezers come in all 'ammer and tongs an' get big…just to lose it all when the black dog bites."

Hearing Peter's Australian accent, Hammer had asked, "Wot's them little baby kangaroos called wot goes into their muvva's pouch?"

"A joey."

"Well, Joey, you ain't got no muvva's pouch in "ere," he'd laughed hoarsely. And so Peter's prison name was born.

Arriving outside the visiting room, Peter was subjected to a body search, and then escorted to row D, chair 4. Chair 4 was bolted to the floor in front of a small desk, which had another chair opposite. Guards watched from the gallery.

Peter had no idea who, or what, to expect. Who had found him, and more disturbingly, why?

Once the prisoners were seated, the visitors were allowed into the room one at a time. The very last to enter was a tall, slim man dressed in a navy blazer, white shirt, and a red cravat. In the grim surroundings, he looked ridiculous. The man's hands fluttered between the brass buttons on his blazer and a piece of paper in his hands. He consulted the piece of paper, and walked hesitantly down the aisle to Peter's table.

Peter did not make it easy for him. With a carefully schooled look of indifference, he kept his head down and waited—trusting his peripheral vision.

Eventually the stranger spoke, "Ah. Er…I say, are you Mr. Jan Pieter de Jager?" The plummy southern-counties' accent was as out of place in Belmarsh as his ridiculous attire.

"I was."

"Ah, yes. Now known as Mr. Peter Jacobs, I believe."

"And who are you?"

"Yes. Sorry. Toby Cheeseman." He offered his hand but withdrew it when Peter ignored it. The man affected a cough to cover his embarrassment. "I am the technical manager of the London branch of your father's company."

"How did you find me?"

"Ah, not easy. Didn't know about the name change. People have been chasing after you for nearly two years, ever since your father died."

"What!"

"Since your father died," Cheeseman trailed off. "Don't tell me you didn't know."

Peter was silent for a while…then put his head in his hands.

Cheeseman folded his lanky frame into the opposite seat. "Look, er…I'm terribly sorry."

"How did he die?"

"He died of a heart attack in Australia, at his home in Perth."

Peter was numb with shock. The old bull he had defied for so long was dead. What did he feel? *Relief? Joy? Sadness?* At this stage, he simply felt disbelief.

An awkward silence followed.

Eventually, Peter shook his head to clear it of the ghosts of the past, and asked roughly, "How did you find me?"

"Well, I got word that people had been trying to track you down…and didn't much care, to be honest. But then things started to happen, and I felt obliged to at least try and find you to let you know what's going on."

"How did you do it?" Peter persisted.

"Ah." Cheeseman twisted awkwardly in his seat. "I'm rather good with computers, you see. I explored a lot of options…and eventually tapped into prison records. Found a likely name with a likely date." He paused. "You, didn't make it very easy."

"I didn't intend to. Who else knows I'm here?" Peter failed to keep the anxiety he felt from his voice.

"Just me."

"I'd be grateful if it stayed that way."

"Look, old chap, I don't care a fig either way. I'm only here because of your father. You may be a complete hoodlum, but I owe it to your father to tell you that his company is being ripped off… and that I'm handing in my notice because, in all conscience, I can't stay in my position any longer."

None of this made any sense to Peter. He'd never involved himself in his father's business. In fact, he had despised it. For as long as could remember, mining interests had consumed his father's time and energy every moment of his waking life.

"I haven't a clue what you're talking about," he said roughly. "Why do you feel you owe my father?" Peter found it difficult to believe that anyone could owe the despot anything.

"Your father was a hard man, but he was also generous. A year after he appointed me to his London office, he gave me an interest-free loan to purchase a flat in Brompton. He said it was an investment." Cheeseman shrugged. "I've never forgotten."

Peter shot him a glance. "How does all this affect me? I've spent a good part of my life trying to distance myself from my father."

Cheeseman chewed on his bottom lip. "Um…before I, er, tell you… Hang it." He drew a deep breath and tried again. "Before I decide to tell you, I need to know if you are worth helping, or whether you are a complete waster. Why have you changed your name and hidden from your father? I'm not going to help anyone who will work against everything he's built up."

Peter didn't react to Cheeseman's rudeness, and suspected from the way he blushed that it did not come easily to him. Peter massaged his temples. Rudeness was easy to ignore. The request for him to tell his story was not.

So here it was. This was the story he had never told—and thought he never would. A complete stranger was now asking him to talk of the tragedies and storms that had defined his life.

Peter worked his mouth, trying to conjure the words. "Mr. Cheeseman, what you ask is not easy for me. When I've told you, you will have to decide for yourself whether I am a hoodlum or a complete waster." He saw Cheeseman wince as his insults were reflected back to him.

Peter continued. "My father came from South Africa, but moved to London for work. There, he met my mother, an English nurse. They married, and I was their only child. Just after I was born, my father took us to South Africa. My early years there were happy. However, his world, and mine, came crashing down when our home was robbed…and my mother was raped and murdered."

Cheeseman opened his mouth.

Peter pressed on brutally. "That event changed my father. He did two things. First, he left his business partner in charge of the African side of his company, and relocated to Perth, Australia. He said he wanted me to grow up in a safer location. The second thing he began to do, ironically, was to beat me. He would lose his temper." Peter looked Cheeseman in the eyes, challenging him with the truth of what he said. "There were beatings, and beatings, and more beatings. It seemed I could never measure up. No matter how well I did at school—and I did quite well—it was never good enough. He became a bitter man." He paused. "Do you know what a South African police baton looks like, Mr. Cheeseman?"

Cheeseman shook his head dumbly.

"My father kept it ostensibly to protect against burglars, but it was only ever used on me. It is black, two feet long, and made of hard rubber. There is a thong through the handle to keep it from being jarred out of your hand." Peter paused. "The pain is shocking. It's unbelievable. You never get used to it. I was always hit on the thighs so it wouldn't show."

Silence hung between the two men for some time. Peter continued.

"My father threw all his energies into developing his business. From the age of twelve, I was brought up by a succession of house-keepers—none of whom stayed for very long. Naturally, I came to hate my father, and rebelled. I left home at sixteen, and worked at the fruit markets. I pushed trolleys, unloaded trucks, and ran fruit stalls every morning before taking myself off to school at 8:30 am. I managed to earn enough to rent a single room behind a garage, and put myself through my final year at school. Tell me; does that make me a complete waster, Mr. Cheeseman?"

"Er...I say, er...no."

"But am I a hoodlum? Quite possibly. Certainly, I was a bit of a hothead. I did not react well to perceived injustice. My father was the first to discover this. It didn't take him more than a day to find me in my little bed-sit. We had an almighty row, and he started to hit me with his fists. But I'd grown, and for the first time, I hit him back with all the strength I could muster. His response was to give me the biggest thrashing I've ever had. For the first time, he hit me in the face and laid me out unconscious. That scared him. I woke up to find him standing over me, asking if I was all right. When it was evident I would live, my father walked out of my flat. I never saw him again. Looking back on it, I think he realized I was safer on my own than with him. I certainly didn't want anything to do with him, and swore to cut my ties with him completely. On my eighteenth birthday, I changed my name to Peter Jacobs."

Cheeseman nodded. "But your new name still kept some semblance of your old name, Jan Pieter de Jager. Perhaps you didn't want to cut yourself off as much as you thought." Cheeseman paused. "I was able to find you."

Peter avoided the question and continued. "I did well enough at school to get into university, where I did a business degree. By then, I was sharing a house with a couple of mates, and was making money with an Internet company."

"What sort of Internet company?"

"I created a virtual office, and designed web pages for businesses."

"Ah."

"When I finished my degree, I traveled to England to begin a tour through Europe before finding a job. I have dual nationality, so I'm able to work here." Peter held the edge of the table, seeking its support. He forced himself to continue. "I got to London, and met a girl at a party. We'd been going out for a few days, when we decided to go to a pub to celebrate the New Year." Peter swallowed. "I had a few beers…and ended up killing someone."

There was a long pause.

Peter continued. "It turned out that the guy I'd killed was a promising footballer trying out for Tottenham Hotspur. I was given three years for manslaughter with a non-parole period of twenty-six months. I get out in two weeks time." Peter drove his forefinger into the desktop. "I thought I was an ordinary sort of guy, but I ended up killing someone." He turned away, unwilling to say more. He wanted this interview over so he could hide back in his cell.

Eventually, Peter said, "Does that make me a hoodlum, Mr. Cheeseman?"

Cheeseman looked around him and shivered. "What's it like being in here? I can't imagine it."

Peter gave a bitter laugh. "It's a nightmare."

"How do you survive?"

"You get used to it."

"With your, er, hot temper, have you been…"

"No, Mr. Cheeseman, I haven't. For the last twenty-six months I have shared a cell with one of the most violent men in Belmarsh. I have long since learned to control my temper."

"Oh, I see."

No you don't, you have no idea.

"But what do you do to stop yourself going mad?"

Relieved to be on a safer subject, Peter said, "I read mostly and work out in the gym. I also write letters for the prisoners who can't do it for themselves."

Up on the gantry, a PO was listening in to his radio. Peter saw him push the klaxon button and bawl, "Time's up."

"I say," protested Cheeseman, "we've hardly got started."

"Forget it," said Peter. "There's a ruckus somewhere. The guards are needed elsewhere."

"Sod it!" Cheeseman unfolded his lanky frame from the seat. He eyed Peter up and down and then held out his hand. "You are neither a hoodlum nor a waster. May I come and see you next week —same time? I think there are some things you ought to know."

Peter shook his hand, and nodded his assent.

"Ah, one more thing: the executor of your father's estate will want to know of your whereabouts. They've been badgering our London office for news of you, although we've not heard from them for a while now. What do you want me to do?"

Peter froze with apprehension. He dropped his head and said, "I don't want people to find me. Not here. And I'm not sure I want anything to do with my father's estate."

"Then might I suggest something? Let's tell no one other than your father's executor, and I'll ask him to forward any relevant details to my solicitor, who can reach you through me—just for the first month after your release. After that, you can do what you like."

"I'd appreciate that. Thanks."

"Next week then." With that, he sketched a wave, and threaded his way to the exit.

Back in his cell, Hammer greeted Peter with, "Only the tax-man or a jilted lover would 'av found ya in 'ere. Which was it?"

"To be real honest, Hammer, I don't know. It was some bloke from my father's company. We had to break off early. There was some drama in High Security. I just had enough time to say some slanderous things about you."

Hammer chuckled, "You couldn't say nuffink that ain't already been said. Wotcha say then?"

"I said you were one of the most violent men in Belmarsh, and that you'd taught me to control my temper."

Hammer made his way across to the toilet. "I never taught you nuffink, young Joey. You had your head screwed on from the start. If you hadn't, I would have chopped it off," he laughed.

Hammer finished his business with a prodigious fart, from which he evidently derived some satisfaction, and continued to philosophize. "I ain't really violent, you know. Them idiots what lose their bottle and cut you up for hardly no reason—they're violent. If I work someone over, I'd have thought about it first. You know. It's just a job, like. What do you think, Joey? Is someone who loses their bottle violent, or is it someone like me?"

"You ought to go to philosophy school, mate. Let's just say I'd rather have you with me than against me."

Hammer smiled, "I'm glad you've worked that out, Nipper."

Chapter 2

Trevor Whitman watched his twin brother through the café window. He was looking old. Alex's white hair and walking stick added a decade or more to his sixty years.

Across the road from him, the finger-like spire of an old church pointed to God. It had long ceased to be the tallest building in the street, dwarfed as it was by towering office blocks. Other gods were worshiped now. It didn't bother Trevor much. Although he called himself a cultural Christian, he didn't have anything to do with church—unlike his brother. Alex was devout. The two of them discussed religion from time to time in an academic, gentlemanly sort of way. But he hadn't fared well in their last debate, and the memory of it was still raw.

Trevor had begun the argument by insisting that all religions were expressions of humankind's spiritual hunger for a meaning beyond death. No one religion was right. All beliefs were legitimate and should be tolerated.

Alex had said that the worship of Molech and Baal in 700 BC required the sacrifice of a first-born child, and asked whether that religion should be tolerated as a valid expression of spirituality?

"Of course not," he'd replied. "Only those religions that are not morally flawed are legitimate."

"And who determines which are legitimate, and which are not? Who puts themselves in the place of God and decides?"

And so the debate had raged.

Alex walked into the café, paused to look around, and spotted Trevor by the window. He waved, and made his way to where he was seated.

Trevor usually enjoyed seeing his brother, but he felt apprehensive today. Alex had promised to bring something he felt Trevor should see.

He wasn't sure he wanted to see it.

The particular sticking point of their last conversation occurred after Trevor had disclosed that he was a member of the Freemasons. Trevor felt that by joining them, he was helping society and upholding all things decent.

Alex's reply had shocked him. He'd said that Freemasonry was not compatible with Christianity in any way.

Trevor was affronted and demanded to know why.

Alex had ticked off the reasons on his fingers. "Because Freemasonry says that all gods are equally valid; because it claims Jesus didn't have to come and die for us; and because elements of Freemasonry are involved in worshiping anti-Christian gods."

Trevor was outraged and mentioned that a lot of senior clerics were Freemasons.

Alex had replied that Christianity and religious institutions never did have much in common—and then refused to continue the conversation any further.

Trevor was furious. It had taken him two days to calm down to a point where he could ring Ernest Wheeler, Grand Master of the Grand Lodge, and question him about Alex's assertions.

Wheeler had assured him that Alex's ideas were based on nothing but fanciful conspiracy theories concocted by those who were ignorant. Such critics had no idea of the sincerity of Lodge members or the good works they did for society.

Trevor had been relieved...but ever since then, he'd been plagued with nightmares.

Alex noticed his haggard state. "You look dreadful."

"Good afternoon to you too."

"What's up?"

"You're late."

"Sorry. I'm a bit slower these days." Alex hooked his walking stick over the back of a chair and sat down. "What's the matter?"

"I'm feeling wretched. And it's your fault, you blighter. You got me all worked up with this Freemasonry thing. I had a chat to the Grand Master of my lodge. He says your ideas are poppycock."

"Hmm."

"What do you mean, "hmm?""

Alex unzipped his portfolio, took out a sheet of paper, and slid it across the table. "One of the benefits of being an historian is that I have access to old documents."

Trevor picked up the piece of paper without enthusiasm. But as he read the heading he became alarmed—*JAHBULON*. He directed a sharp look at his twin brother. *Jahbulon* was a name that should rightly be known only by Freemasons. It was the secret name of the Grand Architect that was revealed in a special ritual of The Royal Arch. Alex should not have known about it.

"You shouldn't have this."

"Read on."

"I can't see the relevance."

"Read."

Speaking patiently, as if to a child, Trevor said, "*Jahbulon* is simply a composite name made up of many gods which we use to refer to the Grand Architect of the Universe."

"Read on."

"Look," he sighed, "the masters of the Craft have always assured us that there is nothing anti-Christian about the name."

Alex did not respond. Trevor frowned, hunched forward, and began to read.

The document appeared to be a series of notes compiled in 1836 by the committee who composed the rituals used by the Royal

Arch. Goodness knows how Alex had got hold of it. The notes explained that the name *Jahbulon* was a composite of the three gods of the three original Grand Masters of Freemasonry: King Solomon, King Hiram, and Hiram Abiff. He scanned the page until his eye caught a name that shocked him. *Baal.* The document stated plainly that the god worshiped by Hiram was none other than Baal.

He furrowed his brow. *Wasn't Baal bad…really bad?*

Alex was watching him and said quietly, "Baal was the ancient fertility god of the Canaanites, and later the Phoenicians. Fertility ceremonies associated with Baal worship often included human sacrifice and temple prostitution. The prophets of the Old Testament had to battle against Baal worship for centuries. So, I'm afraid *Jahbulon* really does incorporate a very anti-Christian god—and those who designed the Craft knew it."

Trevor fiddled with the edges of the paper. When it came to issues of historical accuracy, Trevor knew better than to doubt his brother. Alex was a history professor who worked at the British Museum. After a long silence, Trevor said stiffly, "Thank you, Alex. I'll deal with it. Let's order some tea."

When it arrived, he didn't enjoy it and chose to bring their meeting to an early end, pleading his need to work late at the office.

He went straight home, and pushed open the front door. "I'm home," he yelled as he hung up his coat. There was no reply. He dumped his briefcase on the study floor, and went in search of his wife. Surprisingly, there was no light on in the kitchen. He flicked the switch and discovered a note on the bench. It told him that his wife had gone to her bridge night, and that his dinner was on the stove. *Of course.* He'd been so distracted, he'd forgotten.

Trevor ignored the dinner, and made his way back to the study. He sat at his desk and pondered what he'd learned. At first he tried to convince himself that Wheeler, Grand Master of the Royal Arch, had simply been ignorant of the real intentions and convictions of those who had set up the 'Supreme Degree.' But he knew it wasn't true. Wheeler was the undisputed expert on the history and symbolism of the Royal Arch. Trevor was forced to face the fact that Wheeler had fed him lies, and the thought of that galled him. Secrecy was one thing. Deception and obfuscation was another.

Trevor put his head in his hands. If the Craft insisted on a life-time commitment, there had to be truth. He didn't want to be patronized with fairy tales, damn it. He kicked his chair away from the desk, poured himself a whiskey, and knocked it back in one gulp. The fiery liquid coursed through him, helping to cement his resolve to have it out with Wheeler once and for all. But he was under no illusion that it would be easy…or that the consequences of doing so could be dire. Much of his social life, and many of his business connections, came through Freemasonry. He banged the whiskey glass down on the desk. It was probably just as well he was planning to retire from his banking career.

That night Trevor battled with nightmares again.

***

Ernest Wheeler viewed the scene with contempt. A blindfolded, bare-breasted candidate with a rope noose around his neck, was swearing the oath of an Entered Apprentice:

"…*under no less a penalty than to have my throat cut across, my tongue torn out by the root, and buried in the rough sands of the sea at low water mark, or a cable's length from the shore, where the tide regularly ebbs and flows…*"

Fools. They were innocents, posturing idiots playing dress-ups with no comprehension of the significance of the Craft. He reflected with irritation on his earlier conversation in the antechamber of the United Grand Lodge with a Craft member from Manchester. The buffoon had been bobbing up and down ingratiating himself to everyone on his first visit to Great Queen Street. Seeing Wheeler's regalia, he had stepped across with his hand outstretched, offering the secret handshake and quoted the Freemason's dictum: "Every Master Mason is his brother's equal, eh! So let me introduce myself. Brother Michael Tyler."

Wheeler deigned to shake his hand, but accompanied it with a glare, saying, "Brother Ernest Wheeler, Grand Master, Holy Royal Arch."

Comprehension slowly dawned on Tyler's face, and he scurried away to waylay someone else.

At the end of the ceremony, Wheeler walked across the black-and-white tiled floor, through the heavy doors, and out into the foyer. Digby Allington, Master of the Grand Lodge, was talking to the porter at the front desk. "Not staying for the social, Ernest?" Allington inquired.

"No, Digby, I have..." he wanted to say 'better,' but elected to say, "other things to do." Wheeler passed through the foyer and made his way down the steps into the wet streets of London.

Ten minutes later, the taxi dropped him at the doors of a modern office block. His assistant, Carl, gave a deferential nod as he passed the reception desk and made for the elevator.

Wheeler walked through to his private office and shut the door behind him. He moved behind his desk to the velvet curtain hanging between two pillars, and pulled the drapes aside to reveal the metal door of a strong room. Very few people knew of its existence. He unlocked the metal door and collected two box files. After backing his way through the drapes, he placed the boxes on the desk. His priority now was to review the progress that had been made and calculate his next move.

Half an hour later, the internal telecom buzzed. Wheeler stabbed at a button. "What is it?" Carl had instructions that he was not to be disturbed, but Wheeler knew better than to admonish him. Carl stood six-feet two-inches high, but didn't look tall. Those who met him tended to notice his physique rather than his height. He was competent and knew when he should, and should, not interrupt.

"Sir," Carl said softly, "Trevor Whitman is at reception. He insists on seeing you, and says he will not leave until he has. He rang earlier to ask if you were here. I can put him off, but you might prefer to see him. He seems agitated, but I don't believe he is a threat. I can wait outside if you wish."

Wheeler suppressed his exasperation, and looked at his watch. 10pm. *Damn the man.* Whitman had been asking some probing questions about the Royal Arch in the last few weeks, and was showing the classic symptoms of someone wavering in their commitment to the Lodge. Wheeler tapped a finger on the desk. "Tell him to come in. I'll see him in the outside office."

However, his last words were lost in the sound of crashing and some muffled exclamations coming through the phone. "What's going on?" he demanded.

"Sorry, sir, the office cleaner tipped over a pot plant in the foyer with his vacuum cleaner. I'll bring Mr. Whitman up."

"To the outside…" but Carl had hung up.

———

Trevor did not feel comfortable getting into the lift with Carl. He'd only met him a few times before, and always found him unnerving. Carl's polite demeanor never reached his eyes. Trevor shivered, unable to dispel a sense of apprehension over what he knew he must do. It was as if the monster under the bed, previously understood to be myth, had suddenly crawled out to confront him—and he couldn't tell how it would behave.

Carl pushed a lift button and said, "Mr. Wheeler has agreed to see you in his office." He smiled. "That's unusual. Very few have the privilege of meeting him there."

He was ushered out of the lift, through a reception area, and into a luxurious office space dotted with modern armchairs. Impressionist paintings hung on the walls.

Carl knocked on a heavy door, opened it, and said, "Mr. Whitman to see you, sir," and ushered Trevor through.

The door closed behind him, and Trevor found himself, surprisingly, quite alone.

The office was like no other he'd ever seen. Whilst the offices outside were the last word in crisp, modern minimalism, Wheeler's office was decorated in a classical Greek style. A dark blue velvet drape hung between two ancient-looking pillars behind the desk. It was bizarre.

Where was Wheeler? He must have stepped outside for a while.

The office was dim, lit only by a desk lamp. There were shadows and secrets. Trevor shivered. Looking down, he saw a gold ring lying next to a crystal paperweight on the desk. Beside it was an old-style desk blotter. The edges of some pieces of paper that Wheeler had hidden under the blotter were just showing.

Trevor felt that he'd had quite enough of secrets. In irritation, he pulled the pieces of paper out and looked at them.

What he saw didn't make a great deal of sense, but what he read on the footer of both pages shocked him to the core. He gaped in disbelief. Could this be true? Was it real?

He fought down a rising sense of panic and realized that he needed evidence to show his brother—indeed, the world. Knowing that Wheeler could return at any moment, he took out his mobile phone, moved the two pieces of paper under the desk lamp, and photographed them.

As he did, he heard scuffling noises coming from behind the velvet curtain. A wave of panic washed over him. He tapped the papers together, and pushed them back under the blotter. *What now?* What should he do with the evidence now in his possession? He was under no illusion as to its significance. Trevor ejected the tiny Micro SD card from his phone, but couldn't think what to do with it. The tiny flat piece of black plastic was half an inch square.

Suddenly, Wheeler was there, appearing as if by magic through the velvet drapes. He seemed to take in the scene in an instant.

Wheeler held out his hand. "This is a restricted area. Please give me your phone."

Too shocked to protest, Trevor handed over his phone, and stammered, "I was just about to call home to say I'd be late."

Wheeler said nothing. He checked the message log on the mobile phone and scrolled through the pictures stored on its internal memory.

Trevor's skin appeared to burn where the Micro SD card lay hidden between the base of his thumb and the first finger of his left hand. "Hey," he said. "That's my private property."

"And so is this place. I was to meet you in the outside office. How did you get in here?"

"Carl let me in."

Wheeler frowned, and placed the mobile phone on the desk.

It was the latest camera phone, and Trevor hoped Wheeler did not understand all its technical features. He changed the subject. "Mr. Wheeler, I appreciate it is late, but I needed to see you alone at a time when we would not be disturbed."

Wheeler looked at him levelly. "What do you wish to say? I am a busy man."

"I want to say…" *What?* He paused. What could he say now? Trevor swallowed. "I want to say that I have had enough of being deceived about the true values behind the Royal Arch, and I'm not sure I want anything more to do with it."

Wheeler's face remained stony. "Trevor, please take care not to denigrate the Craft. You have sworn loyalty to it. You've enjoyed the patronage of your fellow brothers in business, and benefited from our networks. We have guaranteed the continued private education of your children in the event of your untimely death, and you have shared in philanthropic acts that have benefited society." Wheeler sniffed. "We don't deserve your censure."

Trevor pressed on, "Last time we talked, you assured me that the word *Jahbulon* was not a composite name that contained any anti-Christian god. I have since seen records of the committee tasked in 1836 with establishing the ritual of Royal Arch, and have learned otherwise. Therefore, I cannot, in all conscience, continue as a member of the Lodge."

Affecting weariness, Wheeler said, "Does the name really matter? We rarely use the term any more in the Royal Arch."

"It is part of our heritage, for goodness sake. We claim ours to be the 'Supreme Degree.' We alone dismiss the Craft's Third Degree as incomplete, and the one thing which sets us apart is our claim to know the true name of the Supreme Being, *Jahbulon*."

Wheeler sighed and began speaking with exaggerated clarity, "Brother Trevor, there are some things that can only be learned over time. A child of three cannot be expected to understand calculus. So it is with the mysteries of the Craft. If things are hidden, it is because we do not believe you are ready to know its full secrets."

Trevor held up his hand. "No, please don't go down that path.

If you are inviting people to join, there must be transparency. How else will anyone know what they are getting into?"

Wheeler compressed his lips. "Trevor, if you want to know the truth, then you need to be very sure you have discovered it. The fact of the matter is that the term *Jahbulon* is not a compilation of specific gods. If you do the research, you will learn that JAH is the Chaldee name of God signifying 'His essence and majesty.' It is also the Hebrew word for 'I am and shall be.' BUL is a Syriac word meaning 'in heaven,' and ON is an Egyptian word meaning 'Father of all.' In other words, they are titles of respect, not specific gods."

Trevor slapped a hand on Wheeler's desk. "Dammit, Ernest, I was there for the Mystical Lecture. I was shown the three syllables of the word written on a triangle with the letters A, B, and L set at the corners. I was there when the lecturer explained that these letters can be juggled to spell the divine incantation, BAL. It wasn't until someone told me about Baal that I made the connection—which is now blindingly obvious."

Wheeler's face remained impassive. "Historically, the Royal Arch companions may have linked the word *Jahbulon* with Baal, but we don't do so any more—not that it would matter if we did. The word Baal does not necessarily apply to a specific god, but to deities generally that existed in the Middle East at the time of the Canaanites. Only later did the name Baal become appended to the anti-Jewish God."

Trevor erupted in anger, "Are you seriously trying to tell me that Baal was not known to be an anti-Christian god by those who set up our code? Your capacity to bend the banally obvious, so that you can call black 'white,' simply beggars belief. It is no wonder that you can call Lucifer 'pure, virtuous, wholesome, and innocent.'"

At this, a chilling frisson crossed Wheeler's face.

The Grand Master eased himself into his chair and put his elbows on the desk. He stared at Trevor over the top of steepled hands. Finally, he looked down at the edges of the pieces of paper protruding from underneath the blotter. He pulled them out, and placed them on top of the desk.

Trevor knew in that instant that he was in great danger. In his passion, he had betrayed what he knew. A dreadful menace now hung in the air. What had he provoked? He reasoned desperately that whilst the secret he had learned was shocking, it could not be so important as to threaten his life. Desperately seeking to keep his rising terror in check, Trevor plowed on. "I want you to know that I hereby resign from the Royal Arch—and from every aspect of Freemasonry."

Wheeler reached forward and picked up the gold ring from the desk, and slid it on his finger. "Why, Mr. Whitman, hasn't anyone told you? No one can un-swear the oaths of the Craft or betray its secrets without consequence. Surely you remember: 'buried in the rough sands of the sea at low water mark, or a cable's length from the shore, where the tide regularly ebbs and flows.'"

Trevor knew then that he was going to die. Affecting a small cough, he put his left hand to his lips and transferred the tiny SD card into his mouth.

Wheeler called, "Carl."

Trevor swallowed the card.

Chapter 3

Peter heard the screams and ranting from the next cell as he joined the prison officer in the corridor to be escorted to the visiting room. Two guards were standing by the door of the neighboring cell. One of them was cursing whilst wiping some filth from his lapel. "Bastard. He got me."

From inside, screams of, "I'll get you, screw," were accompanied by savage kicking of the closed door and the crashing of what Peter could only surmise was a chair against a wall.

Jonno, the sole occupant of the cell next door, was playing up again. It was not an uncommon occurrence. His behavior had resulted in him being placed in a single cell—as much for his own protection as anything. His fellow inmates were heartily fed up with his antics.

In the previous week, Jonno had attempted to throw boiling water over a guard. He had sweetened the water with sugar to make it stick to the skin. The guards hated the fact that prisoners were allowed their own kettles to heat water. Jonno's abuse of this privilege simply resulted in his power being switched off two hours before his cell was unlocked in the morning, so that no hot water was available to him.

However, Jonno only invented more creative ways to express his displeasure. This morning, he had elected to throw feces at the guard unlocking his cell. One of the guards was banging on the closed door in irritation as he called out threats. As Peter walked past with his warder, the aggrieved prison officer snapped at Peter in frustration, "Can't you bastards sort him out?"

Peter paused, and glanced at the guard. "I can try."

He stepped across to Jonno's door and called out, "Hey, Jonno. It's Joey. What's the matter, mate?"

The guard stepped back, and rolled his eyes, making it clear this was not the 'sorting out' he had hoped for.

The screams of abuse rose to a new crescendo. Peter tapped on the door, and continued to shout. "Jonno, you daft bugger. It's me, Joey. What's ticked you off?" Peter knew enough to understand that prisoners' complaints were often very trivial. It was easy to lose perspective in prison. He'd once seen someone knifed, simply because they had spent too long on the phone. If issues could be fixed quickly, potential drama could be diffused.

For a moment, there was silence, then Jonno called out, "Joey, is that you?"

"Of course it is. Who do you think it is? Geeze, you've made the place stink."

There was silence.

"Jonno," said Peter. "I'm opening the hatch. Talk to me, mate." He opened the inspection hatch to find Jonno's reddened, angry eye staring back. "How can we fix it for you, mate? What do you want? Because, sure as hell, what you're doing isn't going to get it for you. Let's see if we can make it work."

There was silence as Jonno's face slid down out of sight. He had sunk to his knees at the base of the door. Soon, the noise of sobbing could be heard. Jonno whimpered, "My oldest boy 'as got himself banged up in the Scrubs." The sobbing rose to a heart-rending level, before subsiding again. "And I need to see him. I don't want 'im going wrong like me."

"Mate, I'm sorry about that," said Peter. He was quiet for a while, before continuing, "How about we get the 'Pie' and the 'Care Bear' to see what's possible?"

More sobbing followed, and Peter had to repeat his suggestion. Eventually, his proposition seemed to give Jonno some assurance. "You fink that'll 'elp, Joey? It's just that them pillocks said it was never goin' to 'appen 'cos I've been too much trouble."

"Yeah, well, let's leave it to the guys who really know, eh? Let's give it a shot. Get the place cleaned up, so they'll let you out for exercise. We'll talk more then." Peter stepped away from the door, and waited for his prison officer to lead him to the visiting room.

"That was well done," said his PO.

When they arrived at the visiting room, Peter was ordered to go to seat C6. He found the seat, and waited for Toby Cheeseman.

Cheeseman was one of the first visitors to enter the room. Surveying the hall, he spotted Peter, and made his way to his table. Today, he was wearing a Tweed sports jacket and a mustard-colored waistcoat. He was scowling as he sat down.

Peter was wondering what he'd done wrong, when Cheeseman bounded back to his feet, and held out his hand. "Terribly sorry, old boy. Er, hello...again." Having repaired his manners, he flopped back into his seat.

It was difficult for Peter not to smile. "What's the matter?"

"Ah, yes. Am a bit browned off actually. Hmm...where to begin?"

Peter waited patiently.

"Yes. First, good news: my solicitor phoned your executor. They were a bit pleased evidently, as they'd nearly given up on you. They've agreed for my solicitor to represent them, and read you your father's will once you've given concrete evidence of your identity. Call to make an appointment on your, er, release." He handed Peter a business card. Peter took it carefully, giving the guards a chance to see it clearly to allay any suspicions about it being the means of transferring illegal substances.

"I'll do that. Thank you."

"I've also written my phone number on the back."

Peter nodded his appreciation.

"I'm afraid that the rest of the news is not so rosy."

Peter waited for Cheeseman to go on.

"Do you know your father's business partner in South Africa, Mr. Manier Gobler—or 'Manny' as he prefers to be called?"

Peter shook his head. "I heard his name mentioned, but I never met him."

"I see. Both he and your father set up Mining Management Systems. Your father was the brains, of course, but Manny Gobler had the contacts." Cheeseman drew a deep breath. "Anyway, the partnership worked out well, and the company set up offices in South Africa, London and Australia. We design computer programs to keep track of all maintenance schedules, stock, and equipment for the mining industry. Our programs have saved companies millions through improved efficiency and timely maintenance." He sniffed. "I head the team that writes them in the London office."

Peter said nothing.

"Er, anyway, despite the company's success, it never went public. Both Gobler and your father each held forty percent of the shares. The other twenty percent was given to key staff members who helped start the company. Each share carries one vote at the company's AGM. Since your father's death, his voting rights have not been exercised, and Gobler has had absolute control."

Cheeseman sighed. "I'm sorry to say that in the last eighteen months, he's been milking the company—using it to purchase luxuries for personal use, particularly here in London. More importantly, we've won no significant contracts in the last nine months, and are just subsisting by maintaining our old contracts." Cheeseman grimaced. "Staff numbers have dropped, and I am the only senior person left in the London office. Gobler has sacked most of those who have challenged his behavior. He maintains that he is simply exercising his right as the founding company director."

Peter waited for Cheeseman to get to the point. When it was evident that he was not going to be told anything more, he prompted, "It sounds very regrettable, but why are you telling me this?"

"Ah, didn't I tell you? Your father set up his will in a very particular way: as a discretionary testamentary trust. He did it for tax purposes. What this means, is that on his death, his appointed executor operates the trust on behalf of the named beneficiaries."

"And who are the beneficiaries?"

"Just you! I'm instructed to tell you that you are the sole beneficiary of your father's estate. This means you own forty percent of Mining Management Systems." He paused. "In other words, you're my boss."

Next morning, at five am, a naked man turned slowly in the chilly morning wind, hanging from the neck by a rope suspended under Blackfriars Bridge.

Chapter 4

Professor Alex Whitman looked up in awe at the massive Babylonian masterpiece. He'd flown into Berlin that morning to examine it. The Ishtar Gate was certainly impressive. The gate was designed to do just one thing: intimidate all visitors entering the city.

Alex reflected on the contradictions of the Babylonian kingdom. Nebuchadnezzar II, had been responsible for the famous hanging gardens, the temple of Marduk, and the colossal walls of Babylon —wide enough to allow two chariots to pass side by side along their ramparts. And yet he had also popularized crucifixion.

The professor made his way over to the ancient wall. Its flank was covered with glazed blue tiles. Golden bas-relief images of lions, wild oxen, and dragons ran along its length.

He ran his fingers over a dragon. This was what he had particularly come to see. It had the head of a snake which had a single horn and a crest on top. The scaly body had the hind feet of an eagle, the front feet of a lion, and the tail of a cheetah. Of all the beasts featured on the walls, the dragon was the only mythical one —and the professor suspected there was a significance to it that had not yet been fully understood.

He peered at the dragon's long, scaly neck and noticed it wore a collar. The beast had been domesticated—probably pressed into the service of the Babylonian god, Marduk.

Alex took out an ancient drawing he'd brought with him. It was a depiction of Marduk with a dragon at his feet. But this dragon had two horns, not one. Horns, he knew, often represented kingdoms. *So what was the other kingdom? Who were the...*

Alex felt his phone vibrate, fumbled for it in his jacket pocket, and answered the call.

"Professor Whitman, this is Detective Sergeant Allan Jenkins of London CID."

"Um, hello Detective." Irritated by the interruption, Alex's mind continued to work. *Could that kingdom be Assyria?*

"I'm afraid I have some bad news."

The detective's comment snapped him out of his reverie. He pressed the phone hard against his ear.

The detective continued. "There's no easy way of saying this: your brother has died. I'm very sorry to have to break this to you. I understand that you and Trevor were close, and that he was your twin."

Alex's head began to spin. "What! How could he be dead? I only saw him yesterday and he...Was there an accident?" The professor groped his way toward a bench seat at the end of the museum hall.

Jenkins continued. "Your brother's wife and daughter are understandably distressed, and with his son being in America, we were hoping you could come and formally identify his body?"

Alex couldn't process the fact that Trevor was gone. Trevor, the most consistent feature of his life: the one who had shared his mother's womb and so much of his life—was dead. Shock masked the reality of loss. But the beginnings of grief's fury began to flicker like lightning before a storm.

"How did he die?" he asked.

"Possibly foul play, but we can't rule out suicide." There was a lengthy pause before the detective inquired again. "Are you able to assist by identifying the body?"

The professor pulled himself together. "Aah, of course. I'm not actually in London at present. I'm in Berlin doing some research. I'll see if I can get a flight back tonight. One way or another, I should be with you by tomorrow afternoon."

"Thanks, Professor, and again, I am very sorry for your loss."

"You mentioned that you could not rule out suicide. I believe you can. I knew him well. He has never given any indication of being suicidal."

"Yes, sir, I suspect you are right. People don't usually take their clothes off before they hang themselves. We'll talk more tomorrow."

A prison guard escorted Peter to 'stores.' There, Peter's meager belongings were returned to him, and he was taken back to his cell so he could change into civilian clothes. He hadn't worn them for two years. He was shocked to find that he couldn't do up most of the buttons on his shirt because he'd bulked up so much.

Hammer watched Peter fold up his prison clothes, and place them on the end of the bed. "I'm sad to see ya goin', young Joey." He scratched his crotch. "I've got another nine months before I join ya. Warn the girls at Wapping to get ready for me." He screwed up his face as if struggling to find words. Eventually he said, "I'd wanna say it was okay to mention my name if ya find yourself in trouble dahn the East End." He laughed coarsely, "The trouble is, 'alf of 'em would kill ya on the spot. Better to say nuffink." So saying, he slapped Peter on the arm, lay back down on his bed, and turned over.

Peter was led along the landing, down the spiral staircase, to the office of the prison governor. There, he was given his discharge allowance of sixty-four pounds plus the seventy-two pounds he had saved. Finally, he was given a rail ticket for anywhere in the country. Peter had simply shrugged and said, "Central London," and signed for his cash.

After being escorted to the gatehouse, he gave his name, signed again, was checked against a photograph, and led to a huge gate. It opened electronically only to reveal another gate—closed. He walked between the two gates, and stood in the 'no man's land.' The first gate clunked shut...and the second opened With a sense of unreality, Peter walked outside.

Looking out over the dismal gray London morning, Peter felt intimidated, displaced, and very lonely. It was terrifying. There was no one to give him orders. However, he relished the fresh morning air, and the sight of his foggy clouds made by his breath. Part of him wanted to shout to those blithely going about their normal business that this was an incredible day. The other part of him wanted to hide.

Peter made his way to Plumstead railway station. He hadn't the courage to get on the first train and let it pass by as he stood immobilized by fear. He spent the next forty minutes conjuring up the courage to board the next train.

He got off at London Bridge, and caught the tube to Stepney Green. Peter couldn't believe that he'd once navigated these tasks without thought.

He walked to a budget backpacker's hostel that had been recommended, found a pay phone, and made three calls. The first was to Cheeseman's solicitor. He would be happy to see Peter at 11am on Friday at his offices. The second was to Toby Cheeseman himself.

"Mr. Cheeseman, Peter Jacobs speaking. I've, er, been released. Can we catch up for a chat?"

"Ah, well...I suppose so, old chap. I leave the company in two weeks time, so I've got a lot of tidying up to do. But I could fit in a coffee at the *Phoenix*."

"What is the *Phoenix*?"

"It's an old sailing barge that's been converted into a floating café. You'll find it moored in St. Katharine's Dock, just a few hundred yards from my office." He paused; Peter could hear him tapping some computer keys. "I can see you there at 3pm, Friday."

"Thanks. I'll see you then."

Finally, Peter rang his probation officer to establish contact and arrange a meeting. She was keen to meet with Peter as soon as possible, having been told, evidently, that Peter had no family, no supportive friends, no immediate job prospects, and a paltry prison payout that would only keep him in temporary accommodation for a few days. Could Peter suggest a place to meet, preferably tomorrow morning?

Peter's mind raced, "Er, yes—10:30am at the *Phoenix*. It's a café on a sailing barge moored at St. Katharine's Dock."

"Fine, I'll see you then."

Alex looked down at the pale face. "Yes, that is my brother Trevor." Anguish welled up within him. Part of his soul felt ripped out, and the hole it left behind ached and bled. Trevor, once so vital, once so passionate, and full of life—was dead.

Death was so uncompromisingly final; such a cruel ending of dreams, opportunities, learning, and love. Screwing his eyes shut, he fought to keep a grip on his emotions. The words of the Welsh poet, Dylan Thomas, came to him: *'Do not go gentle into that good night.'*

Alex bowed his head, and made a silent vow. *Trevor, I will not accept your death gently. I will 'rage, rage, against the dying of the light', and I will do all that is within my power to uncover the evil behind your murder.* Alex looked up to blink the tears away. Life was such a precious gift—such an unlikely, delicate thing. That anyone could so summarily dismiss it, was an obscenity against the miracle of existence.

But then, as he stood there in his hurt and anger, a deeper call reached his heart. It was as gentle as a zephyr, and as insistent as a parent calling a child—it was an invitation to prayer.

After three minutes, Detective Inspector Allan Jenkins gave a discreet cough. It was enough to bring Alex back to the grim realities that had to be addressed.

The detective led Alex to the lift, and escorted him to an office where he rang through for two mugs of tea to be brought to them. "How many sugars?" Jenkins asked.

"Er, one, thank you."

"Professor, we are treating the death of your brother as suspicious. Do you know of anyone who would have cause to wish your brother ill?"

Alex answered the questions as best he could, assuring the detective that Trevor had no money problems, no gambling addictions, or family or business quarrels. He had been—in every respect—a model citizen. Why anyone would want to kill him was a complete mystery.

The detective nodded. "We can track his movements until 9:30pm two nights ago. As best as we can ascertain, he left a perfectly ordinary investment meeting with a group of clients, but never made it home. We found his car in its usual place in a city car park."

Jenkins clicked the end of his ballpoint pen a few times and then asked, "Professor, have you heard of Roberto Calvi?"

Alex shook his head. "Why do you ask?"

"Roberto Calvi was an Italian banker who was found hanging under Blackfriar's Bridge in 1982. He was chairman of Italy's second largest private bank, Banko Ambrosiano. His bank was under investigation for illegally exporting twenty-seven million dollars out of the country in violation of Italian currency laws. It was later discovered to have debts estimated to be between seven-hundred million, and a billion American dollars. Much of the money had, evidently, been siphoned off via the Vatican Bank. The Vatican was embarrassed enough to pay two-hundred-and-twenty-four million American dollars to the creditors in recognition of its moral obligations."

"And do you think there is a link between the death of my brother, and this Italian banker?"

"I doubt it. But I can't help asking the question. In 1982, Calvi disguised himself, and fled from Rome to Venice with a false passport. From there, he hired a private plane to London. At 7:30am on Friday the eighteenth of June, 1982, a passing postman found his body hanging from scaffolding beneath Blackfriars Bridge. Calvi's clothing had been weighted with building bricks, and he was carrying around fifteen-thousand pounds worth of cash in three different currencies."

"Could there be a connection? Was anyone charged?"

"Your brother's hanging was different in many respects, and there may not be a connection. As to who was involved, nothing could be proved. It could have been the Mafia, but there is another possibility. Calvi was a member of Italy's most powerful Masonic Lodge, *Propagands Masonical*, also known as P2."

Alex frowned. "Tell me about them."

"The Grand Master of the Lodge was a textile manufacturer, Licio Gelli. When his house was raided during an investigation into a false kidnapping, they found a list of Lodge members that contained the names of forty-three MPs, forty generals, eight admirals, the police chiefs of Italy's four biggest cities, and some of the nation's top financial leaders—including Roberto Calvi."

"What made the police suspect the involvement of P2?"

"The P2 members referred to themselves as *frati neri*—black friars."

"Blackfriars Bridge."

"Exactly."

The professor hesitated before saying, "Would you mind telling me if you are, or ever have been, a Lodge member, Detective?"

Jenkins grimaced. "I can assure you I am not—although I can't help thinking sometimes that it might have helped my prospects if I had been."

Alex nodded slowly before he said, "My brother was a member of the Lodge. We used to argue about it. But I have to tell you; whilst Trevor was a banker, he was not a big player in the financial world. I certainly can't see him being involved in any shady Freemasonry deals. He was highly principled."

Jenkins picked up a mustard-colored envelope from his desk, extracted a small plastic bag, and placed it in front of the professor.

"Do you know what that is, Professor?"

Alex picked up the bag and looked at the tiny piece of black plastic inside it. "No, I'm afraid I don't."

The policeman pointed to the bag. "It's a phone's memory card." He paused. "Can you tell me why we would find this in your brother's stomach?"

Alex was startled. "I haven't the least idea. Trevor was certainly up with the latest gadgets, but I haven't a clue why he would swallow a memory card. Have you been able to see what's on it?"

"We have. It contains a number of photos—most of no significance. But the most recent one is interesting."

Alex raised an eyebrow.

Jenkins continued. "It's a picture of two pieces of paper. The resolution is not great, but we have blown it up as much as we can." Jenkins slid a photograph out from the yellow envelope and passed it over to the professor.

Before looking at it, Alex said, "Detective, I can assure you that my brother was neither eccentric nor careless in his actions. If he needed to swallow something in order to hide it, he would have had a very good reason for doing so." He bent down and examined the photograph. It was a picture of two sheets of paper—one partly overlapping the other. They were fanned out; presumably on a desk, as the corner of a crystal paperweight could be seen.

One piece of paper contained a carefully reproduced pencil drawing of some Egyptian hieroglyphs chiseled on a piece of stone. The header of this page simply had the name 'Beatrice' written on it. The second piece of paper contained some sort of list. Most of it was obscured by the top page—except for its footer. He could see some tiny writing on the bottom of the page.

The professor turned to Jenkins. "Do you have a magnifying glass?"

Jenkins opened a drawer on his desk, and extracted a magnifying glass. "We still keep some of Sherlock's tools here," he said with a clumsy attempt at humor.

The professor focused the magnifying glass on the tiny writing. Swimming into focus, he read the words, *Lucifer: pure, virtuous, wholesome, and innocent.* His face froze as he stared at the words.

"Does any of this make sense to you?" asked the detective.

"No, it doesn't, but I would like to have a copy of this picture so I can investigate it further."

"I'm not sure that is wise. I should probably tell you, professor, we've been to the British Museum to talk with your colleague,

George Daintree. He tells me that the hieroglyphs on the front page say"—he consulted his notebook—"*Ramses beloved of Aman, like the son of Osiris, has placed on his obelisks the secret identity of the ultimate one.*" The detective looked up. "He also suggested that my involvement with you regarding the investigations should be minimal as you would be too emotionally…er, disturbed."

"He did?"

"Yes."

Strange. The professor drew in a deep breath. "Detective, if you had looked carefully at the bookshelf above the filing cabinets in my colleague's office, you would have seen a small leather case."

"A Freemason's case?"

"They have a policy of not actually telling you these things."

Jenkins drummed his fingers on the envelope in front of him. Then he picked it up and handed it to the professor. "Don't flash it around. If you have experts that can give us any further information, let me know. But let me do the work. Is that clear?"

The professor nodded, saying silently to himself, *Forgive me, George.* The professor knew very well that George Daintree kept nothing more sinister than a set of miniature carpet bowls in the leather case. But, the fact that it had once been a Freemason's case was a slight concern. Alex folded the envelope and slipped it into his jacket pocket. He would do some investigations of his own. However, to do so, he would need the help of one particular person —someone who was an expert in her field.

Chapter 5

B eth Anderson picked away with a needle at the grains of sand encrusting a piece of Egyptian glassware. It was a tiny double-handled vase dating from the New Kingdom period of 1786-1085 BC. The technical skill required to make this exquisite vase would not be matched in England for another fifteen-hundred years. It was incredible.

She'd tied her hair up in a loose bun. Some of the strands had escaped, so she tossed her head back and blew them away. As she did, she caught sight of Kingsley on the next bench looking at her with his puppy-dog eyes. He was, ostensibly, cleaning an Egyptian necklace with a tiny brush.

Beth had long since ceased to be troubled by his lovelorn looks. She knew that Kingsley was happier inhabiting his world of fantasy —safe from having to negotiate the more complex waters of reality.

Her phone rang.

She pulled out her flip-top mobile. "Hello, Beth speaking."

The distinctive voice of Alex Whitman came back at her. "I'm still missing my best post-doctoral research student, and bewailing the fact that she is throwing her life away doing restoration work rather than engaging in serious historical research."

"As you very well know," she countered, "I'm learning restoration so I can go for the curator's job here and become your boss. What's up?"

"My boss, eh?" Alex chuckled. "Then it should come as no surprise to you that I need your superior expertise in hieroglyphics—Ramses II—your doctoral research area."

"Sure, I can come up if you like."

"Er, no. This is an off-the-record private thing. I'm actually ringing from home at the moment, taking a week off. Um, is there any chance of catching up for lunch tomorrow—my treat?"

"Great! Let's make an extended lunch of it. Usual place?"

"Thanks. Let's say 12:30."

One mile away, another phone rang. Ernest Wheeler picked up the phone. "Yes?"

A voice replied, "The police have a photo. I've seen it. Without the context, it can't make much sense to anyone. Lose the desk and the paperweight. Everything else can be managed. I'll contact you later."

The phone cut dead.

Peter used his first afternoon of newfound freedom to visit a shopping center. He bought a pair of respectable trousers and two shirts that actually fitted him. But he found it a harrowing experience that left him feeling bewildered, emotional, and very vulnerable.

Next morning he reviewed his finances. After buying his clothes and paying for one week's board—he only had thirty-one pounds and twenty pence left. He sighed and made his way down to the hostel common room, where he hoped to find someone who might know the way to St. Katharine's Dock.

Discreet inquiries resulted in a young man yelling across the room, "Hey, Kym, don't you work down at St. Katharine's? A bloke here wants to know how to get there."

A diminutive girl with short black hair was standing by the window, shrugging her way into a duffel coat. As she pulled the edges of her coat together, she said, "Well, if 'the bloke here' wants to know, tell him to ask me." She spoke with a broad Australian accent.

Peter made his way across the room and introduced himself. "Er, sorry to be a pain, but I'm new here, and I've got a meeting at the *Phoenix*. I thought I'd go early to see where it is. My name's Peter Jacobs."

"Well, Peter Jacobs, if you move your arse, you can come with me. I've got a waitressing job across the way from the *Phoenix*. But we need to go now if we're going to catch the bus."

"I'm ready."

She looked him up and down. "I'm Kym Leesman."

"G'day, Kym."

The bus was crowded, and those getting on had to scuttle about in order to find a seat. Peter stepped aside to make room for Kym to be seated. He saw a young man with a hard-bitten face try and compete with Kym for her seat. Peter stepped forward, apparently innocently, to place himself in his way.

The man scowled and moved to the back of the bus.

Enough people got off at the next few stops to finally allow Peter and Kym to sit together. In the careful opening round of questions, he admitted that he came from Perth, and learned that she was from Adelaide. She had trained as a chef at Regency Park, and worked with some success in one of Adelaide's more hip restaurants that specialized in native seeds and fruit.

"You have no idea some of the amazing flavors you can get from the Aussie bush." Kym sighed and reflected sadly, "The café I work in now is just an up market grease spot. It churns out unhealthy carbohydrates in unimaginative forms. We only get business because we're down by the docks where the tourists go."

"Why do you stay?" asked Peter.

"I want to move on as soon as I can. But any job is better than nothing. I'm moving into a flat with some friends next week, and I need the money."

They stepped off the bus onto the narrow, congested streets. After five minutes of dodging the shoulders and elbows of people hurrying to work, Peter glanced at the view that appeared between two tall buildings. What he saw caused him to stop in amazement. There, looking down at him regally, stood the Tower of London. Its famous White Tower could be seen clearly rising above the castle wall.

"Pretty cool, eh!" said Kym. "And you'll see Tower Bridge when we get down to the dock."

They continued on, passing between brown-brick warehouses, most of which seemed to have been converted into apartments. When they arrived, Peter could see that St. Katharine's Dock was split into two main pools: a western and an eastern dock. The western dock was largely occupied by a modern marina. It was crowded with luxury sailing boats that, judging from the flags flying from their sterns, hailed from every nation on earth.

The eastern dock contained a collection of marine vessels from days gone by. One-hundred-year-old spritsail barges, with their characteristic leeboards, nestled against each other in the shadow of a renovated warehouse. Across the other side, an old light-ship was berthed, presumably as an historical curio. Pubs and coffee houses dotted the walkways and roads. Even in the gray morning light of London, it was a charming sight, a celebration of all things maritime that promised to tell stories he wanted to hear.

Kym pointed out the mast of one particular wooden barge. It had a green tarpaulin draped over part of its decking to offer protection for dinner guests going down below for a meal. "That's the *Phoenix*." She then pointed beyond it. "I work two hundred yards down that road at a mock Tudor pub called 'The Anchor.'"

Peter expressed his thanks.

With a deprecating wave, Kym turned and strode away.

For a moment, Peter forgot his anxieties concerning his imme-diate future and breathed in pure freedom. He was on his own—and he had a whole morning to himself. But then, like vanishing rays at sunset, his sense of exaltation was again overtaken by dark anxieties about the future.

He berated himself for his fear and taking a deep breath, began to explore his new surrounds. Peter walked past the lock gates toward the esplanade that ran along the bank of the River Thames. Navigation was made easy by the looming splendor of Tower Bridge. Peter stared at it, wondering how it could appear so untouched by the dramas of two world wars. Its two concrete piers and pseudo-Gothic architecture gave it a sense of permanence.

He wondered, fleetingly, whether time really could heal the ravages of history, particularly his history.

Peter turned and made his way back to the dockside where the *Phoenix* was moored. Taking a deep breath, he stepped across the gangplank onto the wooden deck.

The old barge had the feel of uncompromising strength and utilitarian purpose. He glanced at an information board by the gangplank. It told him that the vessel was eighty feet long, twenty feet wide, and carried four-thousand square feet of sail. Despite its size, it was designed to be sailed by just two men. Peter, who knew a little about sailing, found it hard to believe.

The barge's mast and boom soared aloft, kept upright by shrouds tensioned by deadeye blocks. Up at the bow, the jib boom had been canted up into the air, presumably to protect it from damage whilst the barge was moored.

Peter was charmed by what he saw. Almost reluctantly, he made his way down the stairs into the hold. Inside, he saw that almost the entire length had been converted into a café containing booths, like those in old Victorian coffee houses. Running right through the middle of the cabin, along the entire length of the hold, was the barge's massive keelson block. It protruded above the floor and provided a convenient shelf for tourist brochures and display stands.

Only two booths were occupied. A young couple sat in one midway along the length of the cabin. An elderly man with snow-white hair occupied the other. He was getting to his feet with the aid of a stick. The man's face held Peter's attention. He had seen the expression in prison—and recognized it in himself. It was the face of someone crushed by life; someone in deep grief.

Peter paused on the steps to give the elderly man time to limp up to the counter. The woman standing behind it began to operate the hissing pipes and taps of a coffee machine to make the man his drink. Peter queued behind him.

When the woman handed the man his coffee, he smiled his thanks and limped back to his booth. Peter could tell the man had been crying—the tops of his cheeks were wet.

The barista reached out to him to protest that he had not paid for his drink. Peter put his finger to his lips and signaled for her to keep quiet. "I'll pay for it," he said softly, "and may I have a cappuccino, please."

When told how much the drinks would cost, Peter was appalled. He resolved to drink just half his coffee and let the rest linger while he worked out what he could say to his probation officer. He would need to say something convincing to give her assurance that he could manage life outside of prison.

After fifteen minutes of unproductive thinking, Peter saw the elderly man get up, and limp his way over to where he sat. "Forgive me for disturbing you," he said, "but the waitress has just informed me that you paid for my coffee. I am deeply embarrassed that was necessary. I can get a little forgetful at times. I want to say thank you, and buy you a coffee in return."

"That's not necessary, but to be truthful, I'd welcome another coffee. I've let my last one go cold."

The man glanced at Peter's half-filled cup. "Cappuccino?"

Peter nodded.

Calling over to the young woman behind the counter, the elderly man said, "May we have two more cappuccinos, please?"

The woman replied, "You need to place your order at the counter, and then wait for your coffees."

At this point, a large man came through from the kitchen behind her. Peter immediately noticed three things about him: an impressive girth, a black piratical beard, and a booming voice. "What on earth are you thinking, woman?" he yelled. "Can't you see that he walks with a stick? It's Alex. He's a regular here." The pirate shifted his attention to the elderly man, and said, "Of course…" but he got no further. The waitress interrupted him.

"Don't you shout at me! Who do you think you are? You told me the rules. Don't blame me if I'm just doing what I'm told."

It became apparent that the pirate was not a man to bear such retorts. He shouted, "You daft woman. Haven't you a brain in your head? Don't you have eyes? Can't you show some initiative— perhaps even some care? Good grief—" Again, he was interrupted.

"I'm not taking this sort of crap from anyone."

"You will, if you want any future on this barge."

"I don't want a future in this bloody barge. You can't treat me like this. I quit."

To which the pirate shouted, "Good riddance! You were only employed because of your husband, anyway."

At this point, a gaunt young man dressed in a dirty white chef's uniform came out from the kitchen. The female hellcat continued to scream, "And he quits too. Where I go, he goes." She continued to hurl insults at the pirate suggesting things that were anatomically improbable. When she'd run out of words, she reached under the counter for a shoulder bag, grabbed her husband, and marched to the steps. Once there, she turned, spat on the floor, and propelled her man up the stairs.

A deathly hush hung in the air.

"Sorry about that, Alex," said the pirate. "I'll get you your cappuccinos. Just give me a moment to wipe the floor."

As the large man wiped the floor, the young tourist couple edged past, and fled up the stairs.

The elderly man who was with Peter began to apologize. "Lenny, I am sorry to be the cause of this. I didn't…"

The pirate waved him into silence. "Forget it, Alex," he rumbled. "She was hopeless. And to tell you the truth, her husband wasn't much of a cook. However, it does leave me with a problem. I've got people coming for lunch in a couple of hours—including you and Beth, incidentally, but I've got no cook."

The old man pursed his lips. "We can easily go elsewhere,

Lenny." He turned, faced Peter, and held out his hand. "Perhaps I'd better introduce myself. I'm Alex Whitman." He pointed to the pirate. "And this is Lenny, the owner of the *Phoenix*."

Peter shook Alex's hand and nodded to Lenny. "I'm Peter Jacobs."

As Lenny busied himself behind the counter making the coffees, Peter and Alex sat down together in a booth. Peter noticed that Alex was not as old as he first thought, probably in his early sixties. It was the snow-white hair, thin frame, and limp that aged him.

"And what made you pay for my coffee, Peter?" The man's candid eyes appraised him.

"Um, you looked distracted—as if you were in some sort of distress." Peter paused, then added, "I hope whatever it is resolves well."

"Thank you. My twin brother has just died. We were quite close. I came here so I could get out and do some thinking."

"I'm sorry for your loss." It was the standard phrase, but he didn't know what else to say. He sought to disguise his embarrassment by asking, "And what made you buy me a coffee? You didn't have to do that."

Alex smiled. "You looked to be distracted and in some sort of distress. I, too, hope whatever it is, is soon resolved."

Peter dropped his gaze, remembering his shame. Eventually he said, "Mine is a difficult story. Let's just say that I'm looking for a way ahead, and can't seem to find it."

Above them, a gust of wind caused the barge's rigging to thrum. The sound reverberated through the hull.

Alex nodded. "Well, Peter, I am a stranger who can be no threat to you. There is nothing you could tell me that would either shock me or make me regret buying you a coffee. So, if it's helpful to talk about it, please do."

Peter kept his head down and said nothing.

Alex sighed. "If it's grief—there is always hope. And if it's shame, then it can be a springboard for change." He shrugged. "Alternatively, you can allow both to destroy you. It's a choice."

Peter was shocked. He was shocked that he was so transparent to this man; shocked that he was understood. A flash of anger flared up. Words were easy. What if Alex knew the truth? Would he be so kind then? Life was not pretty; he was not pretty. He threw a bitter challenge into the stranger's face, one calculated to make him back off.

"Yesterday, I came out of Belmarsh Prison where I served twenty-six months for manslaughter."

"Then you can look forward to a whole new beginning. I wish you well, Peter. Do you take sugar?"

Alex's response stunned Peter. He had shown his worst side and been met with grace. The rebuff he had engineered had not at all resulted in what he expected. He was speechless…and understood he'd been given something very precious: the gift of acceptance. Bewildered, he lowered his head.

Lenny came across with their coffees and failed to notice the tenor of the conversation going on between Peter and Alex. He placed the coffees in front of them and, unbidden, eased his bulk into the seat next to Alex. "Dammit! What the hell am I going to do? I've put a call through to the agency and no chefs are available. They might have someone next week. Fat lot of use that is! I'll have to shut the *Phoenix* down." He put his head in his hands.

Peter was glad of the chance to change the subject. He contemplated Lenny's doleful form and asked, "Lenny, how much would you pay for a good chef with formal training and five years' experience in a good restaurant?"

Lenny glanced up and said, "Anything they wanted right now."

"Seriously."

"Seriously?" Lenny appeared to reflect on this for a moment, and then gave Peter a more carefully considered figure. "That would be for cooking lunch six days a week and dinner four days a week."

"Do you have menus for both lunch and dinner?"

Lenny waved at the counter. "Behind the counter. What's on your mind?"

Peter slid out of his seat and said, "I'll be back in ten minutes." So saying, he collected two menus, and ran up the stairs. Once on the dock, he made his way along St. Katharine's Way to 'The Anchor.'

Peter didn't even need to go inside the pub; Kym was outside wiping tables. She recognized him, and waited for him with hands on hips—her expression hovering between defiance and curiosity.

Peter did not waste any time. "Hello, feisty one."

"What do you want?"

Peter handed her the two menus. "Can you cook most of this stuff?"

Kym looked at the menus scornfully. "It's basic crap. Anyone can cook it. Why do you ask?"

"Would you like a permanent job on the *Phoenix* as chef, cooking lunch six days a week and dinner four days a week?"

"What's the pay?"

When he mentioned the salary, Kym whistled.

"Are you serious?"

"Deadly."

"When would I start?"

"In two minutes."

"Seriously?"

"Seriously."

Kym's answer was decisive enough. She took off her apron and walked inside the pub. Peter followed behind her. Kym marched up to a balding man behind the bar and thrust the dishcloth and apron at him. "Freddy, I quit." Without waiting for a reply, she turned, and walked outside.

Back at the *Phoenix*, Peter introduced Kym to an incredulous Lenny. Terms were agreed, and Kym immediately went behind the counter to the kitchen. She'd only been there ninety seconds before she yelled, "This place is filthy. I need a day this week where everything shuts down and we clean this place from top to bottom. And your food selection sucks."

Lenny stared at her in disbelief.

Peter cleared his throat. "I think you'll get used to her in time." He paused before continuing. "There is, um…a small price to pay for taking Kym on as your chef."

"What's that?" said Lenny, without turning his head.

"That you take me on as a waiter."

Lenny turned and stared at him.

"From what little I've seen, I can vouch for his people skills," said Alex.

Lenny looked Peter up and down.

Peter immediately regretted saying anything. *Be invisible.*

Silence.

"Well then, young fella, you'd better learn to operate Big Bertha here." Lenny pointed to the coffee machine. "Follow me."

Peter stayed where he was and eyed the steps—*escape.*

Chapter 6

The first coffee Peter made was for his parole officer, Margaret Templeton. She'd come into the *Phoenix's* great cabin, looked around the booths, and saw all were empty except for Alex. She'd then hailed Peter and inquired if a message had been left for her from a Peter Jacobs.

Peter admitted that he was, in fact, Peter Jacobs.

She looked him up and down as he stood in his black apron. The apron had a line drawing of a Thames barge on it, making it obvious that he had some connection with the *Phoenix*.

"You work here?"

"Um, yes. I think so."

She furrowed her brow and gestured to a booth where they might talk.

Lenny looked across to him and raised an eyebrow.

Peter's newfound confidence suddenly evaporated. He was convinced that once Lenny learned the truth about his past, his employment would come to a sudden end. However, Peter was equally sure that he wanted to work without the fear of his employer finding out about his past. Drawing a deep breath, he said in a voice for all to hear, "Lenny, Alex, this is my parole officer, Margaret Templeton."

Lenny growled, "Parole Officer? You didn't tell me anything about being on parole, young Peter."

Peter looked down.

Alex nodded. "Would it change anything, Lenny?"

"My oath it would." Lenny turned to Peter and growled. "How do I know I can trust you?" Silence hung in the room. Lenny continued on, brutally. "Can I trust you?"

"Yes," said Peter, not looking up.

"What were you 'done' for?"

At this point, Ms. Templeton protested, "He is not obliged to tell you, and I don't think..."

Alex put his finger to his lips and said, "Do go on, Peter."

"I got into a fight. Someone was killed."

"Did the other guy start the fight?" demanded Lenny.

"Yes, but he was drunk."

"Were you drunk?"

"I was slightly drunk."

"Is drink a problem for you?"

"No. I will never drink alcohol again."

"Is losing your temper a problem for you?"

"No."

"Then make the lady a bloody coffee, boy."

For the second time that morning, Peter felt a surge of relief and liberation. It left him giddy and grateful beyond words.

Once the coffee was made, Peter sat opposite Ms. Templeton.

She told him that he was required to meet with her every month for six months, and that his continued release was contingent on him not breaking the law. He would also need to convince her that he could manage life outside of prison. This meant either getting a job or being enrolled in an approved training course. If that wasn't enough, he was required to find stable accommodation—a place where he could be contacted.

Peter was lost for words. It was all too much. He looked away from his parole officer to the massive deck beams above him. The one above his head had the barge's registered tonnage carved into it. The barge shifted and creaked like a living thing.

Lenny had sat himself opposite Alex in a booth across the aisle, trying not to be obvious in his eavesdropping.

Ms. Templeton continued remorselessly, "How much money do you have access to?"

"Twenty-four pounds and sixty pence."

"I don't mean in your wallet, I mean your entire savings."

"Twenty-four pounds and sixty pence."

There was silence.

Peter was surprised to see Alex struggle to his feet and step over to his booth. Turning to the parole officer, Alex said. "Excuse me, ma'am." He then turned to Peter. "Did you pay for my coffee knowing that was all the money you had?"

Peter nodded.

Alex shook his head, turned around, and returned to his seat.

Ms. Templeton said, with just a hint of acerbity, "May I ask you not to interrupt, gentlemen. This is a private and confidential conversation."

Peter acknowledged that the restricted space of *Phoenix's* hold did not make private conversations very easy.

The parole officer turned back to Peter. "Am I to understand that you have a job in this, er, cafe?"

"Yes, ma'am, he does," said Lenny from across the aisle, completely unfazed by the parole officer's remonstration.

"How much do you earn?" she continued, affecting to ignore Lenny.

"I have no idea." Turning to Lenny, Peter asked, "Lenny, how much do I earn in a week?"

Lenny got up, motioning to Alex to join him as they both sat down in the booth next to the parole officer. Ms. Templeton rolled her eyes in exasperation.

"It seems to me, ma'am," said Lenny, "that a whole lot of things would get done quicker if we were involved—considering that we are involved."

The parole officer pretended not to hear him and continued to question Peter. "Where are you going to live? You can't afford to keep living at the backpacker's hostel."

Peter dropped his head. "I'll manage. I have a job, and I will find something I can afford. My expenses won't be great."

She continued, "It's not just finances. You need to be with people who care."

Although Ms. Templeton had meant to challenge Peter with this remark, it was soon evident that her challenge had found a very different target.

"Sorry to interrupt again," said Alex. "Peter may not have told you yet, but he has been offered accommodation, at minimal rent, in a spacious riverside flat in Bermondsey just across the river. It is the home of a professor who works at the British Museum." He turned to Lenny. "Lenny here can vouch for him."

The parole officer frowned. "Can you?" she asked.

"I sure can," said Lenny with a grin.

"And who is this professor?"

Alex gave a deprecating cough. "It's me." He turned to Peter. "But only if you want to. What do you think?"

Peter opened his mouth in disbelief, unsure if he'd heard rightly; not daring to think such a possibility could exist.

Alex smiled. "I take it from that vacant expression, that you are saying yes." Turning to Ms. Templeton, he continued, "Peter can be contacted at my flat on Bermondsey Wall East." He gave the details.

At that point, a crowd of lunchtime visitors started to clatter down the steps. Lenny brought his meeting with Ms. Templeton to an abrupt close. "Peter, get to work. Settle people in. Get orders. Do drinks first, then offer the menu. Go, go, go."

Peter stood up in disbelief. Lenny pushed him into the aisle.

Peter drew in a deep breath and made himself face his first challenge. After two years of keeping a low profile and hiding in shame, he was now required to engage with people. He doubted he could do it and cursed himself for his own headstrong folly in thinking that he might.

Alex seemed to sense Peter's hesitation. "Just be yourself, Peter, and don't worry. You may not know it yet, but you're good with people."

With severe misgivings, Peter headed for the counter.

It wasn't long before the job swept him along, and he found himself too busy to be nervous.

Just occasionally, he felt the need to glance at Alex in order to maintain his courage. The professor was still sitting with Margaret Templeton. He was staring distractedly at the table whilst she spoke. When he lifted his head, the harsh neon light showed a face lined with grief. Yet, on seeing Peter, he smiled, and gave a nod of encouragement.

The parole officer was making it clear that she was not happy. She scowled at Lenny behind the counter.

Lenny beamed at her sweetly and said, "You're a very attractive lady, Ms. Templeton. Are you married?"

A blushing Ms. Templeton hurried toward the steps.

The lunchtime custom at the *Phoenix* was busier than expected and, notwithstanding the Herculean efforts of Kym in the kitchen, orders soon started to fall behind. Peter waited on tables and, when he could, helped Kym in the kitchen. Lenny attended to the drinks, dividing his attention between the till, the bar, and the coffee machine. Alex made his way behind the counter and offered to help Lenny by grinding fresh coffee and stacking the dishwasher.

Peter was in the process of collecting plates when another set of feet could be heard coming down the stairs into the cabin. He looked up in time to see two shapely legs. The rest of her was wrapped in a short coat—but her face was not. And it was beautiful. She had finely chiseled features and perfectly curving lips. Auburn hair fell over her shoulders. Peter suddenly felt awkward and out of his depth. He forced a smile. "Welcome to the *Phoenix*, ma'am. Are you on your own? I mean—sorry—how many seats are you looking for?"

The woman smiled back. "I'm meeting someone for lunch, but I'm a little late. He will have booked a table under the name of..." At that moment, Peter, still an amateur at holding six empty plates, was unable to stop a potato, liberally covered in gravy, from falling onto the woman's shoe.

Handicapped by his perilously stacked plates, Peter was powerless to do anything. "Oh, I'm so sorry. I'll get a cloth."

The woman reached over, took a paper napkin from a vacated table, and wiped her shoe. Then she retrieved the errant potato and put it back on Peter's pile of plates. "All sorted," she said.

He stammered his thanks and made his way back to the kitchen.

———

Beth watched the wide shoulders of the waiter as he walked away. But it was the memory of his face that she particularly dwelt on —the serious expression, the brown eyes, and hair that was far too long.

She hauled herself back to reality and began to look for Alex amongst the booths.

"Over here, Beth," called Alex.

Beth was amazed to find the professor doing duty behind the counter at the end of the barge. She hurried over to him.

"There's a bit of an emergency on at the moment," explained Alex. "There's been a complete change of staff in the last two hours, and I have been pressed into service. Both Peter and I are a little unpracticed at it, I'm afraid."

The handsome waiter came out of the kitchen door with arms full of desserts.

Alex nodded toward him. "Oh, and this is Peter, by the way. He's just been employed here."

She looked at him and smiled.

"Hello," he said, before hurrying on.

A call came from behind the kitchen door. "Hey, Pete, move your arse back here when you can. I need some more salad chopped up."

Alex continued, "And that's Kym, also employed here as of a few hours ago." He leaned forward and confided, "She's terrifying."

Beth noticed the smudge of ground coffee on the professor's cheek and shook her head in disbelief.

Another call came from the kitchen. "Hey, Alex, tell Peter I need him. Now!"

Alex looked up and surveyed the cabin. Beth also turned and saw Peter only halfway through clearing a table, with some new customers standing beside him.

"Oh dear," said Alex quietly.

Seeing the impossibility of the situation, Beth pushed through into the kitchen and said to the dark-haired woman at the bench, "Hi, Kym, I'm Beth. Not much experience, but willing to do the donkeywork. Where do I begin?"

"Darling, you're a beautiful sight. There's the lettuce. And there are the tomatoes, onions, avocados, and capsicums. Put a sprinkle of basil on the top. Seven plates of salad, please ready for lasagna."

"What's a capsicum?"

"A pepper; use the red peppers."

"Right."

She set to work.

Two hours later, with the last customer gone and the kitchen in some semblance of order, Lenny, Alex, Kym, and Beth sat around a table exhausted. Lenny brought over a chilled bottle of champagne and a fist full of glasses. "I hereby absolve you all of any sensible responsibilities this afternoon."

Beth took her glass gratefully. "So this is what a girl can expect when she's invited to lunch with you, Prof."

Alex gave a tired smile. "I promise I'll make it up to you."

She noticed, now the excitement was over, his face had become pale and haggard.

"Complimentary meal whenever you want it," said Lenny. "You guys were amazing. Kym, you're a champion. If you leave me now, I'll cut my wrists."

"Just keep paying me, darling. But I'm not having this again. We need more staff."

Lenny took a swig of champagne. "Nah. It's just bad luck that two businesses decided to drop in unannounced for group lunches. I doubt it will happen again."

"Trust me, matey: it will if I've got anything to do with it."

Beth stole a covert look at Peter, who was still behind the main counter. He seemed a bit edgy, out of place, and at a loss for what to do. She heard him say, "Boss, do you want me to scrape together a few nibbles to share?" He turned to Kym. "Would that be okay, Kym?"

Kym leaned back and stretched. "Don't leave a mess."

"Brilliant idea," said Lenny.

A few minutes later, Peter came in from the kitchen carrying a dish of antipasto.

Lenny raised his eyebrows, nodded his thanks, and grabbed a hunk of pickled eggplant. Speaking with his mouth full, Lenny asked Peter, "Where's your drink?"

Peter stammered, "I, er, didn't know I could get myself one."

"For goodness sake, Pete! Grab a drink whenever you need one. Don't ever ask again." Shaking his head, he continued, "I'll tell you soon enough if I think you're taking liberties."

Beth wasn't sure she understood the context of what was going on or why Peter was so diffident. *A strange man.* Nonetheless, she was grateful for his antipasto. She was hungry.

Peter fetched himself an iced tea from the fridge cabinet and sat down. For such a powerfully built person, he contrived to be as inconspicuous as possible. She wondered why.

Beth was squeezed between the professor's lean frame and Lenny's significant bulk.

The conversation that followed came easily from Lenny and Kym, hesitantly from Peter, and barely at all from Alex.

Eventually, it was time to leave. Beth looked at her watch and announced, "Sadly, I have to get back to work." Turning to Alex, she continued, "Do you still want to catch up, Alex?"

Alex brought himself back from where his mind had taken him with obvious effort. "Er, yes please. I am sorry. When are you next free?"

"I can come around to your place after work on Friday?"

"Come for dinner."

She nodded, gathered her handbag, and stood up.

Alex stood up with her and accompanied her to the foot of the stairs. Before she could climb them, Alex laid a restraining hand on her arm. He took an envelope from his inside pocket and gave it to her. "You'll find some hieroglyphics in there. Can you tell me exactly what they say and anything else you think may be significant about what you see?"

She furrowed her brow. "Sure." She made to open the envelope, but the professor forestalled her.

"Later. And can I ask you to keep it to yourself? It's fairly important that you tell no one at this stage."

She gave Alex a searching look. "Okay," she said slowly.

"Thanks, Beth."

She leaned forward and gave him a kiss on the cheek. For some reason she added, "Please take care."

Peter watched Beth disappear up the stairs with a strange sense of loss.

Alex, readying his walking stick at the foot of the stairs, called back to him. "Peter, I'll pick you up from here at 5pm the day after tomorrow. That will give me two days to sort things out." Then he turned and climbed the steps.

Peter turned back to Lenny and asked, "What's wrong with Alex's legs?"

"No idea. He doesn't talk about it."

What a day it had been. Peter looked around the cabin. "What now?"

Kym stood up and prodded him in the chest. "Your day has just begun, old mate. You have some serious scrubbing to do."

Lenny started to smile until Kym aimed her stubby finger at him, "And you and I are going to look at this crappy menu, make it simpler, tastier, and more nutritious. I want to double your food budget, double your prices, and double your profit. With limited space like you have, you can't afford to sell low-budget meals. We need to go boutique—seriously upmarket."

Lenny turned to Peter. "I blame you. I used to be master of this vessel."

But he didn't seem too unhappy with the cruel hand life had dealt him.

Chapter 7

Ernest Wheeler looked up as Carl stood in front of his desk. He nodded, giving him permission to speak.

"They've found it," said Carl. His level of animation never rose beyond the demeanor of one of Madam Tussaud's waxworks, but there was a hint of triumph in his eyes.

Wheeler allowed himself a smile. "Well, that was easier than expected. I take it that the reported position was fairly accurate."

"Yes, only about half a mile out. It was behind the Margate Hook. The mud banks have moved over the years and she's under about six feet of silt. They'll start sucking it away in four days time."

"Tell *Grayling* I want them to report every day at 9pm from now on. They will report to you. You brief me."

Carl nodded. "They need to take on some equipment. Our people have organized for them to use the wharf at *HMS President*— nice and private."

"Keep me informed."

As Carl left, Wheeler pushed his chair out from the desk and savored what he'd heard. They had found the *Beatrice*.

At last!

The ship had rounded the North Foreland and entered the

Thames Estuary on a foul, stormy night, on October 13th, 1838.
The storm had battered the ship and driven her onto a sandbank
where she was pounded to pieces. There was only one survivor—
Edward Burles, personal clerk to the archaeologist, Richard Vyse.
He'd managed to swim across the Gore Channel to the rocky beach
at Birchington. Burles had not survived long. He died a few days
later—probably from exposure and exhaustion.

The thing that scandalized the residents of Birchington at the
time was that Burles refused to reveal his name. He simply gave his
initials. The villagers had therefore buried him in a pauper's grave
on unconsecrated ground outside the village. However, before he
died, he'd penned a brief note asking that it be delivered to an
address in London.

That note now lay in the vault behind Wheeler's new desk. In an
untidy, spidery hand, Burles had written, *The stone, lost one mile off
Birchington*. It was signed simply, *EB*.

Burles' wife had received a house and a generous pension for the
rest of her life. She always supposed it had come from her husband's
employer, Richard Vyse.

The streets of London wore their scruffiness as a badge of honor.
The buildings in any particular part of London often shared the
same history and were built of similar materials. Like school
uniforms, they advertised each other's identity. Peter couldn't help
but contrast this with his hometown of Perth that reflected the
fiercely independent character of its people. There, every house was
different. It was as if they refused to talk to each other. Mock Tudor,
Queen Anne, colonial, and contemporary stood side by side,
shouting their independence.

Peter got off the bus and made his way along the grimy streets
toward the docks. So much had happened yesterday that he wasn't
at all sure he could believe it. He had trouble believing that the relationships he'd formed yesterday would still be intact today. And
there was also the misgiving about sharing a flat with someone he

hardly knew. What he did know was that Alex was unlike anyone he'd ever met.

Peter's own experience with his father had left him wary of older men. So why had he agreed to share accommodation with Alex? As he reflected on it, he decided that he was not so much wary of older men, rather, of those wielding power. Alex exuded gentleness and understanding. But paradoxically, Alex did it in a way that seemed to empower him. It was bewildering.

He made his way around the edge of the dock until he could see the *Phoenix* with its impressive mast and rigging. Lenny was on deck wrestling with a huge pile of canvas. As Peter approached, Lenny leaned wearily against the mizzenmast.

"Need a hand?" asked Peter.

"This isn't strictly café work."

"Then let's agree not to be strict about anything."

"You'll get filthy."

Peter saw that Lenny was covered from top to toe in brown stains. He looked as if he had crawled out of a primeval swamp.

"Will it wash?"

"Yeah, but it's messy. The sails are preserved with ocher and cod oil. It comes off onto everything. If you really want to help, grab some overalls from under the bunk in the stern cuddy. You'll find the door behind the stairs. Whew! I'm knackered."

Peter crossed the gangplank and was going downstairs when Lenny called out, "Keep out of Kym's way." He pointed to a white van parked on the quayside. Yellow hoses spilled out of the back of it down into the fore hatch. "She's got some industrial steam cleaning mob down there. And this afternoon, we're getting a new fridge installed."

"I take it we are closed for business today."

"Yeah. But we've got plenty to do."

Down below, Peter could hear the hissing sound of a steam cleaner at work. Kym was behind the counter, throwing things into boxes.

"You seem happy in your work," he said. "I'm helping Lenny on deck for a bit. Let me know if you need a hand with anything down here."

"Nice of you to turn up," Kym said, ignoring the fact that Peter was, in fact, an hour early for work. She waved him away. "Buzz off. But I'll need a hand to get rid of these boxes in a bit."

Peter nodded and pushed through a door into the stern cuddy.

The tiny cabin had old-fashioned wooden bunks built in on either side. A chip-burning stove stood between them, its flue going up through the deck-head. The cabin smelled of tar and linseed oil.

Peter stripped down, donned some paint-splattered overalls, and padded back on deck in bare feet—careless of the cool spring weather. He was soon helping Lenny heave the heavy canvas sail out to the mizzenmast where he lashed it into place.

The barge's massive, spade-like rudder streamed behind her shapely stern. Peter looked around him. "Do you actually sail this thing, or is all this rigging stuff just for show?"

"Of course she sails!" Lenny snorted. "Well, to be honest, she sails once a year in the annual London barge race. She's a bit creaky, but she still goes like the clappers on a beam reach."

Peter learned that the *Phoenix's* engines had broken down two years before, and the barge now had to be towed through the lock into the Thames for the race. Evidently, it was quite a complicated business. Peter was pleased to think that the barge could still sail. "It must cost a fortune to keep her afloat," he said.

Lenny tugged at the final lashing. "Sailing is like standing under a cold shower tearing up one hundred pound notes." He grinned. "The only thing that makes it workable is that I get my berth for free, as I'm considered to be a tourist attraction." He pointed across to the cafés on the wharf. "If you compare my costs with renting a café, it's about the same—even if I have to do a lot more work." He shook his head. "Six years ago, I was in marine insurance…but I burned out and lost my marriage. I decided on a sea change and bought this boat." He slapped the mizzenmast. "Now I work twice as hard but, curiously, don't burn out."

At morning tea, they sat around a table in one of the booths to plan the rest of the day. Kym asked, "Do either of you guys know your way around a fruit and veg market?"

"I used to work in one," said Peter.

"Brilliant. You and me—5:30 tomorrow morning. Here. We're going to suss out the markets." She turned to Lenny. "Can I take your van tonight? I'm going to need it."

Lenny nodded. "I sure won't be using it at that time of day, lass."

"I'm not sure about the buses that time in the morning. Do they run that early?" asked Peter.

Lenny shrugged. "No idea." He scratched his beard. "The easiest thing is for you to stay aboard the *Phoenix* tonight. It's pretty rough, but there are blankets under one of the bunks. You should be comfortable enough."

Peter accepted gratefully, glad for the chance to avoid another night at the hostel.

Kym prodded Peter's chest. "I need your body this afternoon, mate. You need to help me carry the cooking gear we're going to buy."

Lenny looked over the top of his coffee mug down the length of the main cabin. "What about this seating area? If we're going upmarket, do we need to do anything with it?"

Kym and Lenny started swapping suggestions and arguing.

During a lull in their conversation, Peter ventured, "I'd never seen the *Phoenix* until yesterday, so I think I can tell you what it was about the barge that caught my imagination."

This comment succeeded in getting Lenny's attention. "What?"

Peter searched for the right words. "I…loved the ambience—the whole wooden boat thing. So if you're redecorating, I reckon less is best. Let the boat sell itself. Get rid of all the kitsch, the pseudo-nautical stuff, and keep as much natural wood around the place as possible."

Peter tapped the massive wooden keel block. "I'd clean and renovate this with buffing oil and turn it into a feature." He turned around. "I'd go for top quality tablecloths and settings. And why not get rid of the neon lights and put a small oil lamp in each booth.

The soft light would create a sense of intimacy and make the varnished wood look great." He smiled. "Intimacy is what this place does best."

Silence followed.

Eventually, Kym said, "Wow!"

Lenny cocked his head and nodded appreciatively. "Peter, old son; your budget is one thousand pounds. You work with me, but essentially, you're in charge of the main cabin. You've got three days." He leaned back. "That goes for both of you. We need to be back in business in three days."

Kym and Lenny left the *Phoenix* for their respective homes, leaving Peter alone in a world of boats, timber, chaos, and new beginnings. He listened to the boat halyards tapping against the masts above the hum of the city traffic and felt he'd been reborn into a whole new world.

Taking advantage of his freedom, Peter decided to explore the local area. He ambled along Mews Street and then turned left down St. Katharine's Way. The road ran parallel to the Thames.

Although the walk was interesting enough, he was frustrated at not being able to see through to the river. Buildings, usually converted warehouses, stood in the way. All of them seemed to be made of the same brown brick. The five-story warehouses typically had car garages on the ground floor and unrelieved flat brick walls above, pierced by unfussy windows. Peter was pleased to see that the renovators had made no attempt to hide their utilitarian origins.

As he passed the pillared portico of Devon House, he was able to peer through the glass doors to a courtyard and beyond to the Thames which glided lazily on its way. He continued past a notice board and read that the buildings behind were those of *HMS President*, the shore base of the Volunteer Naval Reserve.

As the lingering London twilight gave way to night, the brick buildings, once so charming, began to look a little more sinister. Further on, Peter saw an alleyway leading down to the river. On the far bank, he could see the lights of Bermondsey. He would be living over there with Alex tomorrow. It was hard to imagine.

He walked down the alleyway, but soon found it blocked by an iron gate. Gates: they had defined his life for two years. He gave it a shove. To his surprise, it opened.

Peter made his way through and continued down the alleyway until it ended at a set of steps leading down to the water.

Sadly, the view he had anticipated of Tower Bridge was obscured by the buildings of *HMS President*. He glanced at the two pontoons beside him that pushed out into the Thames. A smart-looking yacht was moored against the nearest pontoon behind a twin-hulled salvage vessel.

The view across the Thames, glittering with a thousand city lights, was enchanting. He sat down, still struggling to believe he was part of it all.

Eventually, the evening chill persuaded him to move on. As he stood, he caught sight of some movement by the nearest pier. The nose of an inflatable dinghy poked out from between the stern of the yacht and the salvage vessel.

A man, clad in black, was kneeling on one of the inflatable's sides attending to something on the stern of the yacht. After a few moments, the man slid across to the other side of the inflatable. Then he stood up and peered through the scuppers of the research vessel behind him.

What happened next seemed surreal. A dark figure loomed above the man and swung at him with what looked to be a metal pipe. There was a sickening thump and a splash, as the man in the inflatable fell into the water. It all happened so quickly that Peter wasn't sure if he had seen it at all. The only evidence was the gentle lapping of the water and the bobbing of the inflatable.

Peter immediately kicked off his shoes, tore off his jacket and jeans, and dived into the water—grateful that his childhood in Australia meant he could swim like a fish. The icy water stung like a thousand bees. He forced himself to ignore the shock and powered across the thirty yards to the inflatable. A body in a wetsuit was floating beside it. Peter turned the body over to get the man's face out of the water. He hooked an arm around the grab-line on the inflatable and began administering CPR.

Head back, pinch the nose, breathe slowly, one breath every fifteen seconds; lessons from a lifetime ago.

Suddenly, the man started to cough and retch. Peter turned him sideways so he wouldn't choke, holding him against his chest.

Above him came a shout—and something crashed against his head.

There was an instant of agony, and then everything swirled into blackness.

Peter fell in and out of consciousness—only dimly aware of what was happening around him. Two figures were hauling him backward into the inflatable. Unconscious again.

A powerful outboard engine. Pounding. And cold. So cold. Unconscious.

Dragged out. Lifted into the back of a van. Brief drive. Mostly conscious.

Lifted out.

Two huge walls on either side of him. Was he back in prison? A prison warder in a new uniform. Green. Brief argument. Calls of "Get them to sick bay" and "Gizmo, get the MO."

A needle.

Relief.

Chapter 8

Peter woke in a darkened room with a chink of daylight streaming in between floral curtains. *Very strange.* The sheets were white. Prison sheets were green nylon. He was also dressed in pajamas he'd never seen before, and a bandage was wrapped around his head. He eased his feet over the edge of the bed and placed them on the floor. His head was sore, but not impossibly so. Emboldened by this discovery, he stood up and made his way gingerly to the window and drew the curtain aside.

He'd expected to see bars across the window. But he didn't. Across a well-tended lawn, William the Conqueror's iconic White Tower reared upward into a perfectly blue spring sky. He could see the characteristic hats on top of the mini-towers at each corner. The idiosyncrasies of history had resulted in three of them being square in shape whilst the fourth was round. Realization dawned on him. He was inside the Tower of London.

The door behind him opened, and an army officer walked in. "Hello," he said. "I'm Captain James Tremelling, the medical officer at the Tower. How are you feeling?"

"Sore."

"What's your name?" he said, tilting Peter's head back and shining a medical light into his eyes.

"Peter Jacobs."

"Well, Peter, look at my fingers and follow them with your eyes." Peter did as he was told. The doctor continued, "You've had a nasty bang on the head. Nothing broken as far as we can see. But you should really get an X-ray to make sure. I'll write you a chit. You should be kept under observation for a day or so."

"How did I get here?"

"Three of the yeomen brought you in. Evidently, you stopped one of them from drowning—but somehow, in the process, suffered a blow to the head." He compressed his lips. "I don't mind saying, there are a few unanswered questions. A couple of the yeomen are outside waiting to see you. I've told them to wait until you've had your breakfast. Scrambled eggs and toast okay?"

"Fine. Thank you." And then he remembered that he should be meeting Kym on the *Phoenix*. "What is the time?"

"Ten past eight."

Peter groaned. "Oh no! I need to make a phone call. I was meant to meet up with someone for an early morning job. She'll be furious. I need to ring the *Phoenix* in St. Katharine's Dock, but I don't know the number."

The medical officer walked to a phone on the bedside cabinet, and asked for a call to be put through to the *Phoenix*.

Lenny answered the phone. "Peter, where the hell are you? Kym has had to go on her own. She's none too pleased. What's going on?"

"Sorry, Lenny, I've had an accident and I...I honestly have no idea what happened. All I know is that I've been unconscious, and that the medical people at the Tower of London are looking after me. I'll get back just as soon as I can." He paused. "I'll put you on to someone who can tell you more than I can." Peter handed the phone to the medical officer. "Can you explain things?"

The medical officer took the phone and with a masterful economy of words, explained the situation.

"Captain James Tremelling, medical officer at the Tower of London speaking. Last night, your man dived into the Thames to save one of my men from drowning. In the process, he incurred a blow to the head that rendered him unconscious. We've patched him up, and he's spent the night with us. He is in no way to blame for his 'no-show' this morning and will be dropped off at his home once he has satisfied me there are no medical complications. He will need two days off work." He turned to Peter. "Where is your home?"

Peter's mind whirled. "The *Phoenix*," he stuttered. "The *Phoenix* actually is my home."

The doctor put the phone back to his mouth. "He'll be dropped off to you, probably mid-morning. Please keep an eye on him for a few days. Ring me if you have any concerns about his condition." He put the phone down and turned back to Peter. "Back to bed," he ordered. "Breakfast will be brought on a tray. Have a brief—and I mean brief—chat with the yeomen. Then I'll assess you again prior to possibly releasing you, and running you back to the *Phoenix*. And I'll rustle up some clothes for you. What size are your feet?"

After breakfast, Peter was thinking he should be getting up when there was a knock at the door.

It took a moment to realize that he needed to answer it. "Come in."

Two middle-aged men walked into the room—both had an unmistakable military bearing. One was tall, fair, and sported a ginger mustache. The other was short, dark, and barrel-chested.

The taller one introduced himself. "I'm Warrant Officer Dicky Chambers. This is Sergeant James Trent. Do you remember much about last night?"

Peter shook his head. The pain made him wince. "Up to a point, yes...but I don't remember how I got here."

"The chap you rescued from the drink last night was Geoff Osborne. He's doing well, but they've taken him to Queen Alexandra's Military Hospital for X-rays. He sends his regards and gratitude, by the way." Dicky Chambers pursed his lips. "We've had a bit of a talk with him this morning."

If ever there were men who exuded power in their bearing,

these two did. The sight of them was deeply disturbing. Peter dropped his eyes and said, "I'm Peter Jacobs." He paused, and then continued. "I'm glad your mate is okay." He leaned back into his pillows. "Can you tell me what's going on? The doctor said that we both bashed our heads." He risked a glance at the two men. "But I remember enough to know that's not quite true. So can you tell me what happened…and why I am here?"

Dicky Chambers grunted. "Well, lad, why don't you tell us what you do remember, and we'll decide what else you should know. Take your time." The soldier must have seen the apprehension in Peter's face because he went on, "And we'll do all we can to ensure nothing happens to you that you don't want to happen."

Peter looked at them both, drew a deep breath, and began slowly. "Well…I was sitting at the end of an alleyway, looking at the lights across the Thames, when I noticed a bloke in an inflatable dinghy doing something at the back of a yacht. He moved across to look at the boat behind it when someone standing above him attacked him. It was all very quick. Your mate got knocked into the water, and the attacker disappeared."

Peter half-closed his eyes and continued. "I slipped off my gear and swam across to find him face down in the water. I hooked my arm around him, and started doing mouth to mouth. Fairly soon, he came to. Then I heard a shout and was hit from above. I don't remember anything much after that."

Dicky Chambers maintained an impassive bearing as he listened. "That shout came from me. I was on watch on the end of the furthest pontoon. And Jimmy, here, was on watch at the other end. We brought you here." He stared at Peter for a while. "I suppose you ought to tell the police about this. It's pretty serious."

Peter said nothing.

"Are you planning to?" Chambers prompted.

Peter hesitated before saying, "I'd rather not, if I could avoid it."

"Why?"

Damn, damn, damn, damn. Aloud, he said, "Because I've just got out of Belmarsh, and I'm on probation. I'd rather not attract the police's attention right now."

"But you're a bloody hero. You've done nothing wrong," said the shorter of the two men in a voice made hoarse, presumably by years on a parade ground.

"Hmm. But it's violence. It makes the police nervous."

"What were you inside for?" asked the ginger mustache.

Peter closed his eyes in anguish. He'd had enough. His head hurt. Strangers were probing into that private part of his heart that caused him horror, nightmares, and shame. It was all too much. Then, appallingly, tears started to fill his eyes. He had not shed a tear for two years. He blinked them away savagely. A young man, leering and drunk—but so very much full of life—dead, at his hand. It was all too much.

Maybe it was the bashing on the head; maybe it was the care he had received from strangers over the last few days. Whatever it was, something inside him unlocked. He started to sob. His grief, so long bottled up, spilled out.

Trying to pull himself together, he sought to explain. "I killed a guy...in a fight. Killed. It was an accident—the worst mistake of my life. I killed someone. How do you live with that?" He wept.

The two men watched Peter behind stony faces.

Dicky Chambers said, not unkindly, "It's okay, son. We'll come back later." With that, they left.

It was a full fifteen minutes before Peter fought his tears to a standstill. He felt emotionally exhausted and ashamed at his lack of self-control. What on earth was happening to him?

There was a light knock on the door before it opened. A smiling face peered around the edge and asked in a soft Scottish brogue, "May I come in?"

For some reason Peter thought the comment absurd. No one ever asked permission to come into his room. Peter wanted to say, *No.*

"Yes, sure."

A middle-aged man about Peter's own size, with hair graying at the temples, came in. He wore a tweed jacket and a dog collar. "I'm Hamish O'Brien, chaplain at the Tower. I've brought you a dressing gown and some slippers." He smiled. "If you're up to it, slip them on and come with me to my quarters to choose some clothes that might fit. I'm told your name is Peter. Please call me Hamish."

When Peter stepped into the morning sunshine in his dressing gown, he found the experience surreal. It was a wonderful spring morning. Groups of tourists were making their way along the paths toward the White Tower and another building Peter didn't recognize.

Hamish pointed to the guards standing either side of its entrance. They were wearing red military coats crossed with straps, and wore massive bearskin hats. "That's the Waterloo Barracks. You go through there to the underground chambers if you want to see the Crown Jewels."

He kept up a running commentary designed, Peter suspected, to put him at ease. "They're guardsmen. Never call them soldiers unless you want to upset them. Proud lot. Ahead of you is The Chapel Royal of St. Peter ad Vincula, our parish church. We share it with a number of distinguished corpses: two wives of Henry the VIII, and Lady Jane Grey, who reigned for only nine days in 1553. They were all executed here."

Two black ravens strutted across Tower Green. "There really are ravens here then," commented Peter.

Hamish nodded. "They've had their wings clipped so they can't fly away. There are seven of them, and each has their own cage. They're cared for by the Ravenmaster, one of the Yeoman Warders." He smiled. "Superstition has it that when there are no longer ravens in the Tower, the White Tower and the kingdom will fall." He looked up at the White Tower. "At least the White Tower is still standing."

A Beefeater, dressed in his blue and scarlet uniform, was clutching a halberd and having his photograph taken with a group of tourists. Hamish acknowledged a salute from the Yeoman with a wave, and then pointed across the lawn. "My quarters are over there beside the Beauchamp Tower. I look out to the place where people had their heads chopped off." He grinned. "It reminds me of the important things of life."

Once they were inside Hamish's quarters, Peter was fitted out

75

with trousers, shirt, and a jumper from the chaplain's wardrobe. He even found shoes and socks that fitted.

"Thank you very much," said Peter, embarrassed by Hamish's generosity. "I'll get them cleaned and give them back as soon as I can. How do I contact you?"

Hamish fished out a business card and gave it to him.

Peter looked at the embossed card in amazement. "Chaplain to the Queen. Is that right?"

"Yes, I'm one of them."

"You actually meet with her?"

"Occasionally. She likes to use the chapel in the White Tower, The Chapel of St. John the Evangelist, for quiet reflection. It's one of her favorite places."

"Oh," said Peter weakly. He was beginning to feel he was living a tale from a child's storybook.

Hamish invited Peter to sit down in one of the armchairs. He sat in the other, crossed his legs, and said, "So, you've killed someone and are unsure if you can live with yourself."

Peter was completely unprepared for the straightforward way Hamish pointed to the demons in his heart.

Hamish went on. "I'm glad it matters to you. But I wonder if you can you tell me why it matters."

Still in shock, Peter stammered, "Of course it matters. People are...are special."

Hamish waited for more.

Peter swallowed and continued. "They have hopes, dreams, and potential. And people love them." He dropped his head. "I've caused a lot of grief."

"Plenty of people kill. Some of the men here have killed," said Hamish.

"But they are soldiers. It's their duty, their job."

"They are human beings like you. And the people they kill also have mothers that grieve."

"But my killing was a senseless, stupid, avoidable accident that happened when I was drunk."

"Then, I'm very sorry for you. It must be hard to bear." Hamish circled one foot in the air. "The question is, will you let your grief motivate you to live life well? I'm not talking about making atonement—that only traps us in the past; rather, use it to motivate you to pursue things which are good…and to pursue them courageously." He wagged a finger. "Every day you allow this tragedy to hold you back from living fully, you simply empower the evil more. Instead, you could choose to disempower it by grieving the past, forgiving yourself, and using the tragedy as motivation to make the best of the future."

"That's easy for you to say."

"It's perhaps easier for me to do," corrected Hamish.

"What do you mean?"

"When I do things stupid, evil, and hurtful, I'm able to access the grace and forgiveness of God." He shrugged. "All of us need God's grace."

They were interrupted by a knock at the door. Hamish got up to let in the two Yeoman Peter had met before. Hamish gestured toward them. "Peter, I gather you've already met Dicky Chambers and Jim Trent. They want a private chat. After that, they'll clear things with the MO and drive you home." He pointed to the card in Peter's hand. "Ring the number on the card for an appointment to see me again. Oh," he said, turning back, "come to the guardhouse. Don't queue with the tourists. Go straight to the counter."

With that, he stepped out the front door.

Peter watched him go and said to no one in particular, "Is he always like that?"

The man called Dicky said, "He's a good guy. Understands men." Clearing his throat, he continued. "Can we have a word before you leave?" The two of them sat down.

Peter nodded to the door. "You guys put him on to me, didn't you?"

"Yes."

Silence hung between them.

"Thanks."

Dicky Chambers nodded. "You're probably wondering what's going on." His mustache twitched as he spoke.

Peter waited for him to say more.

"There's a lot of internal-forces rivalry going on. There always has been and probably always will be." He shrugged. "When soldiers like us get put out to pasture, we've nothing better to do than get up to some mischief."

Peter raised his eyebrow.

Dicky Chambers cleared his throat. "Some years ago, the British military bought three sailing boats for adventure training. The one they gave to the army was called *Royal Blue*. The air force boat was called *Sky Blue,* and the navy's was called *Deep Blue*." He paused. "I don't know if you've noticed, but there are no naval guys in the Tower. That's because they swear loyalty to the navy rather than the Queen. As such, we tend to single them out for a hard time." Dicky stroked his mustache. "They put a nice naval crest on the stern of their boat, *Deep Blue*—which three of us thought would look a whole lot better hanging up behind the bar in our mess here at the Tower. Geoff had just unscrewed it, with Jim and myself acting as lookouts, when he was attacked." He compressed his lips. "So you can see, if you don't want to involve the police, we're happy to cooperate."

Jim Trent interrupted. "But it'll probably mean that some bastard is likely to get away with attacking you and Geoff."

Peter nodded—then wished he hadn't. His head pounded abominably. "First things first," said Peter. "Did you get the navy's crest?"

Dicky smiled, "Already installed in the mess."

"And, er...Geoff is okay?"

"Seems to be."

"Then let's drop it."

Jim said hoarsely, "Of course, this makes you an accomplice—which means you have a right to visit the mess now and again. We stick pretty close together...and you've saved Geoff's life."

"I appreciate that." Peter paused before continuing. "You've seen me weep like a baby, but I'm afraid there's worse to come." Peter looked up at them. "I killed a guy because I was drunk. So I don't drink. If you can cope with that, I'll come."

Jim expelled a slow breath and said, "Well that will make a novel change. Some of us would kill a guy for a drink. But if you promise to be good company and tell scurrilous tales as outrageous as our own, you're welcome." He nodded to the mustache. "Dicky's been a Regimental Sergeant Major, so he's a little bit crazy—we all need to be in order to live here."

Peter shook hands with them both. "Pleased to meet you. Thanks for saving my skin…and getting me help. I appreciate it."

"Let's get you home."

"Just one thing: Am I right in understanding that you guys find it difficult to get out into 'civvy street' from here?"

Dicky answered cautiously, "Yes. The men find it hard to get out and mix it with civilians." He shrugged. "We've become addicted to our own company and culture."

"Do you get a day off?"

"We're on a roster. Most of us try and have Wednesday off."

"Would it help if you guys booked out the *Phoenix*, the floating restaurant at St. Katharine's Dock, every fortnight on a Wednesday? If enough of you could fill it, I think we might be able to reserve half, even all of the seats, on the barge for you. I'd have to check with the boss. We could perhaps send you the menu, so you could put in your order the day before. That would make it easier for us and probably help with the price." He shrugged. "But only if it would help."

Dicky looked at Jim who, after a brief pause, gave the smallest of nods. Dicky said, guardedly, "Young Peter, that might be very useful. Work out what's possible, then talk to us again."

Chapter 9

Peter was dropped off at St. Katharine's Way, so he only had a short walk down the dock to the *Phoenix*. He felt self-conscious with his bandaged head—and because he was looking more respectable in his borrowed clothes than he'd ever looked in his life.

A morning breeze teased the water into a million sparkling lights, and the boats of the marina showed off their clean white livery. So much had changed and was changing. The *Phoenix* now represented a community in which he had a place and was valued. To his left, he could see the top of the Tower of London where Hamish had challenged him to take charge of his future.

As Peter pondered this, an ache for new possibilities started to push its way through the background noise of shame. He was not able to fully define it, let alone understand it. He was just conscious that something was spluttering into light. That's the thing about light, he mused, you only needed a little bit of it to completely change what had once been perfect darkness. New ideas were playing on his mind—teasing him with possibilities.

Kym was on the quayside beside the *Phoenix*, pulling boxes from Lenny's van. When she saw Peter walking toward her, she stood up and watched him with a derisive smile.

"You look like a fugitive from a Miss Marple film set. She flicked the lapel of his tweed jacket. "Quite the lord of the manor.""

"Got dressed up just for you, Kym."

"Yeah, sure." She pointed to the bandaged head. "How is it?"

"It's just a prop to win your sympathy."

"Save your breath, mate. My tastes are elsewhere. She reached up and held him by the jacket's lapels. "Which is just as well for you."

Peter smiled. "You're completely terrifying, you know."

Kym rolled her eyes, stepped onto the barge, and yelled down the forward hatchway, "Pete's here. Let's have smoko."

Peter caught Lenny's muffled reply from down below, "What the hell's 'smoko,' woman? There's no smoking on this boat."

"That's 'morning tea' to you Poms."

Lenny's head popped out of the forward hatch. He gave Peter an appraising look, then said, "Have you finished saving the world, boy?"

"I think the world conspired to save me, actually," said Peter.

"Are you fit to work?"

"Yes."

Lenny eyed him doubtfully. "The doc said you should have a few days off."

"I think I've wasted enough time. We've got two days to get things ready." He glanced at his watch. "I've got to see a solicitor in the city in two hours time, but I'll get changed and do an hour's work first."

Peter began to make his way down the main stairs before he paused and said, "By the way, could we handle a guaranteed booking for lunch every Wednesday fortnight for the Yeoman from the Tower. They could pre-book if we gave them the menu and get special rates."

"Bloody hell," said Lenny, shaking his head. "Boy's a genius."

Dressed again in Hamish's conservative clothes, Peter sat in front of

Mr. Collins of Hershey and Collins, Solicitors. He was a thin man in his sixties, who, despite an ashen skin that betrayed serious health problems, had a sparkle in his eyes.

"Hmm, interesting," he said. "Most interesting—an intriguing situation. Everything changes now you've been found." Mr. Collins looked up at Peter. "As you have no doubt been apprised, your father set up his will as an optional discretionary testamentary trust. This means that you don't have to pay much in the way of tax on your inheritance."

Collins tapped a pile of documents in front of him with his pen. "On the death of your father, his estate was wound up by his executor, his solicitor in Perth. Also on that date, the trust fund legally passed to the named trustee. That's you. However, as you had not been found, your executors were obliged to continue to manage the trust in a way they believed was in your best interest."

The solicitor pulled a face. "No doubt their costs will be considerable, but I have here a financial breakdown of their activities in the last two years." He pointed to a table of figures with his pen. "You will be relieved to hear that they have done well, and the profits made should more than cover their costs. Your father's home has been leased, and has made money. His two cars have been sold, and his goods and furnishings have been packed and put in storage. They are awaiting your instructions as to what to do with them." He leaned back and steepled his hands together. "I'll give you a copy of the deeds to the trust, and a copy of your father's Last Will and Testament. But I must warn you that you could be in for a shock when you discover the extent of the trust's assets. Do you have any idea about the value of your trust?"

"None whatsoever," said Peter. "I had nothing to do with my father's business...and very little to do with my father."

"Then it will come as some surprise to you that the trust is currently valued at five-point-four million Australian dollars. That's not including the shares your father had in his own company. It's not a publicly listed company, so it's a little more tricky getting a share price for those."

Peter wasn't at all sure he had heard correctly. "Come again?"

Mr. Collins cleared his throat. "You, as the sole trustee, are owner and manager of a trust worth five-point-four million Australian dollars."

Peter was dumbfounded.

Mr. Collins continued. "You could elect to close down the trust and cash it all in, transferring the funds to a bank or into shares. Alternatively, you can continue to manage the trust as it stands."

It was all too much. Peter found himself giddy with disbelief. "Mr. Collins, I need help. I haven't a clue what to do…and it's all a bit of shock. Would you act as my solicitor and advise me?"

Mr. Collins blinked and regarded Peter in silence for a while. Eventually, he nodded. "I'm happy to do that. We'll draw up the agreement before you go, if you like. What would you like me to do, exactly?"

Peter put his head in his hands. "I have no idea how to manage funds like this. It will take time to come to terms with it and learn how to use it responsibly."

Collins nodded. "I suggest that in the immediate future, you let the trust fund continue. It is doing very nicely and is generating income. Just take out what you need to help you live now." He smiled. "Perhaps buy a car and spoil yourself a bit, but let the rest earn money from the investments. Do you have a bank account here?"

"No, I had an Australian account which I operated by credit card, but that no longer exists." Peter did not explain that he had emptied the account, and given the entire contents anonymously to the parents of the young man he had killed.

"Then may I suggest you open an account here? I will make an appointment for you, if you wish, with a bank of your choice."

Peter nodded his gratitude. "I will be guided by your wisdom. Please choose one that will allow me easy access to funds in Australia."

For the next hour, they busied themselves with administration.

As they were concluding, Mr. Collins asked, "Do you have any instructions as to what you wish to do with your house in Australia and the goods kept in storage?"

Peter said instinctively, "Yes. Please sell the lot. I don't want any of it. Not a thing. Put the funds into investments."

"Absolutely. If you put that in writing, we'll get on to it."

By the time Peter had finished at the solicitor's and opened a bank account, it was early afternoon before he returned to the *Phoenix*. With some relief, he changed back into his overalls and set about scraping the last of the paint off the sides of the dining booths.

The sense of normality he craved slowly ebbed back as he listened to the work going on around him—and the banter between Kym and Lenny.

Peter's eyes were watering with the dust, and his head pounded as he lay on his back, scraping at the last of the paint from the bottom of a booth. The dust was coming from Lenny, who was attacking the front counter with an orbital sander. The *Phoenix's* insides looked a mess. Dustsheets, debris, and tools lay everywhere.

Lenny's sander switched off, and Peter heard him say, "Don't trip on that power cord." He coughed, and then said, "Are you here to see, Peter?"

Peter rolled over and saw Cheeseman standing at the bottom of the steps looking around in bewilderment.

"Er…yes. But I'm not sure…"

Lenny was looking like a grizzly bear that had been through a sandstorm. He prodded Peter with a foot. "Your visitor is here."

Peter, dressed in a filthy set of overalls and in bare feet, grimaced as he stood up.

Cheeseman looked at him with amazement.

Peter walked to the end of the cabin and removed the dustsheet from the end booth. "Mr. Cheeseman, thank you for coming. Can I get you a coffee?" He turned and called over his shoulder, "Lenny, is it all right for me to take a break for twenty minutes?"

Lenny wiped the sweat from his forehead. "I think we all need a break." He called to the two casual staff who had been brought in to help him in the main cabin. "Take a break for a while, guys, and make a brew."

Peter gestured toward Lenny. "This is Lenny, proud owner of the *Phoenix*, which we hope will shortly rise from the ashes."

Cheeseman acknowledged the big man with a wave.

Lenny called out, "How do you have your coffee?"

"Black...and with as little dust as possible."

"We do coffee, boy, not miracles."

Toby Cheeseman wiped his seat with a handkerchief and sat down. He was dressed in a pinstriped suit.

Peter wondered how he should start. "Um...Mr. Cheeseman," he said, "I wanted to see you to get some sort of assurance that I could continue my life untroubled by anything to do with my past, or by anything to do with my father's company. However"—he drew in a deep breath—"things have happened that have caused me to change my mind."

Cheeseman regarded him without expression.

Peter continued. "You said that my father's company has its AGM in about two weeks time. Can you tell me where it will take place?"

"Certainly. Here in London, at The Tower. That's the hotel beside the dock, next to Tower Bridge. Why?"

"Because my parole conditions prohibit me from going abroad." Peter toyed with the spoon in his coffee mug. "Mr. Cheeseman, I'm going to put an idea to you, and I'd like you to tell me if it's possible. But I need to know a few things. First: who, exactly, holds the twenty percent of the company's shares not held by Manny Gobler or me? Secondly: what is your relationship with those who hold them? Thirdly: are you able to hack into our own company's computers to get evidence of Manny Gobler's financial dealings over the last two years? And finally: can you isolate all company records, client lists, contracts, and financial records from Manny when I give you the word, so he can't operate any business transactions of the company or tamper with its records?"

Cheeseman leaned back and considered Peter in silence. Then he put his fingers together. "I may have knowledge of some of the, er, more controversial aspects of computing, and I can easily let you know who owns the shares, but you had better tell me what you have in mind."

And so Peter did.

Twenty minutes later, Cheeseman was shaking his head and had a smile on his face. "I love it—so Machiavellian. Delicious." He rubbed his hands together. "And worthy of my singular talents. Let's strike a blow for the righteous, eh what!" He leaned forward. "The only tricky thing is that it will take a bit of time to set it all up—time that I was going to use to tidy up my projects before I left."

Peter nodded. "Um, I wanted to speak to you about that too."

"About what?"

"Mr. Cheeseman, will you give me three months? If I haven't satisfied you that I'm able to help the company prosper in that time, then leave with my blessing." He shrugged. "I'm asking you to stay."

Cheeseman said nothing. Eventually he nodded. "Righto, three months. And please call me Toby."

Peter held out his hand. "Toby, this plan stands or falls on your willingness to do what I've asked and your skill in doing it. Don't think for a moment I don't appreciate it. Please call me Peter?"

"Certainly, old boy. Peter it is."

By the end of the day, Lenny pronounced himself pleased with the progress made. The first coat of Danish oil had been applied to the front counter, the booths, and the central wooden keelson. Kym, together with a bevy of tradesmen, had worked wonders in the kitchen. It had been transformed into a well ventilated, stainless steel, ergonomic marvel.

Peter was sitting with Lenny and Kym on the main hatch-cover on deck to escape the smell of the fumes below. He was clutching a mug of tea, trying to calm the pounding in his head. As a day of rehabilitation following a blunt force trauma, his activities left much to be desired.

"Are you okay, young Peter?" said Lenny.

"Fairly moderate."

"Hmm."

A little later, Alex came limping along the dock toward them. He came to a halt, and pointed with his stick at the debris littering the dock. "I rather suspected there would be a few changes about the place. But I wasn't sure it would happen so quickly. Can I have a look at what you've been doing?"

"Not until it's finished," said Kym. "But I will let Peter get you a mug of tea."

"That would be excellent. Just black, thank you Peter. No sugar." He smiled. "I've come to collect you, to take you home. But a cup of tea first would be welcome." Alex made his way across the gangplank.

Peter ducked down below to make the tea. As he did, he was conscious of an unusual emotion. It came from hearing a word he'd not heard for many years: 'home.' It stirred a welter of contradicting emotions: hope, security, fear, and longing. The emotions chased each other around until he managed to wrestle them to a standstill, and appear back on deck under some semblance of control with Alex's mug of tea.

Alex drove Peter to the backpacker's hostel to collect his things, then back down the A11 and across Tower Bridge.

His car smelled new. Peter asked whether it was.

"It is," said Alex. "It's the new Mitsubishi Colt. It's a car I find I can easily get out of with my legs."

Peter ventured to ask, "What is the matter with them?"

"Polio. I was one of the last to be infected before they discovered the vaccine."

"I'm sorry to hear that," Peter said, wishing he had the words to say more.

Alex was soon pulling into a cul-de-sac before a set of modern, two-story flats. The view from the end of the road was spectacular. To the left was Tower Bridge, and straight ahead were the old docks of London's East End. Peter slung his rucksack over his shoulder, and followed Alex into his flat.

A stair chair lift had been installed to give Alex access to his upstairs bedroom. The flat was spacious, tasteful, and looked every inch the home of a bachelor academic. Alex had converted the downstairs bedroom into a study. It featured bookshelves, a picture window overlooking the Thames, and a fireplace in which a fake log-fire gas heater had been installed.

Peter inspected the prints of old-fashioned boats hanging on the walls.

"One of my hobbies is messing around in boats," said Alex. It's actually proved very useful. You can't understand the history of London without understanding the estuary." He led Peter to the stairs. "As far as I'm concerned, the whole place is yours to live in except the study; best leave that to me." He smiled. "Then, I won't have to tidy it. If you go upstairs, you'll find your bedroom directly opposite the landing."

When Peter opened the door to his room, he discovered that he also had a view across the Thames.

His own room—with space and tasteful furnishing! He fingered the sheet folded over the coverlet of his bed. And there was a window—a big window.

It all was too much. He pinched the top of his nose to hold back the tears that threatened.

Alex glided up to the landing next to him on the chair lift. "Are you all right?" he asked.

Peter sniffed. "Yes. It just takes a bit to get used to."

Alex nodded and said nothing.

Peter turned away until he'd brought himself under control. Then he faced Alex again.

The professor affected not to notice, and continued. "I've had a desk put in here for you, and you'll find an Internet connection for a computer beside it. Mrs. Taylor comes in one day a week to clean and wash for me. So it's really only a question of making your bed and putting your washing in the basket on the landing." Alex smiled, but even through the storm of his own emotions, Peter noticed that his face was pale and pinched. Although he was putting on a good front, Alex was obviously in deep grief over the death of his brother.

The professor pushed a button and started to glide back downstairs. "Come and let me show you around the kitchen. I'm sorry to say that I'm a very poor cook, and I sometimes forget to eat at all, so please don't let my absent-mindedness frustrate you. Just help yourself."

Peter watched Alex struggle out of the chair lift, and tried to come to terms with Alex's trust. He cleared his throat. "Why don't you let me cook for you in the evenings? I'd enjoy it."

"Really? I had no intention of burdening you with that."

"It's no burden. How about you let me cook when I'm in. I suspect there will a number of evenings when I'll be out."

"That's very kind of you."

"And, Alex, we haven't discussed the issue of rent."

"Oh!" The old man scratched his head. "I hadn't really expected you to pay any—certainly not if you'll be cooking most evenings. You've got no money, and you won't make much as a waiter. So let's just forget it."

Peter smiled at the ironies of life. "Alex, it would help me to adjust to the real world if you let me pay a third of my salary to you. I opened a bank account today, and can organize an automatic payment."

Alex started to protest but Peter insisted, "Please, Alex."

After some polite wrangling, he prevailed.

Peter went upstairs to unpack. There was so little in his bag that he folded everything twice before putting them in the chest of drawers. He found it a strange experience. When all was packed away, he extracted the file containing his father's will and trust deeds and put them on the desk so he could examine them later.

After showering and changing into fresh clothes, Peter went down to the kitchen where Alex was in danger of spoiling a perfectly good piece of roast beef. He took over the cooking, whilst Alex went into the dining room to set the table.

Fifteen minutes later, Alex returned with a glass of lemonade and bitters for Peter. He sniffed the aroma in the kitchen appreciatively. "I must say: I didn't expect these bonuses to come with sharing a home."

At that moment, the doorbell rang, and Alex limped out to investigate.

Peter called out, "Alex, do you have some wine that I can use for the gravy?" He heard steps coming into the kitchen and a second later was tapped on the shoulder with a bottle of red wine. Peter reached back to take the bottle only to discover his hands covering the slender fingers of a woman.

"I was in some dread of tonight's meal, until I saw you in the kitchen. Hello, Peter. I didn't expect to see you here."

Peter, frozen in surprise, kept his hand on her fingers. "Hello, Beth." He turned around and saw the curling hair, the beautiful face, and the amused smile. She was looking fantastic in black pants, white shirt, and waistcoat. "I had no idea you were coming for dinner. It's…it's good to see you."

"What happened to your head?"

"I was careless."

Alex came in from the hallway, "Beth, did I tell you that Peter is sharing the house with me?"

"No, actually, Alex, you didn't."

"Aah...he is."

"Hmm."

Peter handed her the bottle of red wine. "Why don't you find a couple of glasses and enjoy some of this with Alex. I'll stick with lemonade. Dinner will be a while yet."

She nodded and took the bottle. For just a moment, the tips of her fingers rested over Peter's hands, and he held on to the bottle for a few seconds longer than was necessary. Pretending nonchalance, he let go.

Beth turned and walked into the sitting room to join Alex.

Peter looked down at his hand as if seeing it for the first time. He could still feel her softness.

Chapter 10

B eth sat beside Alex on the couch and grilled him about Peter. What did he know about him? What was he like?

Alex was uncharacteristically evasive. He pleaded an ignorance that Beth only partly believed. From the size of the bandage on Peter's head, it was obvious that he had sustained a great deal more than a bump on the head. There was a lot she was not being told.

She threw herself back in her seat in frustration. In doing so, she discovered that a long mirror on the other side of the dining room enabled her to see into part of the kitchen. Peter could sometimes be seen moving from bench top to oven. He had removed his jacket and his broad shoulders and physique showed well through his loose-fitting shirt. She occasionally caught sight of his face, which even at that distance, seemed to have a hint of sadness, of something closed. She wondered why. Then she reminded herself that most men had inevitably surprised her with some sort of nasty secret, one that always left her crushed. *Guard your heart. Stop being a fool.*

Dinner was a cautious affair. Peter felt himself to be on unfamiliar ground. Beth, he noticed, also appeared reserved. They were both like stray cats meeting for the first time—circling each other—each acutely aware of the other and neither quite sure what to do.

Peter inquired about Beth's job and was amazed to learn that she'd just been awarded her doctorate. He congratulated her and listened as she enthused about the merits of history.

"We all belong to such an amazing story, a story that defines us. It's tragic when we don't know it...or know ourselves."

Peter was incautious enough to say, "Sometimes we'd rather not know about ourselves."

Alex glanced up at him. "Yes, that can require courage."

"It may be a cliché," said Beth, "but I really do believe that there are important lessons to learn from the past that can protect us from making mistakes in the future."

"Didn't someone famous say something like that?" asked Peter.

Alex nodded. "George Santayana. He said, 'Those who cannot remember the past are condemned to repeat it.'"

"Perhaps the only lesson we learn from history is that we are incapable of learning from history," said Peter, with more harshness than he'd intended.

"What a terrible thing to say," Beth retorted. "We can't just give up and retreat into nihilistic despair. Whilst what you say is nearly true, surely we've got a responsibility to ensure that it's not totally true." She pointed at Peter. "Take yourself, for example. Haven't you learned from mistakes you've made in your past?"

Peter toyed with his glass of lemonade. "You may have learned, but sometimes the world doesn't let you change."

"I don't understand."

He glanced at Beth. The candle Alex had placed in the center of the table lent golden highlights to Beth's hair. Peter sighed. He decided that if he were going to lose her friendship, he would rather lose it now than later—before he lost his heart completely.

"Beth," he said, looking at his watch, "sixty-seven minutes ago, I touched your fingers when I handed you a bottle."

He saw Beth stiffen.

"The last time I felt the touch of a woman was over two years ago. I was in a pub with a girlfriend. It was New Year's Eve, and I was slightly drunk." Peter worked his mouth, forcing the words to come out. "A bloke tried to molest her. I hit out with a beer bottle… and I killed someone. I didn't intend to, and I bitterly regret it."

Silence screamed its accusations.

Peter continued. "Four days ago, I came out of Belmarsh Prison on parole after serving twenty-six months for manslaughter." He glanced up. "So, tell me, Beth, will I be allowed to learn from that and move on?"

Beth had her hand up to her mouth in horror.

There was silence.

Peter nodded and got up from his seat. "I'll go and make the coffee."

Out in the kitchen, Peter held on to the bench top to steady himself. His chest heaved as he fought down silent sobs. It was all too hard. He'd been a fool to believe that the happiness of the past few days could last.

Alex limped into the kitchen and leaned against a cupboard. "That was subtle."

Peter didn't answer.

"Probably good to get it out of the way, though. How are you feeling?"

"Not great."

Alex patted him on the shoulder. "Well, Peter, as you have shared a secret, I may as well share mine. You alluded to my somewhat preoccupied demeanor when we first met, and I told you my twin brother had just died. What you do not know is that my brother, Trevor, was actually murdered. He was found hanging under Blackfriars Bridge. I'm afraid it's hit me pretty hard. So will you forgive me if I too appear slightly distracted."

Peter was appalled. "Alex, I'm very sorry." He shook his head. "I was so full of my own problems I didn't think to ask after yours. Please forgive me."

"Don't be ridiculous—there's nothing to forgive. It's just that we need to understand each other if we're going to live together." He nodded toward the doorway. "Beth is here tonight to help me discover if a clue about his death is really a clue or whether it is meaningless. She'll want to know the reason behind my question, so I'll tell her about my brother's murder in just a moment. We're both moving into the study. Perhaps you could give us fifteen minutes before you bring in the coffee—to give me time to tell her." He sighed. "I'm afraid poor Beth will have a number of surprises tonight."

Once Alex had steered Beth into his study, she rounded on him. "Alex," she hissed, "you can't have a person who has killed someone living with you. It's absurd. You don't know what he's like. You don't know if he's honest or if you are safe. What do you know about him? It's ridiculous…"

Alex interrupted her. "Beth, Beth, calm down!"

But she continued. "I know you're driven by commendable principles, but this is plain foolishness. It's too much of a risk."

"Beth, sit down," ordered Alex.

Beth plumped herself down into a chair with mutinous ill grace.

Alex eased himself into an armchair and regarded her levelly. She avoided his eyes. He continued. "Beth, before Peter shared his background, what did you think of him? What characteristics did you see in him?"

"That's not the point…"

Alex interrupted her. "Beth, please, an honest answer."

"Oh, all right." She sighed and thought of his athletic figure. "He looks pretty ordinary." Beth remembered him chatting with the customers, often reading their needs before they were mentioned. "Seems a bit lost for words."

She recalled more than she wanted to recall, remembering that it had been Peter who had made them antipasto when no one else had the energy to move. "Seems to want to ingratiate himself."

She knew she was not being fair or honest about her feelings.

94

The truth was, she felt disappointed…and cross. Her stupid feelings had led her to feel betrayed again.

Beth tried to push the memories of Peter away: his eyes, his physique, and the glimpses of intellect he'd shown in conversation. She shook her head. *Damn it! He was hard to dismiss.* And he'd spoken and conducted himself with an old-fashioned chivalry she'd not seen in anyone except Alex. She lifted her head and said defiantly, "I don't trust him. Men like him always let you down."

"Men like him? What's he like, Beth? If you were in that pub with Peter's arm around you, and a group of drunken louts wanted to paw you, what would you want Peter to do?"

"I wouldn't want him to kill anyone, that's for sure," snapped Beth.

"He didn't intend to. He made a bad judgment and went too far whilst he was drunk. He regrets his action bitterly and is devastated by the shame of it." Alex raised a finger. "By choosing not to drink alcohol, he's doing what he can to ensure that nothing like that will ever happen again."

Silence hung between them.

Alex leaned his head back. "As to his qualities; I have found him to be sensitive to the needs of others, and he has an extraordinary capacity to organize people so that new possibilities occur. Things seem to happen around him." He wagged his finger. "You've heard what he's been responsible for at the *Phoenix*."

Beth said nothing.

Alex continued, "Did you see his head wound?"

Beth lowered her head, slightly shamefaced, and nodded.

"Last night, he rescued someone from drowning, yet he still insisted on coming to work even though he was wounded. What sort of personal qualities does that suggest, Beth?"

Beth objected, "The thing is, Alex, you didn't know more than half of this before you suggested he come and share your house. Admit it."

Alex smiled. "Perhaps. But I had a good feeling about Peter and a conviction I should help him. This can't be done without an element of risk. Compassion, by its very nature, compels people to embrace risk. If compassion does nothing, it is mere sentimentality —and sentimentality never changed anything."

Alex leaned forward and placed a hand over hers. "What is it that has really disturbed you, Beth?"

Beth looked at her old mentor with exasperation. Damn him, he was altogether too intuitive. She pulled her hand away and folded her hands in her lap. "He looked attractive and I noticed: that's all." She shrugged. "So I guess I feel disappointed."

"Aah," said Alex. "Another failed male?"

Beth nodded.

"Following a fair list of failed males."

She threw her head back. "Yes."

"Well, Beth, be careful you don't draw any hasty conclusions."

Silence settled between them. After a degree of peace had returned, Alex cleared his throat. "Beth, I'm afraid I have some distressing news of my own I need to share."

Peter tapped on the study door.

"Come in, Peter," called Alex. "The door's only shut to keep the heat in."

Peter set down the tray of coffee mugs on a small table between the armchairs and made to leave. He glanced at Beth and caught her wiping away a tear. Taking a deep breath, he knelt down in front of her.

She tried to hide her face with her hair by looking down.

"Can I get you some water…a whiskey…a pacemaker?" He shrugged and added with a tentative smile, "Perhaps a Tom and Jerry cartoon? Anything at all? I'm afraid it's been pretty ordinary for you this evening—and I'm sorry for my part in it."

Beth sniffed, tossed her hair back, and blinked away some tears. Peter watched her force a smile and reach for a handkerchief. "No, I'm fine. I am, however, concerned about Alex. Can you persuade him to be careful?"

Alex protested, "Beth, please don't burden Peter with this. There is no danger. I'm simply helping the police by doing some research."

Peter was instantly concerned. "What potential danger are you in, Alex?"

"Oh, it's just a bit of research," Alex said, waving his hand dismissively. "My brother had swallowed a memory chip from a mobile phone before he died. The police found it and printed off the last picture it contained—one they believe may have been taken shortly before he died. As it included some Egyptian hieroglyphics, I asked Beth to examine them. It's her area of expertise."

Peter turned to Beth. "Why would this put Alex into danger?"

"Because the odds are that what is shown on this picture is, in some way, connected with Trevor's murder...and now Alex has it and is digging around to discover its significance."

"Peter, you don't need to get involved in this," said Alex.

"Well that's it, you see: when someone offers you acceptance, friendship, and even their home—it kind of makes you involved." He stood up. "So, what's this evidence you are examining?"

Alex looked at Peter, sighed, and said, "Pull the chair around from behind the desk." He turned to Beth. "Beth, show him."

Beth took a photograph out of her handbag and gave it to Peter.

Peter examined it. "What do the hieroglyphics say?"

"My colleague, Professor George Daintree, says that it means, "Ramses beloved of Aman, like the son of Osiris has placed on his obelisks the secret identity of the ultimate one.'"

At this, Beth looked up sharply. "No, it doesn't, and George should have known this. It actually says, "Ramses beloved of Aman, like the son of Osiris, has placed on his obelisks the secret identity *and power* of the ultimate one.'"

"It's pretty similar," said Peter. "Couldn't it be an honest mistake?"

Alex shrugged his shoulders.

Squinting hard to read the small print on the bottom of the page, Peter asked, "What about this crazy statement about the devil here on the bottom, "Lucifer; pure, virtuous, wholesome, and innocent?'"

"I think that's our best clue. Trevor was a Freemason and statements like that are not uncommon in some branches of Freemasonry. In fact, the American version of Freemasonry, the Shriners, use that very phrase." He sighed. "The general thrust of their sort of Masonic thinking is to recast Satan as God, and recast God as a deeply flawed spiritual being. It's all very disturbing."

"What about the rest of the page, the list of—what are these? Company names?"

Alex shrugged. "No idea. It would probably take an extensive computer search to even begin to make sense of it."

"Hmmm." Peter took the photograph and looked at it again. "Do you mind if I give a copy of this to a friend? He's very good with computers, searches, and that kind of thing."

"You know of such a person?"

Peter nodded.

"You amaze me. Can he be trusted to keep things confidential?"

"I think so."

"Then, I suppose it's okay. I'll scan the picture and give it to you digitally."

Alex took the picture across to the scanner beside his computer and tapped away until it hummed into life. After a little while, he said, "Done. I've stored it on my desktop. What do you want to do with it?"

"May I use your phone?"

Alex nodded.

Peter dialed and waited.

Toby answered after three rings. "Hello, Cheeseman here."

Peter smiled at Toby's strangulated, upper-class accent, "Hello, Toby. Peter Jacobs speaking. Can you switch on your computer? I've got something to send you."

"I'm already at my computer, old boy. What's up?"

"I want to show you a picture—some confidential stuff. Tell me what you think."

Peter emailed the scanned image of the page to Toby.

"Three things, Toby," said Peter. "Can you do a search for that phrase about Lucifer on the bottom of the page and see where it crops up? Second, are you able to enter the words from the list of companies on the same page and see if it matches up with any list that makes sense? And third, can you see the lines and patterns of something on the side of the paperweight?"

"Yes."

"Could you un-distort the image so we can see what it is? Can your computer do that?"

"My dear boy, I have two PowerMac G5 towers linked together. They let me do all sorts of interesting things."

Peter had no idea what he was talking about but took it as encouragement. He turned away and dropped his voice so Beth and Alex couldn't hear him. "And, Toby, keep a record of time spent on this. You will be paid."

Toby laughed. "You don't know my rates, old chap. But I'll have a go. Anything else?"

"Yes. Could you send me a line diagram of our company staff, so I know who they are, who they report to, their responsibilities, and anything you know about their reliability? May I also have a copy of the last few contracts, a list of companies we currently have contracts with, and a list of companies we are trying to get contracts with? You'd better also tell me which countries they are in and the worth of each contract, actual and potential."

"Whew! You've just accounted for every minute of my working day for a month, old bean. Are you sure that's what you want?"

"Yes, Toby. It's important. Put the whole staff on to help you with the non-confidential stuff. Email me what you find to this address."

"My life has certainly become a lot more interesting and a whole lot busier since meeting you."

Peter laughed, "Good night, Toby...and thanks."

An hour later, much of the tension that existed between Peter, Beth, and Alex had eased, and the possibility of new relationships with deeper foundations began to suggest themselves.

They relived the lunchtime drama on the *Phoenix* together.

"Was that honestly the first time you've been a waiter?" asked Beth.

"Couldn't you tell?"

"Other than the falling potato, not at all."

"Trust me, I was the duck paddling like crazy under the water. I was terrified."

Eventually, Beth announced her need to return home.

"And where is home for you, Beth?" he asked.

"It's a dingy little flat behind a plastics factory in Clerkenwell, but it's convenient."

Alex asked Peter to see Beth to the door.

Peter readily agreed. He walked with Beth into the hall and helped her on with her coat. As he opened the door, she turned and looked up into his face. Tentatively, she reached up and touched the edge of the bandage around Peter's head. "I guess we're all a little bit wounded."

Peter didn't move.

Beth continued, "Did the girl you were with ever contact you again?"

"No."

She nodded. "Silly girl."

Beth turned away quickly and crossed the road to her car.

Peter watched her go, unsure of what he should believe.

Chapter 11

Peter was up to his knees in stinking black mud with all sorts of unidentifiable objects scratching his feet and legs. "Remind me why I am doing this again?" he called to Alex, who was sitting on concrete steps beside the sea wall.

"As I recall, you made some facetious comment about history being dusty, boring, and irrelevant. This is your education."

Their good-natured debate had begun over breakfast. It resulted in Alex consulting the tide tables and driving Peter to the north bank of the Thames. There, he'd parked the car—a feat made possible only because of Alex's disability sticker—and the two of them then walked down the footpath leading to the river beside Southwark Bridge. Peter, under instructions from Alex, was now digging around in the mud left exposed by the Thames at low tide.

It was Saturday and Lenny had tried to give Peter the day off in order to help him recover from his head wound. Peter, however, said he'd turn up in the afternoon and do what he could. He had a keen sense of ownership of the project and wanted to see it through. But, for now, he was squelching around in the mud like a ten-year-old child—and loving it.

"I'm finding a lot of really big pieces of animal bone." He held up some for Alex to see.

"That will be the remains of haunches of meat thrown overboard by decades of sailors when this area was a thriving sea port. Keep exploring."

It wasn't long before Peter had an impressive array of broken bits of pottery, tiles, bottles, and bricks lined up on top of the sea wall. Alex tapped his walking stick beside each treasure, telling Peter what each item was and the period of history from which it came. "Tudor, Victorian, Medieval. Hmm…" Alex picked up a broken piece of pottery and examined it closely. "This might even be Roman."

"Roman! You've got to be kidding."

"No, the mud is quite anaerobic, and it preserves archaeological finds very well. Do you concede defeat?"

"Nearly."

"Nearly! Get back out there!"

"No, Alex," Peter laughed. "I concede. I need to clean up as much as I can and get back to the *Phoenix*."

Alex offered to drive him there, but subjected Peter to a running commentary on the historical significance of all the places they passed as he did. As he drove east from Westminster, he said, "We're now entering the City of London—which is really a city within a city. It even has its own mayor, someone quite different from the Mayor of Greater London. Ever since the twelfth century, he's been a figure who wields enormous power."

"Why's that?" asked Peter, more from politeness than interest.

"The City is arguably the wealthiest square mile on earth and is not subject to the Sovereign. In fact, when the Queen of England goes to visit the City, the Lord Mayor meets her at Temple Bar, the symbolic gate of the City. Then she formally asks permission to enter his commercial domain."

Peter was amazed. "I find that hard to believe. Surely she can't allow that. She needs to be monarch of all of the UK. Not just bits of it."

Alex laughed. "Well, if the Right Honorable Mayor controls

most of the nation's banks, including the Bank of England, Lloyd's of London, the London Stock Exchange, and the offices of most leading international traders, not to mention the publishing world of Fleet Street, I think you, too, might think twice about upsetting him."

"Good grief, I had no idea."

"History really does make a difference, eh?"

Peter grunted.

"Just to the north of us is Whitechapel, a district made infamous by Jack the Ripper. Five prostitutes were murdered in 1888. Their throats were cut and their abdomens mutilated. Some had their internal organs removed. All very grisly."

"Come on now, you're an historian. You must have some theory about the identity of the Ripper?" goaded Peter.

"I'm afraid not. Some say he was a deranged medical surgeon. Others say a psychotic killer with a sexual fetish. The genital areas had significant wounding, and the victims were all local prostitutes. A more fanciful claim is that the Freemasons were behind it."

"Why's that?"

"The story is that one of Queen Victoria's grandsons secretly married an illiterate Catholic shop-girl named Annie Crook and fathered a child by her. The nanny, who was employed to care for the baby, later turned to prostitution, and shared her secret with three other prostitutes who threatened to go public. As knowledge of the scandal might have toppled the monarchy and damaged the Freemasons, they were killed."

"Why would that information have caused such a big deal?"

"Because Queen Victoria's son, Edward, was the Grand Master Mason in England at the time. He later became King Edward VII. It was his son, Eddy, who was implicated."

"Wow!" Peter was silent for a while. "Do you think there's any truth to it?"

"I think it unlikely, but it's not impossible."

"Did the Freemasons really have that much power?"

"Well, they had the power of the king." Alex paused. "And..."

"And what?"

"Almost all of the mayors of the City of London have been Freemasons."

––––––––––––

Peter watched Lenny screw the last gimbaled bracket into place. The brackets were to hold the brass oil lamps that hung high on the inside wall of the hull.

Lenny stepped back and put his hands on his hips. "I suppose it's no good me telling you that a sailor has a healthy fear of fire, boy."

"Mate, these lamps have been perfected by centuries of paranoia about fire. They're marine standard and they're safe. You'll see."

"Hmph."

The very first thing Peter noticed as he descended into the long cabin that afternoon was the absence of smell. There was no longer the lingering odor of deep-fried fat, nor the fug of humid, stale air. In its place was fresh air, scented with just a hint of wood waxes and oils. The aroma complemented the unadorned woodwork of the barge's main cabin superbly. The new heat exchange venting system was working well.

"The only smells I want the customers to smell are those I want them to smell," said Kym with a fierceness that brooked no objection. "Smells sell. Fragrance is much more important than people think."

For his part, Lenny had drawn up a new menu with Kym and had it professionally laid out. He had posted them in hundreds of letterboxes in the surrounding apartments and stuck them on the gangplanks at the marina. At Peter's suggestion, he had also dropped them into the main banking, insurance, and media institutions with a note inviting them to have a regular pre-booking arrangement. The invitations included a complimentary meal ticket for two, allowing key people to try out the new menu of the refurbished restaurant.

Lenny had forbidden Peter from doing hard physical work, so

Peter contented himself with taking shots of the refurbished cabin using Lenny's camera. He then hid himself away in the stern cuddy, so he could upload the pictures to the computer and redesign *Phoenix's* website.

Eventually, he was satisfied. When Lenny looked in to inquire if Peter needed a coffee, he was astounded. "Boy, that's brilliant!" He scratched his beard thoughtfully. "Do you think we'll live up to the hype?"

Kym joined them in the cuddy and looked over Lenny's shoulder at the computer. "Of course, we will. It takes nearly as much energy to cook badly as to cook well, so you might as well do it well." She grinned. "And we'll sure have a lot more fun."

The three of them filed back into the main cabin where Peter and Kym began setting the lamps into their brackets. Peter looked up through the skylight and saw that the light was beginning to fade because of the darkening clouds. Moments later, he could hear droplets of rain drumming on the deck. *Phoenix's* hull shivered in the wind, and she began to creak as she pulled on her warps.

Peter fetched a gas lighter and began to light the oil lamps. "Okay, Kym," he called. "Kill the lights."

Kym called Lenny from the kitchen. "Hey, boss, you'd better come and have a look at this."

As Lenny came in from the kitchen, she switched off the main lights leaving only the oil lamps to illuminate the cabin.

Golden light played on the wooden deck beams and the massive keelson. Shadows danced and played with each other, whispering stories of tides, winds and adventures. "Magic," said Kym quietly.

"Brilliant," added Lenny, smiling. "I think we need to celebrate what you guys have managed to pull off…and do it with things unnecessarily alcoholic and calorific. Let's go across to the Dickens Inn for dinner. My treat."

Peter strolled along the sunken lawn outside the massive western wall of the Tower of London toward the line of tourists waiting to gain entry. He couldn't suppress a feeling of guilt as he walked past them all to present himself to the guard sitting behind the counter.

The guard inspected the bag containing Hamish's clothes and passed Peter through a metal detector. Whilst the guards on duty did not have the same intimidating demeanor of the Belmarsh prison officers, Peter instinctively dropped his head and avoided eye contact. This action prompted one of the guards to say, "Don't look so worried. We haven't beheaded anyone here since 1747."

Peter forced a smile.

At that point, Hamish came into the guardroom. "Ah, Peter, good to see you again. I'll sign you in and show you around before we have some tea."

They walked along the cobblestones beside Tower Green. Peter fought the temptation to walk in step with Hamish. The military surroundings seemed to require it. Hamish seemed blithely unaware and continued to chat. "I find it slightly ironic to be a chaplain in the Tower. It's been a place where God's truth, love, and justice have too often been overtaken by bigotry, selfish ambition, and injustice." He pointed to the site of the execution block. "The first person executed was Anne Boleyn, whose only crime was her failure to produce a male heir for Henry VIII. She was executed in 1536 on a trumped-up charge of adultery." He smiled. "Evidently, Henry did feel a small pang of guilt at her murder, enough at least to hire a skilled swordsman from Calais to slice off her head."

"Harry certainly had a unique way with women," said Peter. "Were they always innocent?"

Hamish laughed. "Certainly not. Catherine Howard, Henry's fifth wife, really was guilty of adultery. She was brought to the Tower, where she was obliged to pass the heads of her two lovers mounted on spikes, before being executed herself." He opened the door to his flat beside the Beauchamp Tower, put Peter's bag of clothes inside, and then re-emerged to take Peter across the square.

They walked past a row of ancient cannons and up balustraded stairs into the headquarters of the Royal Fusiliers. Peter uttered an involuntary 'wow' at what he saw. The Fusilier's mess hall reeked of history. Weaponry and banners hung on the walls, filling the place with a sense of dignity and grandeur.

Hamish then led Peter across to the White Tower and up to the chapel of St. John the Evangelist. A row of Norman pillars ran along the flanks and curved around the back of the altar. A second story of pillared archways sat on top of the lower arches, giving the chapel a Byzantine feel. The mellow color of the stonework generated a sense of tranquility. Peter could well imagine why the Queen favored it as a place for contemplation. He also couldn't help but think of the desperate prayers that must have been prayed in this place. The Tower was indeed a place of contradictions.

Eventually, they returned to Hamish's flat. Hamish filled two china cups with tea and handed one to Peter. "How are you going with the demon of shame, Peter? Have you made a decision to be destroyed by it, or to be motivated by it?"

Peter spluttered into his tea, thrown off guard by Hamish's blunt approach. He wiped his mouth and said ruefully, "I thought you English were meant to be reserved and circumspect."

"Here, we have a history of chopping people's heads off if we don't hear the right answers. So, tell me, Peter, how are you going?"

"Mmm, better, I think. Still not easy. What you said made me think."

Peter explained what he had learned about his father's company being in jeopardy, and that he had resolved to try and rescue it. "My father died when I was in prison. He had abused me—beaten me—as a child, so I left home at sixteen and didn't want anything more to do with him." He shrugged. "But then I realized that if I kept running, kept hating, I would always be controlled by the past. So, I'm having a go."

"Good for you, Peter. You've taken the first step toward forgiveness."

Peter frowned. "I have? I'm not sure that's true. I don't feel the least bit forgiving toward my father."

"Perhaps, but forgiveness begins with an act of the will, not a feeling. Feelings follow later." Hamish drummed a finger on the arm of his chair. "Bitterness is one of the most toxic emotions to human well-being—so it's worth avoiding. Forgiveness brings freedom."

"I'm not sure history bears that out. Those who forgive can be taken advantage of."

"That depends on how you define freedom. Freedom from hate is a significant freedom."

Peter rubbed his forehead. He was unused to such language.

Hamish continued. "If God allowed himself to be crucified for our sake, then he knows a thing or two about forgiveness. It also means that he knows a thing or two about ultimate victory." He smiled. "One thing being a chaplain has taught me…is the importance of being on the winning side."

There was a rap on the door. Hamish got up to answer it. Dicky Chambers stepped into the lounge room. "Sir, I am directed by the Yeoman's mess to invite young Peter here to join them for a drink."

Hamish nodded. "I'll bring him over in ten minutes."

"Thank you, sir." Turning to Peter, he said, "We'll also give you a lift home."

"Aah…thanks."

The gathering twilight was beginning to throw the tower walls into silhouette when Hamish led Peter back outside into the square. The tourists had long gone, and Peter could see that the native inhabitants had emerged to reclaim their space. Groups of them could be seen chatting or doing physical training.

"Where did all the soldiers go?" asked Peter, looking for the bright red guardsmen.

"You'll soon see," responded Hamish.

Peter did indeed soon see. He was startled when a fully armed guardsman in combat fatigues stepped out from the shadows in order to satisfy himself as to their identity. After Hamish had waved acknowledgment, he explained, "They change into combat gear. And it's not just dress ups. They take their role here very seriously."

"I can see that," said Peter, as his heart rate began to slow down.

When they entered the Yeoman's mess, Dicky Chambers and James Trent came over from the bar. Hamish left Peter in their care.

The mess was a fair representation of a classic English pub, but with a military theme. About fifteen Yeoman were seated at tables drinking beer, playing dominoes, and reading newspapers. Peter glanced around nervously. He had never before been in a room with men who were so obviously powerful and competent.

He instinctively dropped his head and stared at the floor.

His action did not go unnoticed.

James Trent barked with military abruptness, "S'arn't Major, sort the boy out."

In an equally curt manner, Dicky replied, "Certainly." He stepped across and faced Peter from a distance of six inches.

Peter moved his head back in alarm.

"Son," said Dicky, "no one comes into this mess who doesn't deserve to be here. Everyone here has proved his worth, including you. That means you can look each of us in the eye as an equal. If you fail to do so, we will kick your arse. You don't ever run scared of anyone in this mess. Not even me. Is that clear?"

The sheer power and aggression of his speech was overwhelming. Peter lifted his head and looked at him, straight in the eyes. "Yes, sir."

At this, Jimmy exploded. "You don't call him 'sir.' He is your equal. Didn't you hear?"

Nonplussed, Peter answered, "Then what do I call him?"

"You call him Warrant Officer or Mr. Chambers—we make allowances for civilians." And, if you get away with your testicles still intact, you call him 'Dicky' thereafter."

Peter turned and looked into the intimidating eyes of Dicky, gulped and shouted, "Warrant Officer, you have kept me here for a full two minutes without a drink," which caused some in the bar to cheer.

When the din died down, a man with his head swathed in a bandage came over to Peter and offered his hand. "I'm Geoff Osborn. Call me Ossie. I'm the guy you fished out of the drink. Thanks."

"How are you feeling?"

"I'll live. Doctor says no bright lights or late nights"—he swallowed the rest of his pint of beer—"and told me to go easy on the alcohol."

Peter nodded his sympathy.

Ossie took Peter to the souvenir wall beside the bar. A velvet curtain, about one foot wide, hung in the middle of it. Dicky rang a ship's bell, and having gained everyone's attention, called out, "Young Peter and Ossie will now formally open the newest addition to the mess décor."

Amidst clapping and the stomping of feet, Peter and Ozzie parted the velvet curtain to reveal the Naval Crest so recently lifted from *Deep Blue*.

Peter was then given a glass of lemon, lime, and bitters—which caused more good-natured ribbing. Dicky brought it to an end by barking, "Barman, two bottles please." He drew a line on the carpet with a piece of chalk and handed the bottles to Peter. "The aim, young Peter, is to keep your feet behind this line and to walk forward with your hands on each bottle. The object is to place one bottle as far away from the line as possible, before sliding back with two hands on one bottle. You must not touch the ground in front of the line."

These instructions heralded the start of an enjoyable evening. Dicky and Peter were joined by two other Yeomen. The first was a small, gaunt man, who was simply introduced as Gizmo. "For anything weird and wonderful with electronics, see Gizmo. He was with the Royal Corps of Signals," explained Dicky.

The other Yeoman, Colin, was a fit man with dark saturnine features and distant gray eyes. Dicky whispered to Peter, "Ex SAS. Doesn't say much, but worth listening to when he does."

During the evening's competition, Peter acquitted himself well, losing narrowly to Colin.

Dicky nodded approvingly. "Not many give Colin a run for his money." He glanced at his watch. "Hmm. Pete, we've got this cere-mony we do each evening. You might like to witness it before we take you home."

"What's that?" he asked, massaging the cramp from his hands.

"It's a little thing we've been doing for the last seven hundred years. Not even Hitler's blitz managed to put the kibosh on it. It's the ceremony of the keys. We do it every evening when the Chief Yeoman Warder locks up the Tower."

Dicky and Jim conducted Peter to where a group of tourists were standing to witness the ceremony.

Moments later, a Yeoman Warder, dressed in a scarlet coat, Tudor bonnet, and carrying a lantern, marched into view from the Byward Tower with an escort of four guardsmen. The party stopped to lock up three heavy gates. However, as they approached the archway of the Bloody Tower, a guardsmen challenged them. "Halt. Who goes there?"

"The keys," came the reply.

"Whose keys?"

"Queen Elizabeth's keys."

"Advance, Queen Elizabeth's keys. All's well."

Once the last of the Tower gates was locked, a lone trumpeter sounded the last post. The notes echoed in the barred archway of Traitor's Gate—and into Peter's soul. He found he'd moved a hand to his chest. Feeling self-conscious, he lowered it. As he did, he couldn't help but wonder at a ceremony that continued to celebrate the identity of a nation despite the worst that history could throw at it. This was in stark contrast with himself. He had no idea about his identity.

Dicky jolted Peter from his musings with a slap on the shoulder. "Come on, young Peter. Let's get you home."

Chapter 12

Peter came into the kitchen looking for breakfast and heard Alex talking with Beth on the phone.

"That's kind of you to offer, Beth, but I don't want to trouble you…Okay. If you're sure…Yes…Actually, I'd appreciate not having to wrestle with London traffic today…See you at 9:30 then."

It was Monday, and Peter should have been at work, but he'd asked to have the day off to go with Alex to his brother's funeral. Seeing Alex's haggard expression, he set about making a cheese-and-tomato omelet.

Alex slumped down in his chair at the breakfast bar. "Thanks, Peter, but I'm not sure I'm up to eating this morning. Do you mind?"

Peter looked at the professor's thin frame and said, "Yes, actually. I think it might help fuel you for a testing day."

Alex smiled. "I'll try a bit then." He ate a mouthful. "It's lovely. Thanks." He dug his fork in again. When he'd eaten half, he laid his fork down. As Peter removed his plate, Alex said, "You don't have to go to the funeral, Peter. It won't be much fun being around a grieving family."

Peter paused by the sink. "You are the only family I have, Alex."

Alex considered him for a moment. "Then I'd be pleased to have your company."

———

Beth rang the front doorbell. She could not help but reflect on the last time she had stood there. It was a scene Beth had replayed many times in her mind. Peter had behaved like a perfect gentleman —and yet he had killed. He was one of the most competent people she had ever met—yet one who had moments of shyness and self-doubt. She admitted to feeling disappointed that she wouldn't be seeing him today.

So when Peter opened the door, she stood in shock, not knowing what to say.

She found herself being appraised by dark eyes that seemed to see more than she would have chosen to reveal.

"It's good to see you, Beth." The searching intensity of Peter's gaze made it clear he was speaking more than social niceties.

"Not working today?" It was a crass but safe reply.

"No."

"Hmm." She struggled for something more profound to say. Nothing came. His muscular frame was squeezed into dark formal trousers and a slim-fitting white shirt. He looked disturbingly powerful.

"Beth," he said, quietly. "You said she was foolish not to have contacted me." He left the question unsaid, hanging in the air.

"Oh."

What should she say? Should she claim she had no memory of saying such a thing. But even as she contemplated it, an inner voice screamed, *Tell him the truth, you idiot!*

She swallowed. "I meant it."

Peter nodded slowly. "Thank you. You've no idea how much that means to me."

She searched his face for a long while. Eventually, she said, "Don't hurt me, Peter." Realizing she was voicing what she intended to keep private, Beth added, "I mean...by hurting Alex."

She was mortified to discover that Peter had understood more than she'd hoped. He answered, "I will never knowingly cause you or Alex hurt." Then he opened the door wide for her to enter.

As she passed him, she half reached up to lay a hand against his cheek, but withdrew it. Then the moment was gone.

As Beth entered the church, she offered Alex her arm for support and walked with him down the sixteenth-century flagstones of the aisle. Behind her, Peter hung back and began to edge his way into a rear pew. Alex immediately stopped, hooked his stick over his arm, and reached back to take Peter by the arm. He looked at Peter and then at Beth. "Sit with me, you two. You're family." Then he walked between them to the front pew.

Beth looked up at the Christ figure in the stained-glass window and didn't trust herself to say anything other than 'Thank you.' She was deeply content to be in the company of both men.

In the days that followed, Peter's regime did not waver. After breakfast, he walked the one-and-a-half miles from Alex's flat, over Tower Bridge to St. Katharine's. Once aboard the *Phoenix*, he would help Kym prepare for the day's customers.

He only stopped when Toby came across to the *Phoenix* mid-morning to meet with him. Peter used these times to learn more about his father's company and plan for the upcoming AGM.

What he learned about Mining Management Systems appalled him. But he was also intrigued by what the company was doing. He noticed that just before his father's death, the company had been exploring contracts in Namibia, Angola, Guinea, and Gabon. Unfortunately, the person who had been negotiating these contracts was one of those who had fallen foul of Manny Gobler. When Peter mentioned this fact to Toby, he'd sighed and said, "He was a jolly good chap—great at his job."

"Any chance of getting him back on board?"

"Always a chance if you pay enough. He actually holds five percent of the company shares and has been with us from the beginning. He hasn't sold them yet, so I suspect he still has an inter-est. I'll find out. I do know, however, that he won't come back while Manny is in control of the company." Toby passed a hand over his forehead. "Changing the subject; when do you want me to tell people in the company that you actually exist?"

"I think it's best we keep that quiet for a while—until I find out what's going on." *And work out what, on earth, I'm going to do about it.*

Peter was horrified at the extent to which Manny Gobler had rorted the company assets. He stabbed his finger at an expense sheet. "It says here that in the last two years, Manny has bought a light airplane for his personal use, three luxury cars and"—Peter looked at one line in the company's expenses—"and a penthouse suite here at St. Katharine's Dock." He looked up at Toby. "What's that for?"

Toby shrugged. "He loves London, and that flat is a four-minute walk from our office. I think he intends to relocate here fairly soon. He's married to a woman in South Africa, but he also has a girl-friend here." Toby sniffed. "She comes from Peckham and has, I understand, expensive tastes."

"Wrong side of the river, eh, Toby," he teased gently. "You're such a snob."

"Absolutely," said Toby.

"But the flat is a company asset, not a personal one."

"One and the same thing with Manny, I'm afraid. That's the problem."

"Well, his expenses are crippling the company." Peter picked up another piece of paper and looked at it. "Nothing at all was allo-cated for research and development last year."

Toby shrugged. "I know."

After working a full day on the *Phoenix*, Peter usually elected to jog back across Tower Bridge to Bermondsey East, where he would shower and cook dinner for himself and Alex. He grew to value his time with Alex. Sometimes, Peter would simply sit with him in companionable silence. On other occasions, Alex would draw him into a conversation that required him to ponder things he had never considered before.

One week into his stay, Peter was looking through the window, watching the stars that were struggling to be seen through the loom of London's city lights. He ventured to comment, "It's difficult to think you have much significance in a universe as big as ours."

Alex looked up from his book. "You have more significance than you think, Peter Jacobs."

"That's hard to believe when you learn that the sun in our solar system is one of three-hundred billion stars in our galaxy—which is one of two-hundred billion galaxies in the universe."

"Would it make a difference if you learned that the universe had to be exactly the size it is to allow intelligent life on any one planet?"

Peter looked at Alex disbelievingly.

Alex put down his book. "It's true. If the universe were any smaller, it would have collapsed in on itself through gravity before life had time to develop. And if it were any larger, it would have been too spread out to allow matter to coalesce into galaxies, stars, and planets on which life could form." He smiled. "Science compels us to face the possibility that a higher being may have gone to a great deal of trouble to ensure our existence."

"I thought science and faith were incompatible."

"Not incompatible; they simply answer different questions. Science asks how. Theology asks why. So theology puts science in a bigger picture."

Alex picked up his book and left Peter to struggle with the mystery of his own existence and its disturbing implications.

Peter discovered that Alex's personal life was fairly unregulated. He was extraordinarily flexible in his eating times and thought nothing of sitting down to a meal at 11:30 at night. Peter rather suspected that if he weren't around, Alex would be so immersed in his books that he would revert to his habit of not eating at all. After their evening meal, Peter would usually retire to his room and research the running of his father's company. It was not uncommon for him to stay awake until the small hours.

It soon became apparent that Peter was in need of his own computer, Internet connection, and printer. After consulting with Toby, Peter bought himself an Apple PowerBook G4 laptop. This involved him spending a little of his inheritance. He found it an odd feeling. Peter could not believe the money in the bank account was actually his. As he wrestled with his feelings, he began to form the conviction that his inheritance had been given to him for a purpose. He hoped he had what it took to realize it.

Alex weighed Peter's laptop in his hands. "It looks very sleek and stylish. Does it really have forty gigabytes of hard drive? That's more than my desktop computer."

"It does. Toby tells me that laptops are the way of the future—and they'll soon become even more powerful."

"Goodness gracious." Alex patted the aluminum case. "Well, I'm just delighted there was enough money in your father's estate to allow you to buy something really good."

Peter was not yet inclined to enlighten Alex about how much money there was in his father's estate. In truth, he was reluctant to leave Alex's home, even though he could now afford a very comfortable flat of his own. He felt he'd only just discovered something very special in his relationship with Alex and was loath to lose it. Peter excused the deception by telling himself that Alex needed someone to keep an eye on him—and needed help in his quest to find out why his brother had been murdered.

Ernest Wheeler smiled. The fraternity had gained a controlling interest in yet another finance company in the City—not that it would be evident to anyone else. The shares were spread between three companies, none of which had any connection with each other. All were fronts for an organization that would, one day, blossom to herald a new world power whose authority-base would be a great deal more than politics. Politicians were simply pawns, tools to be used by something infinitely more significant. Wheeler leaned back in his chair. True influence came from controlling two things. He glanced at the *Financial Times* lying on the desk. The first was economic power. The second was spiritual power. He needed a religious mandate that was incontestable and unassailable—one that would give him people's hearts. And for that, he needed the Pharaoh's stone.

Wheeler looked at the ring on his finger. One day, he would be able to wear it in public. He closed his eyes and muttered, *"Give me their hearts and I will give you their kingdoms."* It was a familiar prayer. *Prayer!* He laughed to himself and reached for the newspaper.

Its headlines featured the shock waves being felt by financial institutions as a result of the economic downturn. Many companies were in financial difficulties; they were ripe for the plucking.

There was a tap on the door.

"Come," he ordered.

Carl entered and stood before his desk. He spoke without preamble. "One of the police photographs has gone missing. I think we have to assume that it was given to Professor Whitman."

Wheeler drummed his fingers on the desk. "Give me a threat assessment."

"Whitman was seen in the company of two people at the funeral. One was Beth Anderson. She was his post-doctoral research student."

"That's not unreasonable. I would expect them to be good friends."

"She's an Egyptologist."

Wheeler leaned back in his chair. "Aah."

"What do you want me to do?" said Carl.

Wheeler pondered the issue. He didn't like coincidences, but then again, another death risked attracting undue attention. Whilst he felt sure he could handle it, he judged it to be a complication he could do without—at present.

"I think any action would be an over-reaction right now. Keep the situation under review. And speaking of over-reactions..." Wheeler's voice became icy. "The overzealous fool who attacked the man snooping around the *Grayling...*'

"Has been disciplined," interrupted Carl. "It won't happen again."

Wheeler nodded. "Any other threats?"

"I don't know. The other person with Whitman at the funeral

was a Peter Jacobs. He is a waiter at a restaurant. He's recently moved into Whitman's flat in Bermondsey. We don't know anything else about him."

Wheeler again drummed his fingers on his desk. He disliked not knowing about people of interest. "Find out more and keep me informed."

Chapter 13

Manny Gobler was in a foul mood. The AGM of Mining Management Systems was an occasion when the details of the company—his company—would be laid bare. As both CEO and chairman, he had total control and power, but company law required him to be at least mildly transparent once a year. It irked him. He'd given careful thought as to how information about the company would be presented. Last year's AGM had been chaotic with four long-term employees resigning. Try as he might, the key indicators of the company's progress did not look any better this year. His expenses had increased five-fold, and the company was only just holding it's own financially. He'd forced the retirement of the chief finance officer and installed someone more open to persuasion about what he could do—and what should and should not be presented at the AGM.

On the bright side, Evelyn would be arriving tonight to spend the next two weeks with him in the penthouse suite. With any luck, she would be there, even now, unpacking her bags and making herself comfortable. The thought of stroking the satin skin of her thighs filled him with anticipation. Despite the terrible weather and the expense of living there, he loved being in London.

He stared out of the twelfth-story window of The Tower Hotel. The Trafalgar Conference Room had magnificent views over Tower Bridge. Whilst Manny could do nothing about the weather, the expense of living in London was at least something he could now afford, thanks to the company. He had therefore resolved to move the company headquarters to London later in the year, so he could enjoy more of London society…and, of course, Evelyn's attentions.

The new chief finance officer was busy checking that his presentation was working through the data projector. It reminded Manny that he needed to tell him not to show one of the images. He'd reviewed the presentation on the flight, and try as he might, he couldn't think of a way to make it palatable.

Affecting a geniality he did not feel, he laid a hand on the shoulder of the finance officer and said, "I've decided that you shouldn't show the fourth slide in your report."

"But that's…but we have to. It's the AGM," the man spluttered.

Manny squeezed the man's shoulder until he winced. "It's my company, and I'll tell you what we can and can't do. Do you understand?"

"Yes, sir."

A young waiter came past with a tray containing bottles of Perrier water.

"Give me one of those," demanded Manny. He was still feeling dehydrated from his flight and the two bottles of red wine he'd consumed. The man poured him a glass of water then took up his station at the tea and coffee bar where he began to dispense hot drinks to the shareholders as they arrived.

Manny watched them. Five of the staff from the South African office arrived together. Just behind them, came a larger group, all from the London office.

Toby Cheeseman was amongst them and was, as usual, sounding like a 1950s London fop with his ridiculous accent. Manny decided he would use this London trip to sack Cheeseman. He was asking too many questions and raising too many objections. It was a pity, because he was also brilliant, and almost single-handedly running the technical side of the company. But no one is irreplaceable. *If you don't play ball with me, you don't play ball at all.*

The surprise of the morning came when the last two people arrived for the meeting. Both had flown all the way from South Africa, and both were people he had sacked in the last year. One was Johan Linke, the old chief finance officer; and the other was Christian Steicke, the ex-negotiator for mining contracts in Africa. He was about to object when he remembered they both held a few company shares and had every right to attend. He hoped they had not come to cause trouble.

After glancing at his watch, he strode to the podium and called the meeting to order. Donning his most winsome façade, he welcomed people to the AGM and called for apologies. Only two names were given. The board members and most of the share-holders were present in the room. Following his introduction, the minutes of the last AGM were read out. Manny asked if it was a full and fair record of what had occurred last year. Much to his surprise, no one raised any objections or proposed any amendments.

Manny went on to 'matters arising' and then to the 'financial report.' If there was going to be trouble, this was when it would occur. He presented a highly edited and heavily interpreted summary of the company's financial state. Despite his skill at dissembling, the financial report did not present a good picture. Manny hurried through it, putting the best spin on it that he could, claiming he was laying a solid foundation for the future.

When it was over, he steeled himself for the inevitable objections.

There were none.

Hardly daring to believe his good fortune, he proceeded to the election of the company office bearers, confident that this final agenda item was a mere formality. "Mr. Cheeseman, as our London host, would you be so kind as to take the chair for the election of officers?"

"Certainly, old chap."

Manny bit his lip to restrain himself from biting Toby's head off.

You have only ten more minutes of employment in this company, you ridiculous idiot.

Toby moved to the podium, and called out in his plumy accent, "Nominations please for chairman."

Manny Gobler was proposed and seconded.

"Any other nominations?" asked Toby with bored affectation.

"Get on with it," demanded Manny.

Christian Steicke eased himself out of his chair and stood up. "I propose Peter Jacobs."

"Who the hell is Peter Jacobs?" demanded Manny crossly.

Toby answered, "Ah, he's one of our people in the London Office. He's got a few shares."

Manny glared at the small group of company shareholders that had come from the local office, and tried to work out which fool had just engineered his own sacking.

"Do we have a seconder?"

"I'll second him," said Johan Linke, the old company treasurer. His face was expressionless.

Toby continued, "There will be a vote: one vote per share. The returning officers will be the past and present chief finance officers." He asked that the voting slips be handed out, then instructed those present, "When you vote, clearly record your name and the number of shares in the spaces indicated. Make known any proxy votes."

People immediately began chatting and hissing questions at each other. Who would have the temerity to put their name up against Manny Gobler? Did they know anyone called Jacobs? Manny moved restlessly in his chair. If nothing else, this little voting charade would cement his hold on the company. But, by God, heads would roll afterwards.

The room came to a hush as the company's chief finance officer stood up, and passed a piece of paper to Toby.

Manny saw the ashen face of the finance officer, and furrowed his brow.

Toby opened the piece of paper, and announced: "Mr. Manier Gobler, forty-three percent of all voting shares."

Manny Gobler smiled with relief and got up to resume his place at the podium.

Toby continued, "Mr. Peter Jacobs, fifty-seven percent of all voting shares. The new chairman of Mining Management Systems is..."

"What! Bloody ridiculous!" exploded Manny. "What do you think you are playing at? Only sixty percent of the shares can be voted. What sort of tomfoolery is this?" He pointed a finger at his newly appointed chief finance officer. "You idiot! How do you explain it?"

The finance officer looked as if he wanted the floor to open up and swallow him. He stammered, "I'm terribly sorry, Mr. Gobler. But all the votes were counted correctly. You can check the figures."

Gobler marched across to the desk where the two returning officers sat, snatched the paper summarizing the results and glared at them. "Preposterous. There has been a miscarriage of voting propriety." He waved the papers in the air. "It says here that this Peter Jacobs has forty percent of all voting shares. That's impossible."

Toby Cheeseman's voice suddenly took on an altogether unfamiliar tone of authority, one that shocked everyone in the room. "Mr. Gobler, please sit down, or I will call hotel security and have you removed. Impugning the integrity of the returning officers does you no credit."

Toby's voice cracked on Manny's ears like a whip causing him to sit down in shock. Before Manny could rekindle his anger, Toby continued, "I call on Peter Jacobs to address the shareholders as the new chairman of Mining Management Systems."

Everyone waited for someone to move. After an eternity, the young waiter by the tea and coffee counter made his way down to the front.

"What do you think you are doing, fool!" spat Manny. "Get out of the way."

Unperturbed, the young man continued to walk to the lectern. When he arrived, he took a deep breath and said, "My name is

Peter Jacobs. Before I changed my name, I was Jan Pieter de Jager. I am Kirk de Jager's son."

Peter saw the wave of realization sweep through the room.

As Toby stepped forward to insert a USB into the computer controlling the data projector, Peter continued. "I have something to show you."

With that, Peter launched into a brutally clear presentation of the company's performance over the last two years. With merciless clarity, he showed a graph of the money Gobler had spent on personal luxuries. Superimposed over the top, he showed a graph of falling company profits, falling numbers of new contracts, and the falling level of investment in research and development.

Its impact was shocking.

At the conclusion of the presentation, there was a deathly hush. Peter turned to Manny Gobler and said, "Mr. Gobler, you are summarily dismissed as CEO, as a director, and as an employee of Mining Management Systems. You will be given one year's salary as severance pay. Your actions as Director of the Company over the last two years have been characterized by greed and questionable ethics that, in all probability, should attract the attention of those policing company law. If you leave immediately, no further action will be taken. If you try to access the company computers, you will find that all passwords have been changed."

Peter glanced across at Toby Cheeseman, and saw him nod almost imperceptibly. He drew a deep breath and continued speaking. "The company information on your own computer and backup system has been erased. Indeed, even the computer code on your key to the Company's London penthouse suite has been changed."

Peter hung onto the podium. He did not trust his legs to hold him up during this test of brinkmanship. Just one thing gave him strength—anger. Peter knew its power all too well, and he now knew how to manage it.

It was time to deliver the killer blow.

Peter let go of the lectern. "I also have to tell you that a disgruntled lady, answering to the name of Evelyn, has just left a message saying that you can, quote: 'go to hell,' and that she is returning home. Your bags can be collected from the foyer of this hotel."

Gobler screamed. "How dare you? Who do you think you are, you jumped up lackey? You have no right. That's my computer. It's private property!"

"No it is not, Mr. Gobler," snapped Peter. "It's the company's computer and the company's information. An authorized company member has moved to protect company information from you—a person who has been toxic to the organization's well-being and who is no longer in the company's employ."

Gobler spat back, "The company is nothing without me! How do you think it can operate without my leadership? I'm a founding partner." He pointed a quivering finger at Peter. "What experience do you have?"

Peter could picture an ex-Regimental Sergeant Major commanding him to look into his eyes. He looked at Gobler without flinching.

Gobler was the first to look away.

A crazy, desperate, audacious idea suddenly came to Peter. In the space of a few seconds, he reviewed the risks. He was now on a high, and he knew he would soon crash, leaving him without the courage to try anything. If he was to seize the opportunity, he had to act now.

"The only jobs I've ever had, have been pushing trolleys in a fruit market, and serving as a waiter at a local restaurant." With brutal candor, he continued, "I've had no experience of mining and have never run a company. I suspect that there is a risk that we could go bankrupt within a year. However, none of that is now your concern."

"You bloody idiot. It still concerns me, because I own forty percent of the shares." Gobler turned to all those seated in the room and shouted, "Your shares will be worth peanuts if you let this child...this fool, run the company."

"Then let me buy your shares, Mr. Gobler. I will give you one-million pounds Sterling from my father's estate for your shares."

"Preposterous. They were worth five times as much as that yesterday," shouted Gobler.

"Fine. I'll offer you two-hundred thousand for them in two months time, and believe me, by then, you will be pleased to sell them to me. You will be even more pleased to sell them when people find out that I've spent the last twenty-six months in Belmarsh prison." Peter slapped the lectern. "My offer is one million pounds: now." He paused. "Johan Linke has your share details and the necessary paperwork with him if you wish to sign."

A frisson of shock spread through the room.

Gobler's mouth was open. He shut it with a snap and glared at Peter.

Seconds passed.

Gobler threw his arms in the air and yelled, "I accept." He swung round, and shouted to everyone in the room, "If you let this ex-con, someone with no business experience—a waiter, for good-ness sake, take over the company, it will be worthless." Gobler turned back to Peter and hissed, "At least I'll be a millionaire, whilst you will have nothing other than a lifetime of debts. You can have my worthless shares. This company is finished."

Peter kept an impassive face. "Ladies and gentlemen, please take time to have a tea break. The AGM will reconvene in fifteen minutes."

After signing the share transfer papers, Manny Gobler stormed out of the meeting.

Peter watched him go, knowing that Gobler was yet to learn that all three of his luxury cars, together with his airplane, were being repossessed in South Africa and would shortly be sold off.

He turned back and stared out the window. A shower of rain had just doused the city, but the sun was now peering from between the clouds, bathing Tower Bridge in light.

Johan Linke beckoned Peter over to the table to sign the share purchase papers—and write a check. After signing his name a number of times, Peter returned to the window...and tried to come to terms with all that had happened. Despite the triumph, so many things remained uncertain. He craved peace, acceptance, and safety. He craved…Beth.

"Beth," he whispered. "Where are you? I need you now."

He dragged himself back to reality. The fifteen minutes were up. Taking a deep breath, he resumed his position behind the lectern.

"Ladies and gentlemen, please forgive the recent theatrics." He smiled. "I have to say that, in truth, Mining Management Systems is in very good hands and we are hopeful of making a profit this year."

He nodded to Toby. "I am pleased to announce that Toby Cheeseman will take control as General Manager of Mining Management Systems. Christian Steicke will take over the Cape Town office, and reactivate our push for contracts in Namibia, Angola, Guinea, and Gabon. I will apprentice myself to Mr. Cheeseman and begin to explore markets in America."

He leaned on the lectern. "Whilst I have a business degree, I acknowledge that I have a great deal to learn and will be relying heavily on you all to teach me. I want it to be known that until I believe I am pulling my weight, I will not draw a salary."

He stood up and smiled. "Finally, I would like to propose that Johan Linke be reinstated as the company's treasurer. Do we have a seconder?"

Toby put up his hand.

"Congratulations, Mr. Linke. With the benefit of eighty percent of the voting shares, I can say that it's good to have you back."

For the next thirty minutes, Peter invited those leading different branches of the company to give a ten-minute overview of their department for the benefit of the rest of the shareholders.

When Peter closed the meeting, spontaneous applause broke out.

Peter stood there, bewildered, listening to it. The fact that no one raised the issue of his prison record was, Peter knew, entirely due to Toby's activities during the tea break. He'd busied himself telling concerned shareholders that Peter had served two years for manslaughter, as a result of accidentally killing a thug who was attacking his girlfriend.

Peter felt that it was an overly generous interpretation of facts. In reality, what he'd done was terrible—truly horrible—and had been catastrophic for the young man's family. The shame of it still hung heavily around his neck, continuing to damn him like the *Ancient Mariner*.

Chapter 14

Peter stood at the window in Alex's sitting room, but he was not looking at the view. His mind was miles away trying to grapple with the enormity of what had happened.

Alex spoke from behind his newspaper. "Still wondering about your place in the universe?"

Peter hauled himself back from where his thoughts had taken him, and he reflected on Alex's question. What was his purpose in the grand scheme of things? Did he have what it took to lead his father's company? The doubts that had been kept at bay by the busyness of the day had now surfaced to plague him. Was he meant to be leading a company? Or was this whole life just a monstrous game—a game of chance that mocked humanity's pathetic presumption of significance.

Peter sighed. "Isn't everything...life, all a bit meaningless?"

Alex lowered the newspaper, and studied Peter over the top of his glasses. "Don't you think that the billions of things that had to be precisely right to allow intelligent life to exist on one planet might be a fair clue to the answer?"

"It could all just be a monstrous fluke of nature."

"If you begin with absolutely nothing, even the non-existence of time, then that option is not open to you. Where did the elements come from to use in the giant game of chance that fluked our existence?"

Peter shrugged.

Alex rebuked him. "Peter, these questions need a better intellectual answer than a lazy shrug of the shoulders."

Receiving no reply, Alex continued, "Remember, we are not just talking about the fact of our existence, but the highly unlikely manner of it."

Peter said nothing for a long while. Finally he looked up and said. "Alex, I've just inherited approximately three million pounds from my father's estate—and own eighty percent of the shares of my father's company, currently valued at ten million pounds."

Alex flicked the paper back up. "Then I suppose you're wondering if I should put the rent up."

Peter burst out laughing. All his pent-up emotions poured out, as he doubled over in mirth at the absurdity of everything. Alex dropped the paper and grinned.

Refreshed by his laughter, Peter felt bold enough to ask, "Seriously Alex, how do I handle it? Because I'm not at all sure I can."

"Well, if what you say is the case, you've inherited a huge responsibility…and been placed in a dangerous position."

"Why dangerous?"

"Money does funny things to people. It changes them. Good people become greedy. Modest people become tyrants, and balanced people become workaholics addicted to adrenaline. Money destroys a lot of people." He paused before adding, "Success, as popularly defined by society, is not all that it is cracked up to be. It can be hazardous to a person's integrity and well-being."

"A poisoned chalice?"

"It can be, but it doesn't have to be. I said it was dangerous to handle, not impossible."

"How do I stop it destroying me?"

Alex lifted the paper from his lap, and placed it on the floor. "You need to develop a sense of something bigger than yourself. I, personally, am convinced that means finding who you are in God —but you will have to make up your own mind about that."

Peter frowned and felt way out of his depth. "Can you give me anything more concrete?"

"That is concrete. It's foundational, in fact. But if you want some specific wisdom to keep you living well with money, you might consider this." He ticked off on his fingers: "You will need to intentionally invest in relationships; you will need to navigate hardships well; and you will need to routinely do some sort of humble job of service that will keep you earthed."

Alex stretched out his left leg and began rubbing it. "Surviving success will mean controlling whom and what you allow to influence you. It will mean not being so driven that you lose your joy or the ability to wonder. It will also mean looking after your health. And it will mean remaining accountable to wise people who will keep you honest."

"Whew!" said Peter, and was silent for a while. Eventually he said, "I'm not sure I'm able…" he trailed off.

"But will you try?"

"Will you agree to be that person I make myself accountable to?"

"Yes."

"Will you put up my rent?"

"No."

Alex smiled…and they both laughed.

"Lenny, can I have a chat with you some time this morning?"

Lenny was looking through the order book and rubbing his bulbous nose. He gave no indication of hearing Peter's request. "Business is picking up already. We've got a dozen of your Yeoman from the Tower this Wednesday. I'm going to need more staff."

Peter adjusted his thinking to Lenny's agenda. "Talk to Kym if you want more staff. In her time in London, she's developed a network of people in the hospitality industry. And I'd get her to interview them. You're too soft."

"I hired you."

"Like I said, you're too soft."

Lenny grunted. "I'd just like a little more business to justify it."

"Why not offer breakfast to all the yachties and locals around the dock. Stick a display box containing menus on the gate to each marina pontoon. Have two sittings, early and late. Give a concession to those who book more than twenty-four hours in advance. You could even ring the ship's bell to signal the start of each sitting. It would add to the local color and help develop a sense of community."

Lenny leaned back. "Are you sure you shouldn't be running this barge? Everything that's happened here seems to have come from one of your ideas."

Peter gave a dismissive wave. "Anyone can have good ideas. The trick is working out which ones are worth committing to. Commitment takes courage," he smiled, "and a bit of madness."

"Well, you've got balls, boy, I'll say that for you." He sighed. "I'm just not sure how much longer I'm going to be able to keep you."

Having gained Lenny's attention, Peter again asked, "I'd like to talk to you about that, Lenny. Can we catch up for a chat after the lunch time rush?"

"Sure thing, lad."

Behind them came the sound of someone coming down the stairs into the cabin. Peter turned around to see Toby. Today, he was dressed in a three-piece suit and had a white handkerchief sticking out of his top pocket.

Lenny murmured to Peter, "Here's your 'Burlington Bertie' again. I'll let you two get on with it." He placed a hand on Peter's shoulder. "But I'll need you in twenty minutes."

Peter nodded.

Toby slid into the seat opposite Peter. "I say," he said, "this place really looks spiffing. You've done jolly well. Positive pleasure coming here now."

"How is the London team feeling about the, er, new developments?"

"Pretty good, actually. Some judicial feeding of the rumor mills with the right facts has helped."

Peter looked inquiringly at him.

"Actually," confessed Toby, "I put on a company soiree last night for the local staff and gave them the goss." He smiled. "It went well. I gave them your apologies, by the way, and told them that you had paid for the evening. That earned you a few brownie points. It will cost a bit, but it's definitely worth building good friendships and communications at this juncture."

Peter nodded his gratitude. "That's why you'll make a great general manager, Toby." He toyed with his coffee mug. "I'll try and get into the office next week and introduce myself. When I do, I'd like to visit each person individually at their workstations…and then address the staff together." He paused. "But I'm afraid I won't be much use to you at the office until I finish tidying things up here."

"If you do what you've just said, old chap, you will have done more than Manny did during his entire time as company director." He smiled wolfishly. "By the way, we've had a threatening email from him this morning. He wants his company shares reinstated. He claims he was coerced. I've simply buzzed back to say that there were eighteen people present who can testify that wasn't the case. So don't worry about it."

"He's a bully."

Toby nodded. "I had a chat with Christian Steicke before he left this morning. I've asked him to invest in staff morale, and try and get an early win with one of his contracts so that the African staff start to feel they're part of a successful team again. And I've put in an advertisement for someone to manage the London office. Do you want to be part of the interviewing process?"

Peter nodded. "Definitely." He patted his lips before continuing. "Toby, my parole conditions prohibit foreign travel. Can you get over to Cape Town as soon as possible and help establish the new company culture there?"

Toby raised an eyebrow. "And what exactly is our new culture? You're the one who needs to define it, old boy."

Peter had been giving this some thought and was able to respond immediately. "Reward excellence. Reward risks if they are well considered—even if they fail. Encourage relationships and friendships…and do whatever you can to foster initiative and team spirit. I want open communication, easy access to the boss, and I want to share rewards." He leaned back. "That should do for a start."

Toby patted him on the shoulder. "You'll do, old chap. You'll do. And now for something different." He reached down and fished some papers out of his briefcase. "I've made some progress with the other project you gave me. Actually, it wasn't as difficult as I feared." He laid the papers on the table. "I could have given it to you yesterday, but I thought that taking over your father's company—and making a four million pound profit on shares was probably enough for one day."

Peter smiled ruefully and listened to what Toby had to say.

When they'd finished, Toby asked, "One more thing before I go. Are you still sure you want to be known as Jan Pieter de Jager to company staff and on the company website?"

"Yes please, Toby. It'll help company members and clients feel more secure if they realize that the company hasn't transitioned away from my father's family. Staff and clients can be pretty skittish."

As Toby left, he handed Peter a mobile phone. "If I need to get hold of you at any time, you need this. And here's the number." He passed over a piece of paper.

Peter turned the phone over in his hands. "This doesn't look like any phone I've seen before."

"Probably not. It's a Blackberry. Believe me, it's the shape of things to come. It'll let you view emails, do text messaging, and browse the Web." He smiled. "You'll get used to it."

After Toby left, Peter sat listening to the hull shudder as the wind blew through the rigging. He reflected on his decision to retain his old name in his father's business. It wasn't just a business decision. He knew he wanted to stay as Peter Jacobs for the sake of his relationship with Beth—the relationship he was hoping for, at least. He reasoned that being Jan Pieter de Jager, company director and multi-millionaire, might be an unnecessary complication. Certainly, it concerned him enough to ask Alex not to share the details of his financial position with anyone.

Beth. She was filling his thoughts again. Even now, he could visualize her hazel eyes. They were as mystical as an Irish mist, but could instantly come alive with curiosity and fun. He shook his head. Something was sparking to life within him that he'd never experienced before. He couldn't define it. It was visceral. It was a longing, a tenderness, a pain that was both savage and beautiful. It was terrifying vulnerability. It was not daring to hope, but never countenancing the possibility of defeat. It was compelling and bewildering.

"Move your arse, Peter!"

"Okay, Kym. I'm coming."

The *Phoenix* was a hive of activity over the lunch sitting. A large group of bankers had booked in. Lenny had taken up Peter's suggestion of offering key businesses in the City group bookings at discounted prices.

Kym was delighted, but hungry for more business. She instructed Peter, "Always on-sell, mate. Once they've finished the main course, wheel the dessert trolley to them,and ask what they would like." She grinned. "It's harder to refuse when they are looking at it. And if they don't want dessert, offer them coffee. Take some freshly made coffee to them so they can smell it. It's the add-ons that really boost profit."

Eventually, the last of the customers left, and the cleaning up was done. Lenny nodded to Peter. "Young Peter-me-lad, we're done for now. Make me a coffee and take it out on deck. I'll join you in a few minutes so we can have our chat."

Armed with two mugs of coffee, Peter climbed up onto the deck, stepped over the barge's massive iron mainsheet horse, and made his way forward.

The pennants from the Tower of London were streaming out in the blustery wind. Peter set the mugs down on the forward hatch, walked up to the stem-head of the bow, and held on to the forestay. The cabled rope vibrated like a live thing in his hand as the wind moaned through the rigging.

Peter stretched out his back muscles and lifted his head to the heavens, breathing in the fresh air with relish.

"Hello, sailor. Going my way?"

Peter spun around.

Beth was standing on the quayside.

He gazed at her, grinning foolishly.

She was dressed in jeans, long black boots, a tight fitting polo neck, and an open jacket. Beth looked terrific. Wind whipped her hair across her face. As she brushed it aside, he could see laughter dancing in her eyes.

"You're looking lovely," he said as he moved across to her. He placed one foot on the gunwale and the other on the wharf. "Here," he said, "let me lift you across."

"Shouldn't you be repelling boarders?"

"Pirates, yes; crew, no."

He put his hands around her waist, lifted her across the narrow gap of water and eased her onto the deck. However, he did not let her go.

Beth lifted a hand to his cheek…and then touched his lips.

Peter held his breath.

"Unhand that maiden," growled Lenny as he walked toward them. "All captured wenches and spoils of pillaging are privileges of the captain."

"Hi, Lenny," said Beth, blushing as she eased herself free of Peter's arms.

"Want a coffee? Pete will make you one."

"No, thanks. I must be getting back to work," she said.

Peter reached for Beth's hand. "Why did you come?"

"Oh," she said airily. "I was in the neighborhood and thought I'd drop in for a few minutes."

He said nothing for a while, and then nodded. "I'm glad you did." Not trusting himself to say anything more, he returned the conversation to things more prosaic. "Beth, are you able to come over tonight, late, about 10:30? It's just that I've got some news for Alex, which you might help us understand. I'm sorry it can't be earlier, but I'm working late." Peter searched Beth's eyes, wishing he had the words to say the things he hadn't said.

"Sure. I'll arrive early and bring dinner for Alex. He won't eat otherwise." She stood on tiptoes and brushed the lightest of kisses on Peter's cheek, before walking down the deck to the gangplank.

Lenny laid a hand on his shoulder. "A wench like that might just stop a fellow going to sea." He reached back for his mug of coffee. "Now then, young Peter, what do you want to talk about?"

The kiss had felt like electricity charging through his body. Peter wanted to savor it, to nurse it, and delight in its meaning. No. He wanted to do more.

Instead, he said, "Lenny, I'm in a quandary. I've been offered the chance to be an apprentice at an IT firm. I need to take it up." He paused. "The trouble is, I really like being part of things here. You, Kym, the *Phoenix*...I feel accepted here, and that I've got a place. That's something pretty special, and I don't want to lose it."

Lenny nodded and scratched his stomach. "Well, young Peter; in the short time you've been with us, you've turned everything upside down with your ideas—and worked your butt off to make them happen. So, forgive me for not being exactly thrilled at the idea of losing you. Although, to be honest, it was pretty clear to me that you were never going to stay a waiter for very long."

"I was very happy being a waiter."

Lenny dismissed this comment with a wave of his hand and asked, "Is this apprentice thing full-time, or could you work both jobs part-time—even if it is just one day a week?"

With huge relief, Peter said, "Absolutely. I could do one day a week. Perhaps Wednesdays, if that would suit."

"Right. Let's settle on that. When does all this begin?"

"Next week. The office where I'll be working is just two minutes walk from here, so I'll still be around to sneak a coffee with you now and then."

Lenny grunted. "Will this mob give you enough to live on? Remember, you've got the dragon lady, Ms. Templeton, to convince."

"I reckon I'll manage, Lenny."

Beth put the phone down from speaking with Alex. Her offer to bring dinner had been accepted with an enthusiasm that she suspected had little to do with food.

Dear Alex. He'd always been there for her—through those dreadful days when she'd first worked as his post-doctoral researcher. She put a hand on her stomach. The pain of those days still haunted her; the memory of the time she'd been pregnant; the memory of the boyfriend who'd made it clear he didn't want anything to do with a child.

She'd regretted the abortion immediately and grieved the loss with an intensity she had not anticipated. For nine weeks, she'd been nursing a new life—and then she'd ended it. It had been her child. The miracle inside her already had all its vital organs in place and was growing tiny fingernails. *Fingernails, for goodness sake!*

She'd wept and wept and wept.

It was all too much for the boyfriend. He left.

But Alex had been there with his understanding, and he'd introduced her to a profound level of forgiveness—the forgiveness of God.

She breathed out her anguish. Then, quite deliberately, she took herself to a place of stillness.

Eventually, peace came, and with it a conviction that she was now ready to move on. A new adventure was beckoning.

Why had she visited the *Phoenix*? It must have appeared bizarre to Peter, and yet she knew he'd been grateful. She'd seen it in his eyes. It gave her the confidence she needed to hope.

Beth stripped off her clothes for a shower. She would take a great deal of care in how she dressed for the evening.

As the water played over her, she remembered how it had felt to be in Peter's arms. She'd imagined him stroking her cheek, touching her lips…and more.

Chapter 15

Peter was breathing heavily from his late night jog home from work. He inserted the key into the front door only to find that it would not open. With mild frustration, he rang the doorbell.

A few seconds later, Beth opened the door and stood there looking at him. She gave him a nervous smile. "As we seem to have all our important conversations on this doorstep, I took the liberty of bolting the door so that I could join you here. I've something I want to tell you...in private."

She looked devastatingly beautiful. Her hair cascaded in curls onto her shoulders. The top three buttons of her shimmering aqua shirt were undone.

"Hmm?"

"I need to tell you something of my past." Beth held her arms straight down her side. Her hands opened and closed—her anxiety palpable.

He waited.

"Two years ago, I had an abortion."

Silence hung between them.

Peter could see the anguish in her eyes. He drew in a deep breath. "And now you regret it?"

Beth lowered her head and allowed her hair to obscure her face. "My boyfriend didn't want it." She paused. "I've regretted it ever since."

Peter's emotions were in turmoil. How could he help Beth deal with her demons? What could he say? He cleared his throat. "I'm so sorry for your grief and for the way you were treated… by a man." Peter couldn't think of anything else to say. Very slowly, he reached out, put his arm around her waist, and drew her to him. Beth resisted—her eyes wide. Then she allowed herself to be pressed against him.

He searched her eyes.

She returned his gaze.

He moved his head forward hesitantly, experimentally, then turned away. *No. Too soon.* She wouldn't…?

Beth moved her head, shadowing his movement so that she stayed in front of him. Her lips were just inches away.

Finally, he could bear it no longer. He brought his lips down on hers.

The sweetness of the kiss sent electricity fizzing through his body. It was like nothing he'd ever felt before. He was giddy with delight. It was wonderful…surreal…*amazing.* Her lips were soft, with just a hint of moisture. Unbelievably, they were warm with love. He felt Beth wrap her arms around his neck giving him permission —asking.

A wave of passion rose up within him. He pulled her tighter and kissed her hungrily.

Five minutes later, Beth tilted her head back and laughed. "I think that was our best conversation ever."

Peter nuzzled her neck with the tip of his nose.

Beth murmured something.

"What did you say?" he asked.

"I said 'Thank you, Peter. A million times, thank you.'"

"You're welcome."

She kissed him lightly on the lips, then pulled back. "We'd better go in so you can have a warm shower and not die of pneumonia." Beth towed him into the entryway. "We're in the study. We've eaten, but I've kept some Chinese takeaway for you."

―――――――

Peter came into the study as Beth was laying out pieces of paper on the floor. The fire was burning, and Alex was leafing through a book in his armchair. He looked up and saw Peter carrying a folder. "And what have you got for us, Peter?"

Peter pulled the office chair out from behind the desk and sat down. He placed the folder on the desk. "I've got some information for you about the photograph Trevor took—if you're ready to hear it. I just hope it's of some use."

Alex put the book down and folded his hands.

"First, I've managed to dig up a bit about the company names—at least those we could read. Three could be seen easily, and we've had a guess at a fourth. What they have in common is that they have all changed ownership over the last two years...and all are located in the old city of London. I've a list of them and a map showing their positions. The new owners are various investment groups."

Alex frowned. "What's the nature of these companies? Is there any connection between them?"

"All are concerned with money—mostly finance companies. There's one insurance group, and if we've guessed it correctly, an importing company. Can't say anything more beyond that."

"Well," said Alex. "Trevor was a banker and was involved with money, but I can't see his connection with these companies." He put his fingertips together and closed his eyes.

Only the tick of the clock disturbed the silence.

Finally, Alex opened his eyes and continued the conversation. "There are, I think, only two possibilities. The first is that someone is monitoring the markets in the City for some reason. It has certainly been very disturbed recently with the economic downturn, and there are some predatory groups pouncing on undervalued company shares. If that is the case, we may simply have a list that represents normal economic opportunism."

He tapped his fingers together. "The other option is of greater concern, and that is the possibility that these companies represent some sort of cartel with a common interest. If that is the case, then there is a fairly large economic power base being developed."

Peter shook his head. "Toby has run a search on the directors of the companies we know about, but hasn't found any common thread. I've got them listed here."

Alex leaned over and took the piece of paper from Peter. "You've done well, Peter. Anything else?"

"Yes. The phrase 'Lucifer: pure, virtuous, wholesome, and innocent:' it's only been found once on the Internet, and that was in connection with a Shriner. He used that very phrase in an interview."

Alex nodded. "Yes, I've heard about them."

"Finally," said Peter, "I've got this." He flourished a piece of paper. "Toby was pretty pleased with himself at being able to un-distort the image reflected in the paper-weight. It took him a while." He passed the page to Alex. "He thinks the image is of some sort of medallion, seal, or stamp."

Beth got up from the floor and stood behind Alex's chair so she could see the image. It was very simple—an equilateral triangle with a cross on the apex.

Alex's face went pale.

"What's the matter Alex?" said Peter.

Beth picked up on Peter's concern. "Alex, are you all right?"

"I'm fine," said Alex, sounding anything but convincing. "It's just that I know this symbol." He paused. "It is the symbol of the Golden Dawn. It's an organization that shouldn't exist any more, but this"—he tapped the paper—"may indicate that it does."

Peter asked, "What is the Golden Dawn?"

"It's an order of Freemasonry founded by a group of people headed by William Westcott. They used to hold their rituals in the London headquarters of the Mark Masons. It is a pagan order of Freemasons. Each Golden Dawn temple is presided over by a hiero-phant, a presiding priest who represents the rising sun. The elements of earth, air, fire, and water are evoked during their rituals."

Alex tapped his forefingers against his lips.

"Hmm. Yes," he said, almost to himself. Louder, he continued, "The notorious English Satanist, Aleister Crowley, belonged to Golden Dawn. In fact, if my memory serves me well, Crowley was also admitted as a thirty-third degree Mason into a break-away rite of the Rose Croix."

Beth shook her head. "Surely Freemasonry can't involve Satanism. Isn't it against their creed?"

"Golden Dawn was overtly Satanic. Normal Freemasonry does not claim to be Satanic."

Peter looked closely at the professor. "But you're not convinced?"

"I'm not sure. Some very good people are caught up in it without knowing its full significance." Alex sighed. "It's not surprising. The Freemasons put up a very good philanthropic front. However, its core beliefs, known only to a few, are of grave concern."

Beth furrowed her brow. "What troubles you about them?"

"Many things; many things." Alex closed his eyes and seemed to retreat into some sort of internal space. Peter thought he'd finished speaking but after a moment, Alex continued. "You need to understand that Freemasonry claims to be rooted in the mystery religions of antiquity—including the ancient Egyptian gods of Isis and Osiris. As such, it claims to acknowledge a spiritual reality that is older than Christianity and older than Judaism." He shrugged. "Freemasonry can't, therefore, be contained within a religion like Christianity, which claims to be God's chosen and most adequate form of revelation."

"But my Uncle George is a Freemason, and he's a Church of England vicar," protested Beth.

"Clerics who join generally have theologically liberal views, and feel less constrained by biblical principles. Some believe that Christianity is just one of many alternative cultural badges people use to express their internal spirituality. As such, they have no trouble with Freemasonry."

An uncomfortable silence hung in the room—one that Peter didn't fully understand. He chose to bring the conversation back to the matter in hand. "Well, I think we are starting to get a bit of a picture. If the photo Trevor took was significant, it would suggest that his death is somehow linked with Freemasonry—perhaps even Satanism—and with people seeking financial power."

Alex nodded. "I believe Trevor took that picture to expose something. He and I used to argue a lot about Freemasonry. In fact, I'd just given him some pretty damning information about it." He massaged his forehead. "He thanked me and said he would deal with it."

"What do you think he meant?" asked Peter.

"I think he was going to dig around to determine the truth about it for himself." Alex looked up at him. "I believe he found it." He pointed to the picture. "Trevor took this picture and swallowed the memory chip because he knew it was important—and knew himself to be in great danger."

"I suppose it's plausible."

"It is." He paused. "I think it's time I took what we know to the police. I'll ring Detective Sergeant Jenkins first thing tomorrow. He can look into Trevor's Freemasonry connections and see what he can find." Alex began massaging his legs. "And I think that is quite enough for tonight."

"I had something," Beth said, "but it can wait."

"No, no," said Alex gallantly. "Perhaps we should get some hot drinks, and then you can share it, Beth."

Peter followed Beth into the kitchen and pulled some mugs off a shelf, while she filled the kettle. He found a ridiculous pleasure in doing even this simple task with her. It felt—what? He leaned back against the cupboards and watched her. Natural: that was it. It felt natural.

Beth stepped in front of him, entwined her fingers in each of his hands and straightened her arms down. She leaned forward to rest her head against his chest.

"Hmm, you feel good."

Peter felt her warmth on his chest and didn't trust himself to say anything.

When they went back to join Alex, Beth settled herself cross-legged on the floor among her pieces of paper. She smiled. "Mine is a story of tomb robbers and disaster on the high seas. I've got some stuff on the *Beatrice*."

Alex smiled. "Good for you, Beth."

"What is it?" asked Peter.

"Well, in the early nineteenth century, everyone who could pillage Egypt for its artifacts and relics, did so. There was a mad scramble for them—fueled by a renewed interest in alternative spiritualities, including Freemasonry. Egypt was politically weak and could do little to stop the raids on its heritage—particularly by the Italians and the British. Of the twenty-nine obelisks that still exist, only nine remain in Egypt."

Beth consulted one of the pieces of paper on the floor. "One of the most notorious raiders was Richard William Howard Vyse. He was a military man who then went into politics. But, as a dedicated Freemason, his real love was archaeology. He wanted to collect artifacts representative of the ancient religions the Freemasons claimed as their heritage."

"Why was he notorious?" asked Peter.

"I'm coming to that. Vyse teamed up with a sailor from Genoa called Giovanni Cavigula, who had been employed by some European collectors. Cavigula taught Vyse the art of blasting his way into pyramids using dynamite." Beth sighed. "I can't even begin to think of the damage they must have caused. Anyway, to his credit, Vyse did find four hidden chambers in the Great Pyramid of Giza."

"Blimey! Was there anything left of it after he blasted his way in?" Peter was amazed.

"Yes, he didn't quite destroy everything he touched. In 1837, he discovered the remains of an old wooden coffin inside the third largest of Giza's pyramids. And deep inside the same pyramid, he discovered an ornate sarcophagus made of blue basalt. It was the sarcophagus of Menkaure, one of Egypt's greatest pharaohs. Sadly, the lid had been destroyed, and it had already been robbed of its contents. Anyway, without troubling to tell the Egyptian authorities about his find, he transported the sarcophagus to the coast in order to ship it to the British Museum."

Connections started to be made in Peter's mind. "Don't tell me: the ship was called *Beatrice*."

"Spot on." She grinned. "Honestly, it's 'Boy's Own Annual' stuff. Fortunately, the tomb raiders made a drawing of the sarcophagus before they loaded it aboard." Beth held up a picture of an intricately carved sarcophagus. "It was fortunate, because disaster struck. *Beatrice* went down with all hands somewhere between Egypt and England. No one knows where."

"Wow," said Peter.

Beth looked at Alex. "I think someone is trying to find the *Beatrice* and recover the sarcophagus. People have been talking about finding it for years. Even the Spanish have talked about it. They think it was wrecked somewhere off their coast."

Alex nodded. "It's possible." He tapped the printed copy of Trevor's photograph. "I'd certainly like to know what the link is between '*Beatrice*'—the heading on the page here—and the hieroglyphics below it. Can you throw any light on that, Beth?"

Beth pulled another of her pieces of paper toward her and read from it: "*Ramses, beloved of Aman, like the son of Osiris, has placed on his obelisks the secret of the origin and power of the ultimate one.*" She brushed some strands of hair from her face. "Could it be that someone is wanting to find this place where the power of the ultimate god might be found?"

Alex frowned. "Claiming to know the power of God, is a claim that makes me nervous."

"The hieroglyphics suggest that people would have to examine what Ramses inscribed on his obelisks, if they want to find the secret place." Beth shook her head. "That wouldn't be an easy task."

Alex nodded. "Ramses' obelisks have found their way to half the palazzos in Europe, not to mention Central Park, New York— we have our very own here on the Victoria Embankment at Westminster. Mind you, if anyone really wanted to have a look at Ramses' obelisks, the best place to go is still Egypt. They've got nine."

"Surely the writing on these obelisks must be well documented by now," said Peter. "And if none of them speak of a hidden place where God's identity is concealed, then we can assume it's all a load of rubbish."

"Not necessarily, Peter. Anomalies in the carvings of hieroglyphs are still argued over. It takes a very fine scholar to understand the nuances and significances of everything that is written." Alex smiled. "Someone like Beth. She's one of the world's leading authorities."

"Not that I can help," said Beth. "I'm here, and the obelisks are there." She unwound herself from the floor and collected the mugs. "I think you've had enough for one night, Alex. It's time for me to go home." She made her way to the kitchen.

Peter came to a decision. He leaned forward, and spoke with Alex.

A minute later, Beth returned and bent over to kiss Alex on the forehead.

As she did, the professor cleared his throat and said, "Um, if you could get some time off, would you like to go overseas and explore some obelisks?"

Beth's mouth dropped open. "Alex, you've got to be kidding. You know I would. And if going could help solve the reason behind Trevor's murder..." she trailed off. "But it's not possible. We don't have the finances."

"Aah, well...it transpires that a wealthy businessman—a very good friend of the family, has made some funds available to help solve Trevor's murder. Um, providing I respect his request for anonymity, I'm pretty sure he would fund your trip."

Beth looked at him with astonishment...then suspicion. "Alex, you never lie, but I get the feeling that I'm not being told the whole truth."

She turned to Peter, who had affected an air of detachment and was staring into the fire.

"And you, Peter," she said, pointing. "You look altogether too innocent to be ignorant of what's going on."

Peter protested. "Me? No! I'm sorry. My mind had drifted away. I was anticipating our next conversation on the doorstep."

Peter was about to get up from his desk and go to bed when his mobile phone rang. It was Beth. In a shaky voice, she said, "Peter, my flat has been burgled."

Chapter 16

Peter borrowed Alex's car and drove over to Beth's flat. He arrived in time to be her moral support as the police questioned her. The contents of Beth's desk had been tipped onto the floor, and her computer was missing. The police were sympathetic but philosophical. It was just another burglary.

Peter was less sure.

But he had more on his mind than burglary. He was feeling less than positive at the prospect of meeting with his parole officer, Margaret Templeton.

Next morning, Peter sat in one of *Phoenix's* booths with Toby, nursing symptoms of significant sleep deprivation. The symptoms were in no way lessened by the arrival of his parole officer.

Lenny watched her come down the stairs from behind the bar. "Margaret, me darlin'," he called out. "Welcome back." He looked at her wolfishly. "Tell me, what's your pleasure? Cappuccino?"

Margaret gave him a look, which Peter suspected would freeze hell itself, and replied, "Yes. But I'd like it a little hotter than last time."

"Aah, Margaret," said Lenny. "You're my sort of woman."

"Being your sort of woman," she replied, tartly, "will mean you understand that I need some undisturbed time with Peter—just him and me. Got it?"

"Oh, I get you, Margaret, I certainly get you."

The parole officer rolled her eyes and sat down in Peter's booth.

Toby was dressed as if he'd just come from Saville Row. He stood up gallantly as Peter introduced her.

"Ms. Templeton, may I introduce Toby Cheeseman? He's here for reasons that will soon become clear. I've no objections to him being present for our discussion."

The parole officer nodded and sat down opposite Peter. "Well, Peter, how is it going?"

"Quite well."

When it became obvious that Peter had said all he was going to say, she attempted to draw him out. "Why has it gone well?"

"I have a job, accommodation, and friends."

Ms. Templeton nodded. "Have you had any problems with frustration or anger over the last few weeks?"

Peter remembered the anger he'd felt toward Manny Gobler—for his abuse of power, and the way he'd ridden roughshod over others for personal gain.

"No."

"Have you felt any sense of grief as a result of the hardships associated with adapting to life here?"

He reflected on the intense grief he'd shared with Alex over the death of his twin brother.

"No."

"Any stormy relationship issues?"

"No."

"Then things are going well." She pursed her lips. "Have you had any trouble turning up to work on time?"

Lenny, who was polishing glasses and listening to the conversation, interjected. "Yes he does. He's usually early, and works a good deal more than I pay him for."

The parole officer's face hardened. Peter didn't answer, deeming Lenny's reply to be adequate.

"Can I ask why this gentleman, er, Mr. Cheeseman is with us this morning, Peter?"

"Because I'll be changing jobs next week."

Ms. Templeton raised an eyebrow.

"I'll still be working one day a week here at the *Phoenix*, but for the rest of the week, I'll be doing an apprenticeship at Mining Management Systems under the direction of Mr. Cheeseman."

"Why?"

"Because I've some experience in IT, and I'd like to explore a career in it."

"Does this path have any prospects for you?"

Toby interrupted, "I think, madam, we can say it has."

"And does this apprenticeship have formal accreditation, Mr. Cheeseman?"

"Actually, no. But Peter will learn a great deal with us, and this will stand him in good stead if he, er, moves to any other company."

Ms. Templeton frowned. "I don't want Peter taken advantage of simply so you can get a cheap copy boy to run around for you. I'd prefer it if he was able to gain some formal qualification at the end of it. I want some assurance of real prospects, Mr. Cheeseman."

"I can assure you that if Peter proves competent, he will be able to rise to any position in the company," said Toby, dryly.

The sense of the absurd was not lost on Peter. But to give Ms. Templeton her due, she was trying to do her best for him. Peter had thought earlier about whether or not he should tell his parole officer about his new circumstances, but in the end, could not bring himself to do so. He reasoned that because he would not be earning any more money, there was no need. However, he knew the real reason; he was not yet confident he could make a success of running his father's company.

Ms. Templeton tapped a finger on the table. "Hmm. Well, perhaps give it a try Peter, and we'll monitor the situation. What about salary? Will you still have enough money to live on?"

Toby looked at Peter with a raised eyebrow.

Peter gave a small cough and said, "My salary will match what I currently receive here at the *Phoenix*. My accommodation arrangement with Professor Whitman will remain the same, so I'll manage okay."

"That's all very well, but if your accommodation arrangements fall through with the professor, you'll be in a precarious position financially."

"By then, I hope to have earned a promotion."

Margaret nodded. "Well, give it a try. Good luck." The parole officer stood up and made for the counter. She handed her empty cup to Lenny and said, "Still not hot enough," then turned for the stairs.

Lenny grinned as he watched her go.

At that point, Kym came out of the kitchen and handed Lenny a mug. "What do you think of that?" she asked.

He sniffed the hot liquid inside suspiciously. "What is it?"

"It's lemon myrtle. Tastes terrific. It has a minty, lemon flavor."

Lenny smelled it again and pulled a face.

"Philistine!" said Kym, retrieving the mug. "Trust me, the customers will love it." She walked over to Peter and handed him the mug. "Taste this," she demanded.

Toby got to his feet courteously, looking a little abashed as he stood in front of the pugnacious Kym.

Kym looked him up and down. "Bloody hell, you're a beautiful boy," she said.

Toby spluttered, "Er, hello, madam."

Kym burst out laughing. "Geeze, you're the real deal. Fantastic!" She held out her hand. "I'm Kym. Be nice to me if you want the best meals in London."

"Aah, Toby Cheeseman. I, er, can hardly wait to taste them." With just a hint of panic, he turned to Peter. "Right-ho: must be off."

Peter watched him make a fair imitation of a dignified exit.

Lenny gave Kym a questioning look.

"What?" asked Kym querulously. Then she grinned. "Okay, maybe I'm bi…and keeping my options open."

The Yeomen and some of their wives, trooped down the steps into the main cabin of the *Phoenix*. Peter noticed that the men had their military faces on—stern, detached, and just a bit intimidating. They filled up four of the empty booths with impersonal nonchalance. He collected only a slight nod of recognition from those he'd encountered in the mess a week earlier.

Peter conceded that turning old soldiers into people with a place in civilian life might be a little more challenging than he'd first thought. He chewed his bottom lip. Having to adjust to a whole new life outside of prison himself, he could empathize.

Once they were seated, Peter nodded to a large gentleman with a short, neatly cut beard. The man got to his feet as music began playing loudly from the *Phoenix's* speakers. Then, in a rich baritone voice, he started to sing the song 'Tower Warders' from The Yeoman of the Guard by Gilbert and Sullivan.

"Tower warders,
Under orders,
Gallant pikemen, valiant sworders!
Brave in bearing,
Foemen scaring,
In their bygone days of daring!"

The baritone then raised his hands in front of him, at which, the rest of the diners in the cabin put kazoos into their mouths. The song was finished in a cacophony that bore only a slight resemblance to the real tune.

Peter's initiative had broken the ice. The Yeomen announced free beer for everyone present, and friendly conversation began to be swapped across the aisle between booths. Only the wives of the Yeomen, Peter noticed, remained disengaged as they looked on at their husband's antics.

An hour and a half later, Peter watched the opera singer, a regular patron at the *Phoenix*, being helped off the barge by two Yeomen.

Peter sat at a table in the spring sunshine under a green canvas awning. A line of these had been set up on the Embankment opposite Gordon's Wine Bar. He'd positioned himself strategically so he could see the people coming down the steps to Watergate Walk.

He did not have long to wait.

He watched Beth as she descended the stairs. The sway of her hips betrayed her femininity, and he suspected she was completely unaware of the effect this had on the men around her. When she caught sight of Peter, she smiled—with just a hint of shyness.

"You walked?" he said, lamely.

"Yes." She raised herself on tiptoes and gave him a kiss. "Down Bloomsbury and Monmouth. It's not far from the museum."

After sharing tea and scones, they strolled across the gardens to the Victoria Embankment that ran alongside the Thames. The road beside it was lined with London plane trees, sporting their fresh spring livery. Peter was amazed they could grow at all, given that the ground around them was covered with asphalt and stone pavements.

Beth took him by the hand and towed him over to a monument. It took a moment for Peter to realize what it was. It was the obelisk of Ramses II.

"There it is," said Beth, "Cleopatra's needle." She pointed to the two sphinxes flanking the monument. "No one is quite sure why the sphinxes are facing toward the needle rather than away from it as they usually do. I like to think the workmen involved were just a little absent-minded. But it's just as likely to have a significance that someone's keeping secret."

Peter asked, "What are you looking for on this?"

"Don't know, yet. I know the text of the hieroglyphics pretty well, but I want to have another look in case I've missed something."

He smiled, "I'm in awe of you, Beth Anderson…and amazed you can read this stuff. How does it work?"

She pointed to the carvings. "Ancient Egyptian writing uses over two thousand hieroglyphs, which meant that reading was well beyond the ability of most Egyptians." She pulled him toward the monument. "Each picture character represents either an object, an idea associated with an object, or a sound. This means they could use shapes as an alphabet to spell out a name if it couldn't be represented by a character."

"Sounds complicated. How on earth did archaeologists ever manage to work it out?"

"Aah, for that, you have to thank Napoleon's army. They discovered the Rosetta Stone in 1799, which had messages written on it in three languages—all saying the same thing. It had Egyptian hieroglyphs, classical Greek, and a Demotic language. But even so, it took twenty years for a Frenchman, Jean-Francois Champollion, to translate it."

Peter ran his hand down the edge of the column. "How do you know where to start?"

"Read down the columns. And if the hieroglyphics are horizontal, just look at the direction the human or animal-like characters are facing. They always face toward the start. The Egyptians were obsessed with symmetry, so their writing could go in either direction."

As he began examining the monument, he noticed a small brass plaque at the base. "What's that about?"

"Oh that: it's a very sad story—one of many, I suspect, which could be told about this stone."

He sat down on the plinth, beside it. "Why?"

Beth patted the obelisk. "Despite this thing weighing 186 tons, it has traveled at least five times in its long history. First, it was carved at the granite quarries of Aswan and floated down the Nile—goodness knows how—and erected at Heliopolis near modern-day Cairo in 1450 BC. It originally adorned a temple built to honor the sun god, Ra." She pointed to the top of the obelisk. "In those days, it would probably have had a gold top to reflect the rays of the morning sun."

Peter smiled. The late afternoon sun was causing the highlights in Beth's hair to glow like the embers of a warming fire. He said nothing. How a woman like Beth could give him her affection was bewildering. It left him heady with joy, but it was a joy he was still not able to trust.

Oblivious to Peter's wandering thoughts, Beth continued, "That was just the beginning. As religion was a fairly fluid thing in Egypt in those days, their god, Ra, was amalgamated with Amun, the god of 'Two Lands.' This almost certainly meant that the obelisk was transported by Ramses II to his new royal city of Pi-Ramses in the Eastern Delta."

She wrinkled her nose.

So cute.

"Unfortunately, the tributary of the Nile that watered the city, dried up, and so the royal city, along with its obelisks, had to be moved to Tanis, to the north. There it languished for a thousand years or so until Cleopatra had her little dalliance with Mark Antony. She bore him a son—who the Roman emperor, Augustus, murdered. Augustus then had two obelisks, including this one, brought to Alexandria." Beth chuckled. "He had the audacity to erect them in front of a temple built as a memorial to the son of Cleopatra he'd just murdered."

Peter's interest was now piqued. "All that drama and it still hasn't got to England!"

"Aah," she said, "that's the sad part." Beth sat down beside Peter, and leaned against him.

"In the early nineteenth century, Egypt was part of the Ottoman Empire. The Egyptian Viceroy gave the obelisk to the British in 1819 in gratitude for Nelson defeating the French at the battle of the Nile. The British were grateful, but couldn't think how to move it until the same Viceroy gave a similar obelisk to the French, who managed to move theirs to Paris."

Beth grinned. "This indignity was not to be born, so a group of English Freemasons got together to bring the obelisk to London. Sir James Alexander persuaded a surgeon, Erasmus Wilson, to fund the project. Wilson hired an engineer to put the obelisk in a giant steel tube that could be turned into a small ship. They named the craft *Cleopatra*." She tilted her head. "Appropriate, eh?"

"I suppose so."

"Anyway, it began its journey to Britain being towed behind the steamship *Olga*. Unfortunately, the *Cleopatra* had to be cut loose in the Bay of Biscay during a storm. When the *Olga* sent a boat with six men on board to rescue the crew on *Cleopatra*, the boat overturned and all six were drowned." Beth pointed to the brass plaque. "That's their names listed there." She sighed. "Anyway, the *Cleopatra* was eventually salvaged, and on September 12th, 1878 the obelisk was set up here."

"Blimey," said Peter.

He reflected for a moment on the tortuous sagas of human history—including his own. Then, he got to his feet and began to walk round the obelisk. "It's got a bit battered over the years. Look at all these scratches and gouges."

"You might look a bit battered too if a German bomb had dropped beside you in the First World War." She got to her feet and joined Peter. "All scratches tell a story." She inspected a place where some gouge marks had defaced some hieroglyphics. "Hmm, that's the trouble with hieroglyphics; if you add a mark to the carving, you're just as likely to change the meaning of a word." She pointed to one scarred hieroglyph. "See that? A gouge has turned that square-shaped hieroglyph representing 'a mat' into 'a fish shelter.'"

Beth continued to inspect the weathered carvings until she shook her head. "No," she said. "I can't see anything that could possibly allude to a place where the secret of a god's power might be hidden."

Peter's roster had him working at the *Phoenix* that evening, so he had to go. Although disappointed at not finding any clues, he was deeply content to be in Beth's company. They walked arm in arm to the Embankment Underground where she could catch the tube to Angel. As he was about to leave, Beth reached up and ran her fingers down his cheek. "Do you realize that Alex's mystery benefactor is paying for Alex and me to spend two nights in Paris?"

"Really?"

"Really." She looked at him coyly. "Aren't you insanely jealous that another man is taking me to Paris?"

He reached his hand behind her neck, luxuriating in the feel of her hair, as he drew her to him for a kiss.

"Insanely."

To say that Ernest Wheeler was rattled would be an overstatement. Ernest Wheeler was never rattled. Yet he was disturbed, and he hated to admit, surprised.

Detective Sergeant Allan Jenkins, of London CID, had been politeness personified, yet had managed to convey a warning that Ernest Wheeler was a person of interest regarding the death of Trevor Whitman. It was a shock. Whilst Wheeler was confident the police were only trying to goad him into saying something incriminating, he was nonetheless staggered at what they'd managed to piece together.

Clearly, there were some factors he had not adequately taken into account—and it was that, more than anything, which disturbed him. Wheeler knew himself to be a careful man who rarely failed to factor in all relevant information. He was, however, fairly sure of the source of the police's information—Alex Whitman and Beth Anderson. They were proving to be a nuisance.

Jenkins had peppered him with questions, some seeking legitimate information, others designed to intimidate. The most shocking of these had been the detective asking why the Freemasons might be interested in the sunken ship, the *Beatrice*. Wheeler said he didn't know. Jenkins followed this straight away with the next question: "What is the Freemason's interest in obelisks erected by Ramses II?"

"I can't see that is relevant to anything."

"Was Trevor Whitman a member of Holy Royal Arch?"

Wheeler did not prevaricate. "Yes."

"And you are Grand Master of the Holy Royal Arch?"

"Yes."

"What was the source of disagreement between you and Trevor Whitman?"

"There was no disagreement. He was a brother Mason—an acquaintance only."

"Why would Trevor Whitman be hanged in a similar manner to

Roberto Calvi, a murder to which the Freemasons of Italy's P2 have been linked?"

"I don't know what you are talking about."

Wheeler had found his inquisition two days ago a harrowing experience.

Now, he was looking at the contents of Beth Anderson's computer. There was a lot to look through. She'd obviously been busy over the last few years. And then he saw it—a file entitled, '*Beatrice.*' Wheeler leaned back. There was now no doubt about the source of the police's information. Anderson and Whitman were working together to help the police.

Wheeler drummed his fingers on the table. What should be done? He knew he could not afford to do anything that would attract any more attention to himself. Sadly, this would mean that Alex Whitman could not be disposed of—at least, not yet. But what about Beth Anderson? If she couldn't be killed, perhaps she could be 'managed.'

He stabbed at the intercom button. "Carl."

Carl came in and stood in front of his desk.

"I want to manage Beth Anderson and keep her quiet."

Carl raised an eyebrow marginally.

"No, we can't remove her. It would attract too much attention."

Carl gave the briefest of nods. "What does she value?"

"She values Alex Whitman, her work, and her new boyfriend, Peter Jacobs—the waiter on the floating restaurant."

"Have you managed to find out anything more about Jacobs?"

"No. But he doesn't seem to be a threat. He's got himself another job doing clerical work at a nearby company called Mining Management Systems. I think he's small fry."

Wheeler swung round to his computer and entered 'Mining Management Systems' into the search engine. A moment later, he read the results. "I can't see anything of interest here. They've had a recent change of chairman. It's now a Mr. Jan Pieter de Jager. He's the son of one of the founding directors, evidently." He skimmed through the details. "Hmm, if their company gets any bigger, he might be worth sounding out regarding his interest in the Craft."

"What do you want me to do?" asked Carl.

Wheeler sniffed. "Beth Anderson is the main danger." He leaned back in his chair and reviewed the options. Eventually he said, "Hurt Peter Jacobs. Let's see if Miss Anderson can get the hint."

Chapter 17

B eth leaned across Alex as he pointed out his old friend, Professor Jean-Baptiste Bouchier. The Frenchman was leaning against the stone balustrade of Pont de la Concord.

Beth and Alex untangled themselves from the back seat of the taxi as Jean-Baptiste came over to them. He looked Beth up and down approvingly. "*Mon Dieu!*" he said to Alex. "You said nothing about bringing a beautiful woman. This cannot be Dr. Anderson?"

Alex made the introductions, "Beth, beware. This reprobate is one of the finest French historians, and one of France's most notorious lechers. He is almost single handedly responsible for the reputation of French men throughout the world." Alex smiled. "He is also one of my finest friends."

"Call me Jean. I shall call you Beth." He kissed Beth on both cheeks and then gave Alex an affectionate hug.

Turning to Beth, Jean said. "Now, *ma chere*, I shall take you by the arm and escort you to Place de la Concorde, for I understand you wish to see our Egyptian obelisk." He led her and Alex across the bridge.

Jean stopped halfway across to allow Beth to take in the view down the River Seine. "You cannot love Paris if you do not love its bridges." He pointed past the formal gardens of Tuileries to the dignified buildings of the Louvre. Further away, Beth could see the river island of Ile de la Cité and Notre-Dame.

Beth sighed. She loved Paris. Her mind turned to Peter. How she would love to walk with him across the bridges of Paris and explore the city's secrets together. One day, she promised herself, she would.

"There has not been much concord here," said Jean as they approached the octagonal expanse of the Place de la Concorde. He pointed. "Over there was where the nobility and members of the bourgeoisie were entertained watching convicted criminals being dismembered alive." He waved an arm around. "Louis XV built all this. There used to be a large statue of 'im riding a horse, but it was pulled down during the revolution and replaced by a guillotine. Criminals could then watch the nobility lose their heads."

Beth gave an involuntary shiver.

Jean continued, "The first person to lose his head was Louis XVI. Many others followed, including 'is love-starved queen, Marie Antionette, whom he was most reluctant to bed." Jean drew on his cigarette. "There was also Robespierre. He was the architect of the Reign of Terror that condemned people to death without trial. In the summer of 1794, more than fourteen-hundred people were executed in a single month. The irony was that 'e 'imself was executed by 'madam guillotine' because of his tyrannous behavior." He grinned at Beth. "It's very funny, *n'est pas*? He was executed facing upward so 'e could see the blade coming." Jean made a chopping motion across his neck. "Serve 'im right, eh?"

Beth said nothing.

Bright spring sunshine bathed the square in optimism and hope, as if determined to shrug off its grim history.

They walked onto the Place and made their way across the road to the first of two fountains. Alex sat down on the low wall surrounding it.

The fountain was a magnificent twin bowl affair that sat in a pool surrounded by statues of mythical marine creatures. Another just like it had been built not far away. However, it was the object that stood between them that she had come to study.

She looked up at the two-hundred ton, sixty-nine foot tall obelisk of Ramses II. It had been mounted on a pedestal enclosed within an iron railing.

Alex pointed to the obelisk with his stick and said to Beth, "You go with Jean, while I rest here for a while. I'll catch you up in a moment."

Jean-Baptiste apologized. "I am so sorry, Alex. I am showing off so busily like a schoolboy, that I walk you too fast."

"No, Jean. I am fine and have been greatly entertained by your dark Gallic commentary. I just need to rest for a bit."

Beth looked at Alex with concern. She took out a bottle of water, and handed it to him. "Take your time," she said. "I'll probably be poking about the obelisk for quite a while."

Alex nodded his thanks.

As Jean escorted Beth over to the obelisk, he launched into another monologue. "So, they put an Egyptian obelisk where the guillotine was. Who would have thought that Marie Antionette, when she looked from her window over there in Hôtel de Crillon, was watching the place where she would die, eh?"

"Has the Place's history always been so morbid, Jean?" asked Beth.

"Morbid, *non!*" Jean laughed. "In the early morning one day in 1993, a group of AIDS activists unrolled a giant condom over the obelisk."

Beth laughed. "How on earth did they manage to climb it?"

"Oh, they had ladders. But one man, Alain Robert, 'the Spider-man,' scaled it all the way to the top, using only his bare hands and climbing shoes."

Beth looked up at the monument and shook her head. "Madness."

For the next forty minutes, Beth examined the obelisk with the aid of a folder provided by Jean-Baptiste. It contained a translation of the engraved hieroglyphs extolling the rule of Ramses II and Ramses III.

She knew the history of the obelisk well. The Ottoman viceroy of Egypt, Méhémet Ali, had given the two 3,300-year-old obelisks from the entrance of the temple of Luxor, to the French. With great ingenuity, the French had taken one of them to France. Three years later, in 1836, King Louis-Philippe had it placed in the center of Place de la Concorde where the guillotine used in the Revolution had once stood. The remaining obelisk stayed in Luxor, having been deemed too difficult to move.

The pedestal was decorated with diagrams explaining the machinery used to transport and erect the obelisk. Beth turned her attention to the granite of the obelisk itself. She began examining the hieroglyphics with care, periodically referring to the diagrams contained in her folder. Occasionally, she took out her camera and took a photograph.

As she did so, she noted, with sadness, that modern pollution was doing far more damage to the carvings than 3,000 years of Egyptian history had ever done. It was sometimes difficult to determine what pitting was caused by acid rain, and what was carving. Just for a moment, the pitting and gouges began to suggest fanciful ideas of their own, but reference to the notes and diagrams made it very clear what the hieroglyphics were truly saying.

A gendarme walked over to them wearing his typical round pillbox hat. "*Otez-vous de là!*" he said roughly.

Beth looked over to Jean-Baptiste in desperation.

Jean-Baptiste pulled out an official pass that explained they had permission to be inside the metal railing.

The policeman nodded and walked off.

Alex limped over to join her. He took out a pair of binoculars and handed them to Beth. "I know it looks a little incongruous at such close range, but use these if you really want to see things clearly."

Beth accepted them and resumed her search.

After forty minutes, she felt she had got nowhere.

Just as she was about to give up, she noticed a small mark at the base of the obelisk. It was more of a scratch than a carving. It looked like the top half of a kitchen apron that had been spread out, with an upturned 'V' in the middle of it. The mark was no bigger than her hand. As it was well away from the formal hieroglyphics, she felt inclined to dismiss it. Just to be certain, however, she took a photograph of it.

Jean pointed to the pyramidion that adorned the top of the obelisk. "Do you like its top, eh? The original was stolen in the 6th century BC, so we put a three-meter high hat on it and covered it with gold-leaf. We now have the most cheerful obelisk in the world, *non?*"

Peter sat on the inboard end of *Phoenix's* bowsprit, nursing his coffee, watching the man from the corner of his eye. The man could have passed for a tourist, except tourists seldom traveled alone. Neither did they stay in the shadows rather than the sunshine on a cold spring morning.

Two years of monitoring what was going on around him without apparently doing so meant that such things bothered Peter. The man had a camera with a telephoto lens, and he raised it to take photographs of him when Peter was apparently not noticing.

Peter got up and stepped over to the fore-hatch—being careful to keep his back to the camera. Bending over, he had a conversation with Kym and Lenny down below in the kitchen. He then resumed his position on the bowsprit—and waited.

A few minutes later, Lenny and Kym emerged from under the tarpaulin at the top of the stairs and headed toward the gangplank.

Peter blinked. They were acting like lovers. Notwithstanding their disparity in age, they joined hands, and walked across the wharf toward the warehouse. Halfway there, they paused to take leave of each other.

"I'll see you later, Light of my Life." Lenny's voice carried to where Peter was sitting.

"Oh, believe me, you will…and I'll make it all up to you," came Kym's reply.

Peter recognized the threat in the double entendre and tried not to smile. Lenny was sailing close to the wind.

Kym walked toward the edge of the warehouse where Peter's

stalker stood in the shadows. She greeted the man. "G'day, mate. Beaut' morning."

The man turned away.

"What's the matter? Aren't I pretty enough to be photographed?"

The man turned, and Kym struck a provocative pose.

Peter had to concede that she certainly had the body to do it.

She thrust out her breasts—then bent over, and put her hands on a bollard.

Peter blinked. *She's pole dancing a ship's bollard!*

The stalker stepped toward her and raised his camera.

Kym beckoned. "Get a closer shot." She gyrated her torso.

The man took a few paces toward her and reached out to her.

Peter was now alarmed.

What happened next came in a blur. Kym stepped forward and kicked the man between the legs. "How dare you, you dirty bastard!"

At the same time, Lenny—who had been hiding around the corner—ran to the man and hauled him up by the jacket. "Are you molesting my girl?" He hit the man with a sharp uppercut.

Lenny caught the photographer as he collapsed and dragged him into the shadows.

Kym snatched the camera and started to fiddle with it, while Lenny rifled the man's pockets. He retrieved a wallet, opened it, and inspected it before putting it back.

The stalker began to moan.

Lenny stepped over him, and began to slap his face, helping him to regain consciousness. "Listen gov'nor," he said. "Don't move in on another man's bird if you want to avoid trouble. Now take your camera and piss off. I don't ever want to see you again."

The stalker put out an arm to fend Lenny off.

Lenny hauled the man to his feet, retrieved the camera from Kym, and thrust it at him. "Get lost!"

The man grabbed the camera and scuttled away with a crouching run, still in obvious pain.

"Geez, Kym, remind me never to take you on in a brawl," said Peter.

Kym waved dismissively. "You guys are all the same. Led by your dicks."

Peter heard the bitterness in her banter, friendly as it was, and suspected she'd been hurt in the past. "Not all men are bastards, Kym," He said quietly.

"Bugger off."

It was a warning—one he chose to heed.

Lenny came down the stairs to join them in the stern cuddy.

Peter rounded on him. "I said, 'engage him in conversation'— not kill him! You were meant to ask him if he was waiting to come on board the *Phoenix* and try and find out what he was about."

Lenny plumped himself down on one of the bunks and looked anything but repentant. "Kym spied on him with binoculars and recognized his camera. She said she'd only need a few seconds with it." He massaged the back of his hand. "And I didn't like his intentions toward Kym."

Peter shook his head in disbelief.

"Honestly," Lenny protested, "it all sort of happened…naturally." He turned to Kym. "So, what did you manage to see, girl?"

Kym had her arms folded defensively in front of her. The adrenaline high was leaving her. "Do you think he'll come back?"

Peter shook his head. "I don't think you need to worry about him. If the guy comes back, it will only be to retrieve his testicles from the end of your boot."

"Hmph."

Lenny had pulled out a pen and was writing on the back of his hand. "What did you see?" he repeated.

"The camera was a Nikon D1. It's digital—very nice. I was lent one last year to take casual pictures at a wedding."

"And?"

She sighed. "And the playback feature showed eight or ten shots of you, Peter."

Kym's comment caused everyone to be silent for a moment.

Lenny growled. "Well, boy, someone is either a great fan of yours, or they want someone to be familiar with your face. Is there anything you ought to be telling us?"

Peter didn't like any of the scenarios that suggested themselves. He sighed. "The sneaky way of getting my picture suggests that someone doesn't have my well-being at heart." He thought for a few moments before continuing, "It won't be the parole board. They know me and already have my picture on file. It could be associates of the man I killed two years ago, but I don't think it's likely. None of them would know I've been released." He bit his lip, wondering how much more he should disclose.

Taking a deep breath, he continued. "It may be someone linked to my late father's company. I've inherited some shares, and they may resent the fact that I can exercise the voting rights associated with them."

Peter struggled even more to voice the third option, but he felt he owed it to both Kym and Lenny to be completely candid. "It may also be because I'm associated with Alex. His brother has been murdered."

"And how would that involve you?" demanded Lenny.

"Alex is digging around, trying to find some possible reasons for his brother's murder." He shrugged. "I happen to live with him— that could mean that I'm being checked out."

Lenny rubbed the back of his neck. "Correct me if I'm wrong, but are you telling me you might either be targeted by a bunch of avenging Londoners, a miffed businessman, or a psychopathic murderer?"

"Probably not psychopathic, but yes, that's about it."

"I did tell you that I'd bought this barge so I could live a quiet and generally dull life, didn't I?"

"Sorry, Lenny. I had no intention of involving you or Kym. I can stay at Mining Management Systems and not work here on Wednesdays, if you like."

"Don't be ridiculous. I haven't had so much fun in ages. Just tell me if you ever suspect Kym, me, or the *Phoenix* are in danger."

"I will. Thanks, Lenny."

Lenny pointed to the scribble on his hand. "That's the bloke's name. Write it down somewhere."

"What are you going to do now?" asked Kym. "I can't always be around and be your nursemaid."

Peter nodded. "I think I need to visit a friend."

Chapter 18

Peter stood in front of the prison in a storm of emotions. He wanted to run. The demons of shame and grief screamed at him with fresh vigor. He put a hand against the wall to steady himself, and said over and over again, *I am choosing to be here; I am choosing to be here.* Then, taking a deep breath, he made his way to the entrance.

Peter was met by a further challenge in the reception area. Prison Officer Carter was one of the wardens on duty. The officer patted Peter down with unnecessary thoroughness and then stood just inches from him in an unspoken challenge. "Can't keep away from us, Jacobs?"

The mental image of Sergeant Major Dicky Chambers standing in the same place, came to mind. Peter looked the prison officer straight in the eye and said evenly, "Good morning, Mr. Carter."

It was a win...of sorts.

Peter could see Jack Tanner's impressive bulk sprawled over an iron chair behind one of the desks in the visiting room. He was hard to miss. Peter made his way down the nearest aisle and sat in the chair opposite.

Neither said anything for a moment. Hammer looked at Peter, and gave a small nod. It was recognition enough.

"G'day, Hammer. The girls of Wapping send their love."

"What's the matter, young Joey?"

"Is it that obvious?"

"Our arrangement was that you'd not come near this effin' place again, and that I'd see ya on the outside."

"I've got a job at a restaurant in St. Katharine's Dock. We caught a guy taking pictures of me with a camera using a telephoto lens. He didn't want to be seen. We've looked at the pictures and we know his name. What's it mean, Hammer, and what can I do about it?"

"You 'ave been busy, young Joey. You'd better tell me wot you've been up to."

Peter marshaled his thoughts. "I inherited some shares from my father, and the ex-company chairman, who wants sole control, resents it."

"Is he a hard man?"

"He's a bully, but not violent."

"It won't be 'im then."

Peter nodded. "Nor do I think it's the family of the guy I killed; they're not that sort. There was no real malice in them."

Hammer nodded.

Peter sighed. "I share a flat with a professor whose brother was recently murdered. As best we know, it might be something to do with banking, or possibly the Freemasons. The thing is, the professor is digging around a bit…and I'm helping."

Hammer sighed. "Young Joey, 'ave I taught you nuffing? Don't go poking ya nose in business wot don't concern ya. You know better than that."

"He's a mate, Hammer. I owe him."

Hammer sniffed. After a moment's silence, he asked, "Oo is this photographer geezer, then?"

Peter gave the name to Hammer.

Hammer nodded. "Give me time to make a few calls."

Peter was quiet for a long while. "What's your take on it, Hammer?"

Hammer leaned forward. "It means you've got trouble, mate. Your mug shot will be passed on to someone who's gonna need it to do somefing personal to ya—probably not nice."

Peter already suspected that was the case. He nodded.

Hammer looked Peter over. "Whoever it is would need to be pretty handy, though. You ain't no pushover."

"What do I do, Hammer?"

"Don't have any routines. Never go home the same way twice. Always have a back door you can escape through, or make the front door so bloody strong, they can't get in."

Peter nodded.

Hammer continued, "Never sit in a room where you can easily be snatched. Keep by the emergency exit wiv' ya back against the wall—and use rooms which need several flights of stairs or a lift to get to."

Hammer leaned back. With every appearance of boredom and said in a low voice, "Never go anywhere public on ya own; and don't stand in a busy street near the curb." He tapped the side of his head. "Just use ya 'common,' mate."

"I could use you out there right now, Hammer."

"Bloody oath, you could," agreed Hammer. "I can't 'elp ya much from in 'ere, young Joey, but I'll make a call tonight and see if your photographer is linked to someone." He shrugged. "There ain't much chance of hearin' who's got the contract for ya though. If it's an upmarket mob from the City, I won't know 'em. And if it's a bunch of new hoodlums on the 'Manor,' I probably won't know, either. Can't keep pace with young kids these days."

"Thanks, Hammer."

"Let's have your phone number…and keep away from this bleedin' place."

They talked together for a few minutes more.

"Who are you sharing with now?"

Hammer grimaced. "A pimply faced git oo's been snatching old ladies' handbags. He's scared shitless and got no loaf. I tell you mate, I miss 'aving ya around."

Peter nodded, and asked, "Do you know people who would hear if someone was setting up to do some salvage work on a sunken ship?"

Hammer raised an eyebrow. "Joey, you are full of surprises today. Wot ya talking about? Do you mean doin' the *Mary Rose* thing, like they done in Portsmouth?"

"Probably not interested in raising the ship. That's big money. Just shifting sediment to find something in a wreck, then using a crane to lift it on board."

"Shallow water then?"

"Dunno. Probably."

"Yeah. Well, it's pretty specialized gear, so there's some chance you could find out oo's buying stuff around the docks if it's local. Do you want me to ask?"

"Please."

They sat in silence for a while. Eventually Hammer said, "Time to bugger off, young Joey."

Peter rose to his feet, "Thanks, Hammer," he paused, "for everything."

Hammer leaned back and folded his arms. "Mind your back."

Peter had Alex's car waiting outside the Bermondsey Underground as Beth and Alex returned from their Paris trip. He hugged her and made to kiss her on the cheek, but Beth turned, and kissed him briefly on the lips. It may have been quick, but his head spun. He felt its tenderness, trust, and intimacy. Peter reflected that whilst her action was probably perfectly natural to her, it was still wonderfully strange to him.

He put the travel bags in the boot and opened the back door for Beth. As Peter climbed into the front seat, he watched through the rear-view mirror as she picked up the bunch of red roses waiting on the seat beside her. He saw her smile, smell the roses, and hold them close to her chest.

Peter glanced at Alex seated beside him. He was smiling.

Over a leisurely evening meal at Alex's flat, Beth and Alex told him what they had learned, or more precisely, what they had not learned, in Paris. As the evening progressed, Alex became gray with fatigue, and they were not surprised when he excused himself, and headed to bed.

Peter and Beth curled up on the sofa, and looked out the window at the city lights that shimmered off the Thames. Peter savored the joy of simply being with Beth. Her head on his chest. Occasionally, she would put her hand up to stroke his cheek, as if to assure herself that he was really there.

Reluctantly, he let his mind return to an issue that had been concerning him for some time. "Beth, how do you feel being in your flat after the burglary?"

"Hmm," said Beth sleepily. "I was a bit rattled for a few days, but I've beefed up the security—and the neighbors are terrific. I'm okay."

"Would you mind if I asked a security firm to have a look to see if they can improve things? They're coming to upgrade security here." He added quickly, "It will be at no cost to you. Alex's benefactor has asked us to check our security. Evidently he doesn't want our investigation to be hampered by any fears."

"That's very generous."

"Good, I'll get it organized."

"I wonder who he is," said Beth sleepily.

"I've never met him." They lapsed into silence for another ten minutes.

Eventually Beth asked, "How did your day with the Yeomen go on the *Phoenix*? You never said."

Peter attempted to recall the events of the previous week. "Better than I hoped. To be honest, the whole reason for me staying on the barge on Wednesdays was so I could keep contact with them. They're an extraordinary bunch." Peter paused before adding, "But I'm a bit concerned for their wives."

"Why's that?"

"Well, the blokes let their hair down...but the wives were disengaged...reserved, and sort of..." he searched for the right word, "resigned."

"I expect being cooped up in the Tower, hemmed in by security, tourists, and walls can get to you after a while—particularly if you feel you don't have any real purpose there. The guys go off and do their thing, and they just have to tag along."

After a moment's silence, Beth continued. "Why don't you suggest they come to the British Museum. I could give them a tour of the place and show them things normal tourists wouldn't see."

Peter gave her a squeeze. "You've got a lovely heart, Beth Anderson. I'll ring them tomorrow." He continued, "And a lovely body, by the way; and lovely eyes; and lovely skin; and lovely lips; and a lovely wisdom; and lovely..."

Beth dug him in the ribs. "Wisdom! You'll have to do better than that!"

"Aah, sorry."

She snuggled back down on his chest. "One day, Peter Jacobs," she said, "I'm going to take you to Paris."

Wheeler listened to Carl as he stood in front of the newly installed mahogany desk and made his report.

"I thought it would be better to contract out the job to distance ourselves, but it takes more time to organize—and there are fewer organizations to choose from these days. I'm favoring a Ukrainian team."

Wheeler pursed his lips. He disliked foreigners. However, he dismissed the subject with a wave. Carl had never failed him. He would find a way. "Any other news?"

"Beth Anderson has been in Paris looking at the Egyptian obelisk."

Wheeler pursed his lips. "She certainly is persistent." He tapped his fingers together. *Nothing must threaten the Pharaoh's stone—nothing.*

Leaning back, he said, "I've said you are to do nothing to her here in England. She's too close to us. However, that need not apply abroad." He shrugged his shoulders. "Traveling can be dangerous. Accidents happen."

"I understand perfectly, sir."

Chapter 19

"What am I doing here, Peter?" hissed Beth, as she stepped into the guardhouse.

The guardsmen, dressed in military combat gear, frisked them both before passing them through a metal detector. Another soldier found their names on a computer and rang through to the chaplain.

Four minutes later, Hamish O'Brien entered the room dressed in a shapeless gray pullover, beige trousers, and polished brogues.

The soldier behind the desk greeted him. "Evening, Padre. These two belong to you, I think."

Peter made the introductions. "Hello, Hamish. May I introduce Dr. Beth Anderson, historian and…"

"Peter's girlfriend," finished Beth, stepping forward to shake Hamish's hand.

"Gee, I like the sound of that," murmured Peter.

Hamish raised an eyebrow at Peter before introducing himself. "Hamish O'Brien, Chaplain. Call me Hamish. Thanks for coming. Follow me."

Hamish escorted them through archways and corridors that stood between towering walls, until they came to the castle's inner courtyard. Ahead of them, the White Tower was beginning to be highlighted by spotlights in the deepening twilight.

Hamish explained, "It's good of you to come at such short notice. It's just that the wives are having their weekly meeting tonight, and I thought that Beth's initiative could be put to them." He smiled. "If you present the idea on their home ground, it's more likely to be received well."

Beth nodded.

Hamish continued, "They can be a pretty jaundiced lot and are not always easy to help."

Beth furrowed her brow. "Why's that?"

"Oh, I expect they're just expressing the usual symptoms of being cooped up together. Petty difficulties can easily flare up amongst women who would rather be in their own home." He smiled at Beth. "I jumped at your idea because I suspect it could bring a breath of fresh air for them."

They walked down some steps and came to a door. "This is the residents' common room. It's mostly used by the wives. The men prefer the mess." He sighed. "It's not a great dynamic." He pointed across the green to his own quarters. "That's my place over there. Peter and I will head there once I've introduced you to the women. Just come over when you've finished."

Wondering what on earth she had got herself into, Beth followed Hamish into the common room.

Looking around, Beth couldn't understand why any woman would want to be there. Severe box-like armchairs covered in brown vinyl were grouped around coffee tables. The hall itself was decorated with cream paint above a dark wooden dado. A coffee dripolator gurgled away on a table next to the wall. Two trays of calorie-laden pastries sat beside it.

A gray-haired woman was addressing a group of about eighteen women. Their ages seemed to range from mid-forties to mid-sixties.

The women turned to look at their three visitors with curious but world-weary eyes. The friendliest smile came from one of the youngest women present. She had long blonde hair and a beautiful, doll-like face.

"Oh dear," said Beth under her breath. "These girls need help."

The woman leading the group stepped over to them.

Hamish introduced her. "Wendy, may I present Dr. Beth Anderson—the person I told you about with the interesting proposition." He turned to Beth. "Beth, this is Wendy Chambers. She coordinates these women's nights."

Wendy shook Beth by the hand and led her over to the rest of the women.

Beth chatted briefly to them as she was introduced. As she did, she couldn't help but feel a rising sense of compassion for these women who were forced to make a life in such masculine surroundings. Beth found herself speaking with the woman with the long blonde hair. "Thanks for smiling," she said.

"Oh, did I?" said the woman, laughing. "Well, it's right that I should. It's great to have new people join us. Please call me Bell."

Beth smiled. "Hi Bell." She couldn't think of anything else to say that wasn't banal, so she whispered to both Bell and Wendy, "Tell me; is this place always so severe and masculine. Is this the best the army can provide for you?"

Wendy looked around her, as if seeing the hall for the first time, and said in a deep smoker's voice, "It's pretty awful, but we've sort of got used to it over the years."

"I hate it," confessed Bell.

Beth took a calculated risk. "Don't you think it's time for a women's revolution? Why not change it?"

Bell opened her mouth in surprise.

Wendy stared at Beth for a moment before saying. "Girl, I'm starting to like you." She glanced round her. "This place has always held more than its fair share of revolutionaries. We might as well stick with tradition." She grinned. "Perhaps it is time we really did do something about it."

Beth turned back to Hamish and Peter. "It's time for you two to go. We have got some serious girl-talking to do."

Peter and Hamish were shepherded to the door. It was banged shut barely before they were through it. From inside, Peter could hear Wendy's rallying call, "Right girls, gather around."

Hamish turned to him. "This might be an interesting night. Wendy is Dicky Chambers' wife. She's formidable. If Beth gets her onside, anything's possible."

"I'm not sure what's happening in there," said Peter, "but I don't think they are planning a visit to a museum."

Hamish nodded. "I think we should leave them to it and have a cup of tea."

There was a rap on Hamish's front door. Hamish pushed himself out of his chair, and opened it.

A Guard's officer, dressed in military fatigues, ducked under the low door, and entered. He was introduced to Peter as Captain Jensen. "Sorry to bother you, Padre," said the Captain, "but we have a situation developing with the wives in the common room."

"What's going on?"

Jensen gave a rueful smile. "The women have carried every table and chair out of the common room and heaped them in the court-yard. They are refusing to allow them back in. They've locked them-selves inside with brushes and mops, and are...er, fairly militant...in a friendly sort of way."

Hamish nodded. "I think you have a petticoat rebellion on your hands, Captain." He drummed his fingers on the mantelpiece. "I understand that the tourists tomorrow might wonder at the sight of a pile of armchairs. Why don't you go over to the mess and invite their husbands to carry them off to the old gun room." Hamish smiled. "I'm not sure I'd challenge the women at this stage. I'll wander across in a while and check on things."

"Thank you, sir." The young captain made his way back to the front door. "I'll get on to it. Good night, sir."

Twenty minutes later, Hamish and Peter strolled across the green to the stone steps leading up to the common room. An untidy pile of tables and armchairs was heaped outside on the pavement. They stood for a moment watching a stream of Yeomen carrying them away. Peter recognized Colin, the mess bottle-walking champion, amongst them.

Hamish knocked at the door. He had to do so three times before it opened. The cause for this was not hard to determine. Someone was playing sixties rock music at an impressive volume.

The door was opened slightly by Wendy. She looked at them suspiciously.

Hamish asked benignly, "Is Beth ready to go home yet?"

"Oh, I suppose you'd better come in."

When they stepped inside, Wendy stood with her hands on her hips. "We're fed up with the old décor, so we're changing things."

Peter could see that most of the women had changed into working clothes and were busy with scrubbing brushes and sugar soap. A couple of them were dancing to the music. One was dancing with a mop.

Three others stood in front of a wall drawing on it with a pencil.

Peter found Beth on her knees, sticking some white tape down on the floor. Her hair was awry. She looked up with a grin. "This is going to be an enclosed play area for kids. Most of the girls have grandkids."

Hamish said, "What a brilliant idea."

It seemed to be the right response, because it prompted Wendy into giving them a guided tour.

"The far end is going to have a large screen, and we're going to get a data projector attached to the roof. The other end is going to be a café with healthy food in a chilled display cabinet." She pulled a face. "No more fattening pastry. I'm seeing the catering staff tomorrow."

Peter wasn't sure the catering staff was going to have a comfortable time.

Wendy continued, "What I'd really like, is a good coffee machine rather than that vile dripolator. That's the one thing I'm not confident of getting through army stores."

"Would you know how to use it?" asked Peter.

"Oh yes. We've talked about a program of women's activities for the next six months. The first one is a visit with Beth to the museum, and one of the others is a barista teaching us to make different types of coffee." She pointed to him. "You'd better know that Beth has volunteered you for that."

"I'd be glad to come," said Peter. "But you'd need a coffee machine. Do you have any funds?"

"Not much after we've bought the stuff we can't prize out of stores."

"I may be able to help," he said. "I'll ask my boss on the *Phoenix* whether you can have his old coffee machine." He shrugged. "It's perfectly good, and he's only replaced it because he needs one that can cope with a higher volume of use."

"Do you think he'd sell it?" asked Wendy.

"Why don't you let me buy it for you?" Peter smiled. "It will be my gift to the, er, new order."

Wendy turned around and clapped her hands. "Girls," she yelled, "we've got our coffee machine!"

Whoops of delight broke out around him.

After Beth had received a hug from most of the women present, Peter managed to get her to the door.

Hamish led them back toward the grim portico under the Byward Towers.

They said their farewells in the guardroom and made their way outside into the crisp evening air. Peter took Beth by the arm, and walked with her to the Underground.

"What on earth did you do to set that lot off?" he asked.

Beth hugged his arm. "I didn't do anything. It was all primed to go off anyway. I just made a small comment that seemed to speed things up."

"A small comment?"

"That sparked a revolution." She grinned.

"I think they see you as their Joan of Arc."

"No. Wendy's their leader. I just made a few suggestions."

"Hmm. Are you always going to cause this sort of trouble?"

"Would you mind if I did?"
"I'd insist on it."

Chapter 20

"America!" exclaimed Beth with disbelief. "I'm going to America?"

"If you want...and if you can get the time off. Only for a few days."

Beth was in Alex's office on the second floor of the British Museum. She was standing in front of the window overlooking Montague Place. Below her, she could see three London buses parked in front of the pillared northern façade of the museum. A cool weather front had recently doused London with rain, making the trees of Russell Square Gardens look clean and fresh.

"Your mystery benefactor would pay for me to go to America! Why?"

"It would seem that he's a very determined man. America was my suggestion, incidentally. If we are to make progress, we need to look at the obelisk in Central Park. It's a very significant one." He sighed. "I'm afraid the obelisks are the only real lead we've got."

"But it's a twin of the obelisk brought to London from Alexandria. I didn't learn anything from that."

"Beth, there's no expectation that you will go. I have no right to ask you to traipse across the world looking at obelisks in the faint hope I can get a lead on Trevor's death. I'm just offering the possibility, if you wish." He smiled at her. "You've got a brilliant mind, and you've already done a lot. I certainly don't want to presume on you."

Pigeons were cooing on the window ledge outside. London seemed so normal—and yet, Alex's brother had been murdered in this city. Beth turned to look at her old mentor. He was pushing back against evil using the only weapons he had: his intellect and his friends. There was no question of her not going.

"Of course I'll go, Alex. You know I will." She thought for a moment. "I'm fairly sure that I won't have to take any time off. I could spend a day with an American colleague of mine who's doing restoration work in the Museum of New York. I could make a case that I'll be going to learn some of their techniques."

Alex nodded, then asked: "Do you have any research contacts in Egypt?"

"Why?" asked Beth.

"My benefactor has instructed me to say that he's also agreed to fund your trip to Egypt to look at the obelisk at Luxor." He shrugged. "That will be our final fling. If we don't learn anything there, we'll call the investigation off."

Beth was flabbergasted. "What? Alex, are you sure? I've not discovered anything yet. And I'm not at all sure of my ability to spot things that might be significant. It could all be a dreadful waste of money…" she sighed, "…even though it will be the adventure of a life-time."

"Then have your adventure, Beth." He reached across and patted her hand. "And never doubt your abilities. I believe in you."

Beth smiled weakly and tried to come to grips with everything that was happening. "Where will I stay in New York? I'd better get something organized."

"Already sorted. You will stay in the Excelsior on West 81. It's just a few hundred yards from the New York Historical Society. I've got friends there if you need them. The hotel is only a minute's walk from Central Park."

Beth furrowed her brow. "One day, I'd like to meet this bene-factor of yours."

"I think one day you might."

"I hate to do it to ya, Joey, but I think I need a visit." Hammer's hoarse voice came through the phone without any introduction.

Peter could only surmise that Hammer had some information that was too confidential to share over the phone. He understood that the privacy of prisoners' phone calls from Belmarsh was not something that could be guaranteed.

"I'll come and see you Thursday morning."

Hammer's raspy laugh came down the line. "I'll try and fit ya into my busy schedule."

Three days later Peter was again seated opposite Hammer in the visiting room of Belmarsh prison. His old cellmate watched him through half-closed eyes.

Peter waited. Eventually Hammer folded his massive hands together, leaned forward and said, "The photographer geezer: 'ee's linked to a Russian firm. Very nasty—extortion and prostitu-tion. They're new in the 'Manor' and don't play by the old rules. They want to expand, which means they've got attitude." Hammer leaned back and said, "Joey, old son, you've got major bovva."

Peter was silent for a while, trying to digest what he'd heard. This was just what he'd feared. "How do I stop them?"

"You don't, mate. You stay on their books until the job's done." Hammer shrugged, "That's the way it is, mate. You only stop them if you take out the geezer wot's paying them."

More silence hung between them.

"Any idea who it is?" asked Hammer.

"None."

"Then, mate; you gotta find a whole new way of livin' for you and yours because you ain't gonna get good odds from no bookie."

"You and yours?"

Hammer sighed. "These guys tend to be a bit untidy, like. They will use anyone to get to ya. Savvy?"

Peter nodded his understanding. "My girlfriend's flat was burgled a few weeks ago. Should I be worried?"

"She wasn't hurt?"

"No."

"That's unusual."

A wave of anguish washed over Peter. "But she could be?"

Hammer nodded.

They sat in silence for some time before Hammer continued. "Your salvage stuff: I've got an old 'China' d'han the docks oo's done work for me. He tells me that in the last two months, eleven geezers 'ave been buyin' salvage gear from three outfits around the docks."

Peter took out a pen and pad from his pocket.

Hammer continued. "Two was deep sea stuff; four was for North Sea Oil outfits; and three are being shipped to the Middle East. That leaves two. One lot is being used to do maintenance work on the Thames barrier. And that leaves one, Joey boy—an outfit called CERU."

"What sort of mob are they?"

"It's the Coastal and Estuarine Research Unit at University College London."

"Oh." Peter paused. "I suppose it might not be any of them."

"True. But if your dredging's local, you've got a fair chance. There ain't much wot happens in the Thames that don't get talked about down the docks." The big man shrugged. "Anyway, it's all I got."

"You've done well, Hammer—better than I could have hoped. Thanks, mate."

"You can buy me a beer in three months time."

"I've done better than that, Hammer. I've been given a bit of money from my father's estate, so I've opened up a bank account earmarked for you when you get out." He looked Hammer briefly in the eye. "It's not easy making a new start without a bit of help."

"You don't have to do that, Joey."

"I know."

Hammer pondered the arrangement, and then nodded his thanks. "The dosh'll be handy."

"Any thoughts on what you'll do when you get out?"

"Bleedin' Charlton Athletic have offered me a job as a gym instructor for a junior squad." Hammer laughed hoarsely. "Evidently, I've become a pin-up boy and a shining example of the benefits of their partnership wiv Belmarsh."

"No more 'minding?'"

"Maybe a bit on the side. But kosher. Nuffing dodgy."

"I might be your first client."

"If you're still alive by then, Joey, you won't need no minding. It will be over. So watch ya bleedin' self."

Chapter 21

Beth emerged from the taxi and stood in front of the green-canopied entrance of the Excelsior. She looked up at the hotel towering above her and smiled. It was all so Manhattan.

A uniformed porter carried her luggage into reception. The hotel was trying to portray an image of quiet dignity without being ostentatious. The lounge and dining areas were decorated with old-fashioned wallpaper and were lit by crystal chandeliers. She made her way across the marbled floor to the engraved golden doors of the lifts.

The porter deposited her bags inside her room and hovered until Beth remembered the irritating American custom of tipping. Embarrassed, she hurriedly handed over a note way in excess of what was required.

Beth fell back onto the bed and reveled in the luxury of the room. She wished Peter could see her. *No,* she corrected herself. She wished he were *with* her. Smiling at the thought, she went to take a shower.

Later, she was sitting at the desk, cocooned in the softness of the hotel bathrobe. Beth was due to have dinner in the hotel later in the evening with Dr. Marjorie Bantry from the Museum of New York. Marjorie had left a folder containing information on the Egyptian obelisk at reception, and Beth wanted to study it before they met.

She was intrigued with what she learned.

Ismail the Magnificent, the Khedive of Egypt and Sudan, had sought to curry favor with America by giving them an obelisk. He chose one of the two obelisks that had been made in 1450 BC that the Romans later transported to Alexandria. As England had already been given one of the obelisks, he gave the other to America.

It took nearly a decade to get the obelisk to America. The railroad magnate, William Vanderbilt, financed the enterprise, and Henry Gorringe, a lieutenant commander in the U.S. Navy, was given the job of getting it done. Both were active Freemasons.

Unlike the London obelisk that had been removed from a prostrate position where it had fallen, the New York obelisk was removed from an erect position. This allowed those removing the obelisk to inspect the pedestal, steps, and foundation stones of the monument in Alexandria. Evidently, when they did, they discovered some Roman carvings depicting the tools used by the stonemasons who had prepared the pedestal.

Beth picked up a photograph of what they found and studied it closely. Under some Roman lettering, an artisan had engraved pictures of a ruler, compass, a protractor, a mallet, a square, a plumb line, and what looked to be a bunch of sticks. No wonder the Freemasons had felt excited by this, she thought. The square and the compass form the basis of the Freemasons' logo. She was not surprised to read that Jesse Anthony, Grand Master of Masons in the State of New York, presided over the ceremony in which the cornerstone of the obelisk was laid in place on October 2, 1880. As Beth read the notes, she whistled. It was no small ceremony. Over nine thousand Masons had paraded up Fifth Avenue from 14th Street to 82nd Street.

Her thoughts were interrupted by the phone. Beth picked it up: "Beth Anderson." All she heard was silence and then a click.

Silence.

She put the phone down. A prickle of unease ran up her spine.

Beth rang through to reception. "Excuse me, someone just tried to ring me in my room, but we were disconnected. Do you have the number of the person who rang?"

After a few minutes of searching, the polite American voice came back. "No, ma'am, we can't trace the call because it didn't come from outside. It must have come from our internal system. Do you have a friend in the hotel who might be wanting to contact you?"

Bewildered, Beth replied, "No. No, I don't. Thank you for the information."

"You're welcome."

Beth put the phone down slowly and went to get ready for dinner.

The pollution from half a million exhausts was unable to completely obscure a sunny, spring day. Buoyed by the optimism of the weather, Beth put the disquiet of the previous evening's phone call out of her mind, reasoning that it was probably one of Alex's colleagues who had slipped into the hotel to check she'd arrived safely. She would ring Alex that night to inquire.

Beth walked down West 81st toward the park. She crossed over Central Park West and entered the gates. The obelisk was located on the other side of the park, behind the Metropolitan Museum of Arts, so she set off along the path between the Great Lawn and Turtle Pond.

Central park was a crazy anomaly. It was an eight-hundred-and-forty-three acre rectangle of green in the middle of Manhattan Island—the most expensive real estate in the world. Sky-scrapers surrounded the park, peering down at it as if scandalized by its presence. It was an oasis of tranquility in a harsh moneymaking town. In the distance, she could see a tourist carriage being pulled by a horse along West Drive.

Her thoughts turned to Peter.

She wished he could share this beautiful morning with her. She wanted to share a lot of mornings with him.

My, how you've changed. Was she becoming a vapid, dependent, neurotic who needed a man to complete her? The thought worried her. *No*, she decided. It was simply that she loved being loved, and loved what it felt like to be with him. It was thrilling. It was—she cast around for the right word—*completing*.

Damn! It was all so confusing.

———

The man felt he was ready for most contingencies. He knew that life had a habit of springing nasty surprises—particularly in his line of business.

He was dressed as a jogger, at least for the moment. The green varsity jacket he wore was reversible. It could be turned inside out to look like a smart dark-blue work jacket. At the moment, it was zipped up. He did not want to show that he wore a white shirt and a tie underneath. He liked ties. You could do a lot with a tie.

He glanced down at his black slacks. They were stretchy, and had permanent creases in them. Smart tracksuit bottoms—or everyday work slacks—either. His shoes were beige and had black strips of leather held in place by Velcro. They could be removed in an instant to turn his running shoes into everyday work shoes. Everything was legal and innocuous. Most of it was deadly.

He trailed behind the man wearing a trench coat; the one who was hiding his face in a scarf. The temperature of the day didn't call for a scarf, at least, not one worn like that. More disturbingly, the man was walking forty meters behind Beth Anderson. The suspicion that Beth's follower was up to no good was confirmed by the man looking around just once too often—checking on CCTV cameras.

The jogger watched both of them, confident he couldn't be seen. He was lying diagonally along a low tree branch thirty-yards away—invisible. From this vantage point, the jogger saw enough to know that Beth Anderson would shortly be in trouble.

Beth passed one of the park's beautiful black lampposts. The pearl-shaped light globe on top was caged within an elegant wrought iron bracket. As she admired it, she thought she saw some leaves in the shrubbery to her right twitch and shiver. When she looked, she could see nothing. Beth gave no further thought to it and continued around the curving path until she reached an octagonal-paved area that stood behind the Met. In the middle of the paving, the three-and-a-half-thousand year old obelisk of Thutmose III soared sixty-eight feet into the air. It was breathtaking.

Beth made her way to the metal rail that protected the obelisk and took out her camera. She trained it on the metal crabs that were backed under the base of the obelisk where it sat on the plinth. They looked incongruous. But Beth remembered that the Romans had first used bronze crabs to brace the broken corners of the obelisk, when they re-erected it in Alexandria.

The obelisk was already fourteen-hundred years old at that stage, having first been commissioned by Thutmose III. However, Ramses II had decorated it. Ever seeking opportunities to promote his own glory, Ramses had covered it with his own hieroglyphics two-hundred years later.

She focused the camera on the top of the obelisk and began to translate them as she moved the camera down. *The Horus, Strong-Bull-Beloved-of-Ra*, (click)...*the King of Upper and Lower Egypt*, (click) ...*Chosen-of-Ra; Ra, created by the gods, who founded the Two Lands*, (click).

Beth was saddened at the damage done to the hieroglyphics by the frosts and acid rain of Manhattan. Some of the carving was barely legible. However, she pressed on, absorbed in what she was seeing through her telephoto lens.

King of Upper and Lower Egypt, Men-kheper-ra, who embellishes the house of him who created him, (click).

The jogger watched the man in the coat unsheathe a narrow-bladed knife from his sock and slide it up his sleeve.

Time to move. He crept forward until he was just ten yards away. *Wait for the moment.*

The man in the coat looked about him, drew the knife from his sleeve, and started his run toward Beth.

Now!

The jogger sprang forward and smashed a weighted sock over the head of the man in the overcoat. He caught the man as he fell. The jogger held the unconscious man under his arm and ran him head first into the trunk of an oak tree.

His victim's head snapped back.

Beth completed her photographic record and stood back to wonder at the fact that she was looking at the oldest man-made monument in North America. All two-hundred-and-fifty tons of it had been brought from another continent. *Extraordinary.*

She put the camera into its case, zipped it into her backpack, and retraced her steps. After buying an ice cream from one of the vendors at the park entrance, she headed back to the hotel. She planned to spend as long as possible studying her photographs, before walking back across the park to the Museum of New York. Marjorie Bantry had invited her to come over and have a look at the research facilities there.

Back in her room, Beth transferred the photographs from the camera to her computer, and inspected the images. The responsibility of finding a clue—any clue that would help Alex—weighed heavily upon her. Someone had invested a lot of money to help her find it, and Alex had implicit trust in her ability to do so.

Dear Alex—what a precious man he had become to her over the years. As both friend and mentor, he had prodded her latent academic talent into life and overseen the start of her academic career. She'd experienced hope and forgiveness through his grace…and he'd brought Peter into her life. She found herself smiling.

Her musings were interrupted by the telephone. She picked it up but said nothing, reluctant to give any information until she established who was on the line.

"Hello? Beth, are you there?"

Her heart leaped with delight. It was Peter. "I certainly am," she said, "but I'm getting nowhere…and I'm missing you like crazy."

"Hmm. Do you know how good it feels to be missed? I was spooning honey onto a waffle tonight, and it took me thirty minutes to stop fantasizing about you. It reminded me of the highlights in your hair."

"Just thirty minutes." She laughed. "I'll have to think of ways of holding your attention a good deal longer."

"Stop now, girl, or I am never going to get to sleep. Have you managed to uncover anything?"

"Not a thing. I'm poring over my photographs at the moment. Can't see anything unusual. A lot of the hieroglyphics have been badly eroded. If there ever was something, it may have worn away." She sighed. "I very much fear I'm wasting a lot of someone's money."

"Don't worry about it. You may have moved things on a bit, but perhaps not in a direction you anticipated."

"What do you mean?"

"Has anything happened to you over there that seemed a bit strange or caused you concern?"

She was instantly alarmed. "I had a call yesterday from someone in the hotel, but they put the phone down when I answered."

"Beth, please don't be frightened, but I think we need to take a few precautions. I've just received some information from the American police that you may be in danger. They've caught a guy who had your details in his pocket. I can't say more at this stage, but I promise to fill you in when you get back. Meanwhile, we've worked on a plan to keep you safe here in London."

"Oh," said Beth weakly, but then rushed on. "But what about you and Alex? If this is linked with our investigations into Trevor's death, you two might be in just as much danger as me."

"Unfortunately, we don't have enough evidence to justify getting help from the police, but we have a plan that should keep us safe for a while. In the mean time, we have to assume that there are people somewhere who know what we are doing and who consider us to be a threat."

"And these people kill?"

"Mmm, yes. So the immediate priority is to get you back here where we can keep you safe." He paused. "According to your itinerary, you're spending this afternoon at the Museum of New York with Dr. Bantry."

"That's right."

"Beth, this is important. I know the museum is only walking distance away. But can you get a taxi to the museum and take all your luggage with you?"

"Why?"

"Because you're booked to come home tonight on an earlier flight. It's all been organized. Get a taxi from the museum straight to the airport. I think I can promise that you will be quite safe, if you do."

A million questions clamored for answers but something in the authority of Peter's voice convinced her to follow his instructions. "You'd better have some good answers for me when I get back, Peter Jacobs."

"I'll be there to meet you off the plane and take you to an early lunch. Ask me then, but I warn you, I will probably be incapable of any rational thought once I see you."

Beth laughed and hung up.

That afternoon, Beth enjoyed being in her natural element —exploring the conservation techniques used by Dr. Bantry and her team at the museum. In fact, it was a surprisingly productive time, which helped her feel less guilty about taking the time to come to New York.

Later that evening, she settled gratefully into her seat on the flight to Heathrow. The tensions and demands of the day had left her weary to the bone.

The man two rows behind on the opposite side of the aircraft noticed that she'd fallen asleep even before the aircraft took off.

Chapter 22

Peter and Alex were sitting in companionable silence after their evening meal. Now that Peter was working more conventional hours at Mining Management Systems, meals were eaten at a more regular hour.

Peter knew he'd given Beth the impression that Alex was a partner in the plans he had made to keep her safe when she arrived back in England. It was a generous interpretation of the facts. In reality, Alex knew nothing of his plans, and Peter was working out how to broach the subject with him. He sighed. *Best to come straight out with it.*

"Alex, there was an attempt on Beth's life in New York this morning."

Alex spluttered into his coffee. "What!" he exclaimed. "Is she all right?"

"She's fine. I've just spoken to her, and she will be catching the evening flight that gets in tomorrow morning. I was hoping to borrow your car so I can pick her up."

"Of course, Peter. Take it."

"The tricky thing is, she has no idea that someone was

prevented from attacking her, so I need to persuade her to change her living arrangements for a while, so she will be safe."

Alex gave Peter a searching look. "And just how did you find out about this planned attack on Beth?"

"I employed someone to be her bodyguard. His job was to watch her back without her knowing."

"And is this person's information trustworthy?"

"He is the best, and I trust him implicitly."

Alex bent his head.

When he looked up, Peter was disturbed to see that his eyes were full of tears.

"Enough!" said Alex. "I've put you both in danger. I have to insist that you both stop being involved in the investigation into Trevor's death. I'm sorry I was so foolish. I never meant to put the two of you in danger. If either of you were hurt because of me, I'd never forgive myself."

Peter said quietly, "I'm afraid it's too late, Alex. We are involved. Those we are up against know Beth is a threat to them, presumably because they know what's on her computer."

Alex buried his face in his hands.

"I should also tell you that we caught someone at the *Phoenix* taking pictures of me. I'm told that this person is linked to a European gang who specialize in a number of things, including contract killings and intimidation."

Alex groaned in anguish and said between his fingers, "Peter, I'm so sorry."

Peter got up from his chair, squatted down beside him and put a hand on his shoulder. "I wouldn't have told you any of this, Alex, except that we need to take steps to ensure each other's safety."

Alex gave an indistinct grunt.

Peter continued. "I'll pick Beth up tomorrow morning and take her to her place of safe keeping. Then, at five o'clock, I'll pick you up and take you to yours. If you pack some gear tonight, I'll take it with me in the car tomorrow. Is that okay?"

"Where will we be going?"

"A highly secure flat I've found. I just need to organize a few things first."

Alex nodded in acquiescence. "Thanks, Peter. But how long can we stay in hiding? We have lives to live." He balled his hand into a fist. "What more can we do to bring this wretched business to a close? We've given all we know to the police but there's been no result."

Alex's despair was palpable.

"Then we finish it," said Peter. "We push through until we can give the police enough to shut these guys down." He paused before adding, "I've managed to get a bit more information about people buying salvage gear."

Alex looked up. "What have you got?"

"I've got the name of an organization buying stuff for local use in the estuary. Plenty of outfits have bought gear from around the docks, but only one is for local use. It's the Coastal and Estuarine Research Unit from University College." Peter shrugged. "It's the only lead I've got at the moment. The trouble is, I'm not sure how hard to press inquiries with University College, and I don't know how we can find a stationary boat amongst the hundreds of boats that are in and around the Thames estuary. It seems impossible."

Alex remained still for some time before he stood up and said, "Let's go to my computer. I think I can help."

Peter stood behind Alex as he tapped away on the keyboard. Alex explained, "You should be able to find most ships by using their Automatic Identification System. If you look at this website, you can track the position and movement of any ship in the world." He peered at the screen. "Somali pirates love it."

Alex zoomed into the area covering the Thames estuary. "You see here. These colored arrows show the position of every ship in the estuary. Every ship is color-coded to show what type of vessel it is."

Alex placed the computer's cursor on a red arrow and immediately a little box appeared beside it with figures inside.

"Most of the ships have their details entered into a database. So when you place the computer's cursor over their symbol, you can learn the ship's name, speed, and the direction it is traveling."

"Impressive," said Peter. "But how will it help us?"

"All we need to do is to look for a stationary ship that may not have entered its details in the AIS system. Stationary ships are marked as diamonds rather than arrows. If a ship is stationary for more than a few days somewhere near the likely track of the *Beatrice*, then you've probably got your salvage ship." He smiled. "I'll print off a chart of ship positions each day this week and see what transpires."

"So we're still fighting, then?"

Alex paused before nodding slowly.

"I'll pick you up at 5pm tomorrow," Peter replied. "Bring your laptop."

Peter took full advantage of having both a car and the company of the person he loved. He dawdled along the English roads toward a pub in Windsor. He'd chosen it because of its charm, and because it overlooked the languid waters of the Thames. He was feeling a huge sense of relief now that Beth was back under his personal protection. He'd been haunted by the nightmare of nearly losing her in New York. Nothing, he vowed, would ever threaten her again.

When they arrived at the pub, he kept stealing glances at her as he picked at his plowman's lunch.

Beth reached across and put her hand on top of Peter's. "Peter, I'm really all here…and I'm in pretty good shape. You don't have to keep checking."

"I'm that transparent?"

Beth nodded and then asked quietly, "How much danger was I in?"

Peter knew this question would come, but was still unsure how to answer it. He drew a deep breath. "The police were called to attend a man who had an accident in Central Park. This man had a photo of you in his pocket, together with your name, and the name of the hotel you were staying at." Peter swallowed. "He also had a knife."

Beth looked at him in amazement. "How…how do you know all this?"

Peter toyed with his fork. "I'd given instructions to the hotel that if any issues arose concerning your personal safety, they were to ring me."

Silence followed. Beth gave Peter's hand a squeeze. "Thanks. But how on earth did you persuade them to do that?"

"My name was on the check that paid for your accommodation."

Beth gave him a puzzled look.

Peter shrugged. "Because our benefactor required anonymity, I paid the account and gave the receipt to the benefactor via Alex. I just took advantage of it."

Beth smiled. "Cheeky, but nice. Tell me what happened."

"After the police rang the hotel, they called me and told me that the man they were questioning had a history of violent attacks—not that he'll be much of a threat for a while. He's in hospital with a broken neck. The police asked me if I would know why he had your picture. I said I had no idea. The police were going to talk to you today, but missed you when you left the country a day early. They'll ring you on your mobile tonight."

Beth nodded. "What do I say?"

"The truth." Peter took Beth's hands into his own. "Beth, it seems that our poking about into Trevor's death has put you, Alex, and myself in considerable danger. Alex is devastated about it. This was the last thing he anticipated or wanted for us."

"Us?"

"Someone attached to a criminal gang was caught taking photographs of me the other day. I have to presume it was so I could be identified by people who don't have my well-being at heart."

"Oh no!" Beth looked stricken. "But who is it? Who's behind all this? Who can kill a man in London and organize an attack on someone in New York? Who are these people?"

"People with a lot of influence and money; people who see us as a threat."

"Is it too late to pull out?"

Peter nodded. "Alex and I think so."

"Surely the police can take over now. They know everything we know anyway."

"The police need more evidence, and they also need more information before they can offer any of us protection. Much of what has happened can be explained as circumstantial."

Beth looked out through the window of the old Elizabethan pub. "What about Alex? How safe is he?"

"We have to assume he is not." Peter took a deep breath, "Which brings me to the issue of our safety. I've got a plan."

"What do you have in mind?"

"You have got to be kidding!" said Beth in disbelief. The pale walls of the White Tower soared above the battlements of the Tower of London.

"Beth, I wouldn't joke about your safety. If you're okay with it, you can stay with Bell and her husband Colin. He smiled. "Colin tells me that Bell loves the idea of you staying with her."

"How much do they know?" asked Beth.

"All they know, is that you are in some danger as a result of historical investigations surrounding a murder." Peter got out of the car and pulled Beth's case from the back seat. He smiled. "You should be safe here. I'm told the Tower has been remarkably effective at keeping unwanted people out for the last eight-hundred years."

"But what about my work?" Beth protested.

"Alex has managed to get you a two-week contract to review the maintenance and restoration procedures of the Fusilier's museum." Peter grinned. "So you can cause merry hell with the rampaging wives of the Yeomen for a whole two weeks."

"And what happens then? I can't be a prisoner in the Tower for ever!"

"In the meantime, we work at getting enough information for the police so they can end it."

"Do we have any leads?"

"One. It concerns a salvage boat." He put an arm around her as they began walking toward the Tower. "Let's meet Alex over a meal at the *Phoenix* tomorrow night. I'll pick you up. We'll bring each other up to date and then plan our next move." He looked at his watch. "Once I hand you over to Colin, I'm afraid I need to get straight back to work."

Beth sighed. "Promise me that you'll break me out of the Tower of London."

Peter whispered in her ear, "No wall will ever be high enough to keep me from you, Beth."

Beth rolled her eyes, put her hand on her chest, and said, "Be still my beating heart."

Peter glanced at Alex, trying to work out how he was feeling. The professor looked slightly forlorn as they stood on the plush carpet of the lift, surrounded by mirrored walls and soft lighting.

The lift door opened at the top floor.

Peter shouldered his rucksack and picked up Alex's battered suitcase. Two imposing doors led off from the landing. Peter checked the number on the electronic key and opened one of them.

Alex moved forward a few steps, then stood stock-still. Whilst the opulence of the apartment was staggering, Peter knew it was the panoramic view from the picture windows that had taken Alex's breath away. Peter had to admit; it was pretty amazing. They had a clear view of Tower Bridge to the left, and the Tower of London to the right. Yachts, barges, and luxury cruisers lay at their pontoons in St. Katharine's Dock below them. It was a stunning sight.

Peter showed Alex around the two luxurious bedrooms. Both had marbled ensuites and spas. The kitchen was fitted with top-of-the-range appliances, and the study had beautiful and generous proportions. However, it was obvious that it was the view Alex loved most. He asked, almost shyly, if the table might be moved to the window so he could work from there.

"How on earth did you find this place?" asked Alex. "Who owns it?"

Peter looked up from dragging the table into position. "Well, come to think of it, I suppose I do. It belongs to my father's company." Peter still struggled to think of the company as his own. He went on to explain, "But it's become an unnecessary asset. It's going to be sold."

Alex gazed out of the window. "It must be hard to part with it."

"I've actually not seen it before today," confessed Peter. "Because we were selling it, I've never taken much interest in it." He dragged a chair up to the table and sat down. "The good thing about it is its security, and that it's only a few yards from where I work. He pointed to an Internet socket in the wall. "You'll be able to plug into that from here." He stood and picked up his rucksack. "I'll use the smaller bedroom. You take the master suite." He paused. "I'm hoping all this won't be for long, Alex."

The professor nodded. "We've probably only got a few more rolls of the dice, Peter." He hooked his walking stick on the edge of the table. "So let's do what we can to make them count."

Chapter 23

Peter looked up as Toby came to the door. He was grateful for the interruption to the tedious task of updating the company's email list for Judy, the secretary sitting at the next desk. Peter had to remind himself that it was his own fault. He'd insisted on working from the very bottom of Mining Management Systems to familiarize himself with its operations. However, he always spent the afternoon with Toby, learning how to research markets and manage the company business.

"May I have your attention, everyone," said Toby. "There will be an ice-cream cake for afternoon tea, plus gourmet dips and other irresponsible forms of carbohydrates and sugars. So no heroics or working through afternoon tea. Mild hilarity and levity are the order of the day."

"What's the excuse? Jan hasn't told us anything," demanded Judy.

Toby grinned. "Ah, that's because Jan Pieter de Jager is the excuse. He's won his first contract. I've just heard that his marketing proposition to a coal mining company in Sparta, Illinois, has been accepted. It's a three-quarter-of-a-million pound contract." He turned to Peter. "Well done, old chap. We are in danger of having a very fine year."

Peter smiled. "I'll try and make it if Judy can spare me."

Judy retorted, "Then you'd better hop to it, young man, so you can earn your break."

Peter parked Alex's car in Mining Management's underground car park, and walked with Beth and Alex to the *Phoenix*.

As Lenny showed them to their booth, he whispered to Peter, "Kym said she wants to see you. Something about swapping her culinary best for someone's phone number."

Beth and Alex slid into their seats whilst Peter made his way to the kitchen. A few minutes later, he returned, smiling.

"What's up?" inquired Alex.

"I've exchanged Toby's phone number for Kym's personal oversight of our meals." He sat down. "Poor Toby, I wonder what he's in for."

As they ate, Peter and Alex brought Beth up to date with their thoughts about who might be seeking to salvage the wreck of the *Beatrice*.

"Wow!" said Beth. "Finding *Beatrice* would certainly be a coup. People in England, Spain, and Egypt have been talking about finding it for ages. They've already squabbled over who would have ownership of the sarcophagus if it were salvaged. That's probably why they are a bit cagey about people knowing they are looking for it."

Alex nodded. "With possession being nine tenths of the law, I suspect that the local Freemasons will want to ensure it stays in London."

Peter rubbed his chin. "I wish there was a way we could get into University College and find out about this boat belonging to the research unit."

"That's not difficult," said Beth. "I can go. University College is just up the road from the British Museum. I know some of the people in the history department. My friend Jill works there."

"No, Beth, it's too dangerous," said Alex.

"Too dangerous!" She stabbed the table with her finger. "I think it's too dangerous not to do whatever's necessary to end this." She sat back. "I'm for having a go."

"Beth," said Alex, "someone has just tried to kill you. We've got to be responsible."

"Then let's do something responsibly."

Silence ensued.

Peter cleared his throat. "If you are determined, Beth, I'll go with you as your bodyguard. Just tell me when you want to go, and I'll come and collect you."

"Really?"

"Really." Peter turned to Alex. "May I borrow your car?"

"Of course."

He nodded his thanks.

With the impasse resolved, conversation began to flow more freely. Alex turned to Beth. "Now, tell us about New York. Did you manage to come up with anything?"

Beth wrinkled her nose. "No." She paused. "At least…I'm not sure…Just a wild idea that seems so crazy that I'm reluctant to share it."

"Well, we're all a bit crazy…and a bit desperate," said Alex. "So tell us."

"Okay," she paused as if to gather the right words. "When I saw the corrosion damage on the New York obelisk and the shrapnel damage on the London one, I had the stirrings of an idea." She toyed with her glass of water. "The trouble is, I will need to go to Egypt, to Luxor, to check it out."

Alex briefly laid a hand over Beth's. "If anyone can make sense of any clue on these obelisks, it's you. And if the craziest idea is all that is left when other possibilities are eliminated, then it becomes probable."

"The real issue," said Peter, interrupting, "is your safety. That's of paramount importance. Whilst I'm fairly confident of getting you to Bloomsbury and back in one piece, my parole conditions forbid me from going abroad." He shrugged. "So, I can't go with you."

"Does that mean I can't go?" asked Beth.

"Not necessarily. I'm just saying that your safety is an issue which will need to be addressed if you go." Peter changed the subject. "Why do you think it would help to go to Egypt?"

"Well, I've been thinking about which obelisks would be the likeliest candidates to qualify as obelisks of Ramses II. Then I remembered that the obelisk in Paris used to be the pair of the one in Luxor."

Alex nodded. "We know that. But I still don't see…"

"But don't you see, Alex? Both obelisks used to stand in front of the two huge statues of Ramses II that guard the entrance of Luxor temple." Beth shrugged. "If any obelisks could be called the obelisks of Ramses II, it's those two.

Peter nodded. "And what would you hope to see on them?"

"I think there is a chance that someone has defaced the obelisks of Ramses II in order to ghost another message on them."

"Ghosting?" inquired Alex.

"What's ghosting?" asked Peter.

Beth leaned forward. "Have you ever looked at those eye puzzles with the hidden three-dimensional shapes in them? They can only be seen if you look at them in a certain way."

"What? Do you mean stereograms?" asked Alex.

"That's right. Well, this is the primitive equivalent. You texture the rock surface so certain shapes can only be seen at certain angles."

Peter looked at Beth and saw the excitement in her eyes. It was infectious. *But how could he keep her safe?* He put a knuckle to his forehead and thought furiously. A moment later, he turned to Alex. "Do you think we have enough information to make a case to our sponsor?"

Alex, who was drinking his coffee, coughed. "Perhaps. I'll go up on deck and ring him."

"I'll go with you," said Peter. "I need to make a phone call too. I've got an idea about who would make an excellent bodyguard."

"Who?" demanded Beth.

At that point, Lenny interrupted them by asking if they needed more coffee. "Kym says she's coming out to see you guys in a moment," he warned. "She expects you to be fulsome in your praise."

As Beth gave Jill Covington a hug, Jill whispered in her ear, "Where did you find him? He's gorgeous."

Beth glanced at Peter who was hovering at her side. His dark eyes were ranging around the room. She had to admit, he did look good. He was big, very fit, and looked just a bit dangerous.

Peter and Beth had walked to the Bloomsbury Theatre and found Jill waiting for them in the UCL Union café.

"I'm glad you approve," said Beth, grinning, "because..." She battled to find the right words. Saying 'I'm head over heels' was a dreadful cliché. 'Thrilled' was slightly better, but lame. She needed a word that combined, 'safe', 'cherished', 'at home', and 'complete.' She settled for, "Because I wanted you to like him."

"Like him! If you ever tire of him, darling, send him my way."

After they'd found a table, Peter asked Beth and Jill what they would like to eat.

Jill watched him go and collect their order. "I didn't think they made them like that anymore."

Beth grinned. "I don't think they do."

"So deliciously old fashioned. Where did he learn his chivalry thing?"

"I asked him once. He said he had strict parents."

Peter returned with their salad wraps. "The coffees are coming."

Beth squeezed his hand briefly before hauling her thoughts back to the reason for their visit. "Jill, you've flirted with at least half the faculty of UCL, what do you know about CERU? Have they got a big research vessel working in the Thames estuary?"

Jill Covington raised an eyebrow. "I've no idea. Why do you want to know?"

"Just investigating what options there might be for exploring some of London's marine history. Who would know about it?"

Jill looked around the café. "Arthur would. He's with that group sitting by the window. I'll ask him, if you like."

Before Beth could urge caution, Jill was threading her way between the tables to a party of diners who had the slightly intense, Bohemian look of University professors. Beth watched as Jill kissed one of the younger men on the cheek and spoke to him. The young man looked past Jill to where Peter and Beth were seated, nodded, and rose to follow Jill back to her table.

"Beth, Peter: this is Dr. Arthur Beddington. He cheats at Scrabble, and works in the Geography Department."

"Hi. What do you want to know?"

Beth swallowed. "Do CERU own a research vessel that works in the Thames estuary? I'm exploring what options might be available for some historical marine research."

Dr. Beddington replied, "Yes and no. We can't afford our own research vessel. So what we do is hire *Grayling* when we need to do some research. She's an eighty-five foot long, twin-hulled research ship. She's got lab space, a decompression chamber, and air compressors. We like her because she provides a stable platform to work on." He pulled a face. "The downside is that she is hideously expensive. She's owned by some mob in the City."

"Do you know if CERU are using it at the moment? Is it free?"

"There's a guy doing his doctorate on something to do with Thames sandbank movements. He must have won a pretty amazing research grant, because he's been using *Grayling* for the last month or so. Do you want me to find out the details?"

Beth saw Peter give the tiniest shake of his head.

She replied, "No thanks, Arthur. Our budget is very modest, so I don't think it's possible. However, I'll know where to come if I want to chase it up any further."

"Fine," he said, smiling. "And I don't cheat at Scrabble. It's just that Jill hasn't yet learned that a 'li' is a Chinese mile."

"Is not!" yelled Jill at his retreating back.

Chapter 24

P eter looked out of the penthouse window. Fog, as soft as down, had settled over London during the night, causing the city to look as if it was built on clouds. Only the tallest of buildings thrust their way through the diaphanous mist. In the distance, Christopher Wren's masterpiece, the dome of St Paul's cathedral, rested on a heavenly pillow. To the right, the quirky Gherkin—just recently completed—thrust into the sky, standing guard over the financial hub of London.

He glanced at his watch, sighed, and headed toward the lift. Moments later, he was walking through the foggy gloom toward Mews Street where the company offices were located. Up ahead, he could see the lanky form of Toby, also making for the office. He was clutching a cup of takeaway coffee. By mutual consent, they stood together at the edge of the dock and looked across at the ghostly forms of the boats floating on the water. The sounds of the city's morning rush hour were eerily distorted by the fog.

Toby gestured at the scene with his coffee cup. "It's a fair representation of the state of my brain in the mornings."

Peter gave him a sideways look. "Toby, you portray yourself as a woolly headed, foppish nerd. But I think it's an affectation you use to disguise the fact that you are a genius—and that's something that is not always easy to live with." Peter smiled. "The fact is, I've never known your mind to be anything other than razor sharp…and I've never known anyone more assertive when you have to be. You're a wolf in sheep's clothing, and you don't fool me for a moment."

Toby acknowledged the comment with a nod. "It's mortifying to discover one is so transparent…"

Toby got no further. Behind him a white van screeched to a halt. Three men brandishing baseball bats burst out of it and ran toward them.

Adrenaline turned the next few minutes into slow motion.

Peter's first concern was for Toby.

He did the only thing that would keep him safe: he grabbed Toby's coffee and pushed him off the edge of the dock.

Toby gave a yelp of surprise, flailed his arms in the air, and splashed into the water.

Peter then span round on his feet and ran toward his nearest attacker.

The man faltered as Peter rushed toward him.

Maintaining momentum, Peter hurled the scalding coffee into his face.

With a scream, the man dropped his baseball bat and covered his eyes. Peter grabbed the bat and kicked the man's legs from under him. As he fell, Peter swung the bat and crashed it over the man's skull.

The odds had now changed. But they were still not good. The voice of his cellmate, Hammer, came clearly to mind: *Never do wot they expect. Always keep the initiative.*

Peter leaped off the wharf onto a sloping gangplank that ran to a floating pontoon. He wanted to force a fight on the narrow confines of the gangway where his attackers would have to come at him one at a time.

The two remaining assailants jumped down onto the gangplank, and edged toward him, grim and menacing.

Fighting is mostly intimidation, Joey boy.

Peter roared at them in defiance.

215

The well-muscled man in front appeared completely unfazed by Peter's shouting.

Damn.

The gangplank started to bounce as the man walked toward him. Peter felt the motion and decided to encourage it. He began jumping up and down.

The gangplank's bouncing increased significantly. The big man lurched sideways, momentarily off balance. Peter used the moment to lunge forward, holding the bat like a lance, and jabbed him in the stomach.

The man doubled over.

Peter reversed the bat, swung it up and smashed it on top of his attacker. He followed this up with another brutal swing, stilling his assailant completely.

No half measures, Joey. Be in it with all you got, or don't get involved.

Peter was dimly aware of Toby thrashing around in the water, and a man standing in the bow of a sailing yacht trying to reach him with a boat hook.

Toby yelled at his would-be rescuer, "Throw him the boat hook."

The grizzled yachtsman had the wit to understand Toby's meaning and lobbed the boat hook over to Peter.

Four yards in front of him, the remaining assailant dropped his bat, put his hand in his jacket and pulled out a pistol.

In the time that his attacker took to slip off the safety catch and draw back the slide to cock the gun, Peter had charged forward.

The metal point on the end of the boat hook drove into the man's belly.

The gun exploded as the man let out a scream.

A stinging thump punched into Peter's left shoulder.

The man dropped the gun as he fell on the gangplank.

Peter ignored his own pain and kicked the gun into the water. Then he picked up the baseball bat and sprinted to the top of the gangplank. It took him only a few seconds to reach the white van.

The driver delayed moving the engine into gear a fraction too long. Peter swung his bat, and shattered the van's windscreen.

The van lurched forward and began skidding its way down the road.

Like a man waking after a dream, Peter looked at the bat in his hands—appalled at what he'd just done. He'd understood exactly what he was doing and known the damage he was inflicting. To his horror, he realized that he had very much wanted to inflict it.

———

Peter dropped his head as Detective Sergeant Allan Jenkins stared at him balefully. "You're on parole," said the detective. "You're meant to be keeping your nose clean."

"With due respect, Detective, Peter's nose is scrupulously clean," protested Toby. "I'm his boss; I should know. He was speaking to me outside our offices when a carload of thugs set on him. He did nothing other than defend himself..." he rubbed his sore arm, "... and me, in his rather unorthodox way."

"I agree," said Alex. "Peter needs to be commended for protecting Mr. Cheeseman and beating off his attackers."

Jenkins sighed. "Beating off his attackers is presumably your euphemism for two men currently undergoing emergency surgery for head fractures and possible brain damage. It also, presumably, embraces the fact that a man has just emerged from abdominal surgery for," he looked briefly down at his notes, "a ruptured spleen, liver, and small intestine."

Peter closed his eyes as the demons of guilt began to assail him again. He forced himself back under control and said with a confidence he did not feel, "Fair go, Detective! You did pick up three baseball bats and recover an automatic pistol!"

Jenkins pursed his lips.

Alex had insisted that Peter and Toby contact Allan Jenkins when the police had required them to go back to the station to help with inquiries. He had also insisted on accompanying them himself.

Alex spoke up again. "Detective, the attack on Peter is probably linked with the murder of my brother. I think it's time we filled you in with what's been happening since we last met."

When Alex had finished, the detective sat silent for some time. Eventually he nodded. "I think there can be no doubt now that you three are in danger, and that you have become people of interest to those who are behind Mr. Whitman's death. I therefore strongly advise…" he slapped the desk. "No, dammit! I'm telling you…to cease your investigations and leave matters to the police."

Peter rubbed his forehead, wincing as he did because of his wounded shoulder. "It may be too late, Detective. We can't unlearn what we know about the links between Trevor's death, Freemasonry, and the wreck of the *Beatrice*."

The Detective leaned back. "If you stop now, I am confident of being able to remove the threat coming from the Ukrainian firm of villains who attacked you this morning." He sniffed. "I've ordered that the gang's leader—the father, incidentally, of one of those undergoing brain surgery—be brought in for questioning. If he runs to form, he will turn up with his lawyer and deny all knowledge of this morning's events. However, I am confident of being able to put enough frighteners on him to leave him in no doubt that he will be instantly arrested if any of you so much as trip over a pavement. He knows I've enough on him to make a good case for his deportation."

"That won't stop the people behind it hiring someone else to try again," said Peter. "Do you have any leads as to who they might be?"

"We are making inquiries."

Alex nodded. "Have you made inquiries amongst the Freemasons Trevor was associated with?"

"We are making inquiries," repeated the detective stubbornly.

Alex inclined his head, making it clear he expected to be told more.

The detective reacted. "It's my job to make these investigations, not yours. And it is my job to ask the questions, not yours. If I tell you every detail of our investigation, you might just be stupid enough to meddle. And I won't allow it. Is that clear?"

Alex said soothingly, "I completely understand that, Detective. We'll co-operate in every way we can. I just have one question. I've learned from inspecting my brother's Lodge regalia that he was a

companion of the Holy Royal Arch. I'm sure I could find out elsewhere but it would be convenient if you could tell me: Do you know
the name of the Grand Master of London's Holy Royal Arch?"

Jenkins pursed his lips. "Why do you want to know?"

"Two reasons: I want to know that you know; and I want to
return some of Trevor's regalia to him."

"If I tell you, you must promise me that none of you will make
contact with him, other than to post him your brother's regalia."

"Of course."

"His name is Ernest Wheeler. He's a financier in the City." The
detective shook his head. "Weird guy. He's built two massive pillars
behind his desk."

Peter was in turmoil. He'd not gone up to the penthouse with Alex.
He was too disturbed. Time after time, he replayed all that had
happened—and was appalled by what he'd done. The excuse he
clung to for killing the young man in the pub was that he was drunk
and didn't intend to. But as he reviewed his part in the violence of
the morning, he was not so sure of himself. Maybe he was a killer. It
was a shocking possibility. Peter could not deny his feelings of satisfaction at destroying those who had intended to maim or murder.
But whilst the love of justice was excusable, wanting to destroy was
another.

Demons of guilt drove him into the back streets of London,
where he walked without knowing where he was going. Eventually,
he was lost. Seeing a pub on the corner of a street, he went in.
There were few patrons in the bar—not unusual for mid-afternoon.
The smell of stale beer brought his nightmare back into sharp relief.
The horrors of what he'd been responsible for screamed and
accused with renewed intensity. He dropped his head. Was he no
better now than he was then?

A barmaid with artificially blonde hair was serving behind the
bar. "What will you have, love?"

"A pint of bitter."

She poured it and accepted his money without comment.

Peter took his pint to a corner table and stared at it.

He'd blamed the beer for his actions two years ago, but now he knew he was capable of terrible violence whilst sober. So, was he a killer? Would he always be a danger to people?

He stared at the beer through the concave windows of the glass pot. *Are you my enemy or are you my excuse?* Was it a waste of time to promise that he'd never drink again?

He stared at the tiny bubbles as they made their way up through the golden liquid...and battled his demons.

Finally, with his nerves at breaking point, he dashed his hand sideways and smashed the pot of beer against the wall. Lurching to his feet, he stumbled out the door.

Behind him, he could hear the barmaid yell, "Oi! What's your problem, mate?"

But he'd gone.

Peter found his way back to the apartment, and there, he poured out his hurt and his heart to Alex.

When Peter's torrent subsided, the professor struggled to his feet and made Peter a mug of hot chocolate. This simple act did much to restore Peter's equilibrium.

When Alex sat down again, he said. "I'm quite excited for you, Peter."

These were not the words Peter expected to hear. He lifted his head from his hands and shot Alex a quizzical look.

The professor continued. "All your fears center on two essential questions that many people never get round to asking. They are: 'Who am I?' and 'Is there hope?'" He steepled his fingers together. "If it's true that God exists—as the order of the cosmos suggests; and if it's true that he came as Jesus to rescue us back to himself, then you are not alone, not without meaning, and not without resources."

Peter found himself simultaneously reacting against the possibility of God, and envying Alex his faith. "I suppose Christianity is all right if it works for you," he said cautiously.

Alex looked at him over his glasses. "Don't be patronizing, Peter."

"Alex," he protested, "I wasn't…"

"You're suggesting that my faith is an optional mental crutch people can choose to get them through life." Alex wagged a finger. "The issue is not whether or not it works, but whether it is true. And that's the big question you need to find the answer to."

"Why?"

"Because it will lead you to the grace and hope you seek."

And so the conversation continued.

By the time he went to bed, Peter had arrived at a place of relative peace…and felt ready to resume his quest to resolve the terrible threats still hanging over Beth and Alex.

Beth was sitting at the dining table typing up her notes on the Fusilier's museum when her mobile rang. Frustrated at the interruption, she picked up the phone.

"Beth Anderson speaking."

"How's the Prisoner of Zenda going?"

"Peter!" A wave of delight washed over her. She got to her feet and turned away from the sitting area where Colin was ensconced in an armchair. "I don't want to be rescued for another two days," she whispered. "I'm enjoying myself. But then I expect you to arrive on your white charger."

"Just let down your golden hair and I'll climb up."

"Rescuing me from the Tower will be easy. Rescuing me from the women of the Yeomen will be your challenge. You should see what they've done to their common room. And I'm getting fat. Bell keeps feeding me with scones, and interrupts my study all the time. I've put on two pounds since I came here and been made to feel very much at home."

"I've got some news for you."

"What's that?"

"The last roll of the dice. You're clear to go to Egypt if you wish." He paused. "Do you still want to go?"

"Wow!" She paused. "Of course I want to."

She thought frantically of the many things she would need to do. "I'll get my visa application sorted straight away. Boy-oh-boy, our philanthropist came through again, then."

"Yes. But he's made one stipulation at Alex's and my recommendation."

"What's that?"

"You go with a bodyguard."

"A bodyguard! I don't want to be sharing rooms with a stranger. No way!"

"It's that or nothing. And I can promise you, he's no stranger."

"Who is it?" demanded Beth, jumping to her feet.

"Ask Colin. Goodnight, darling." Peter rang off.

With a cry of exasperation, Beth flung her phone down onto the sofa.

Colin continued to read his book unperturbed.

Beth could not think of a single reason why Colin would know any details about her arrangements, let alone details that even she did not know about. The truth was, she reflected, she knew very little about Colin at all.

Unsure of what to expect, she began tentatively, "Colin, why would Peter suggest you might know who was going with me to Egypt?"

Without looking up, Colin said, "Because it's me."

"You!" expostulated Beth. "But you're a Yeoman in the Tower, for goodness sake. You're not a bodyguard."

Colin put down his book and regarded Beth levelly. "Two years ago, I was an instructor with the SAS at Sennybridge. In one way or another, I've been involved with the SAS for twelve years." Colin picked up his book again. "I suspect that might have something to do with it."

"Oh!" said Beth weakly. She was silent for a while but couldn't help saying, "But the SAS do military things, not bodyguard work."

"We are also trained to keep people alive." Still looking at his book, Colin added, "Who do you think stayed in the Excelsior Hotel with you and watched your back in Central Park?"

Ernest Wheeler sat at his desk unwrapping a parcel marked 'personal.' Peeling open the final wrapping, he found it contained the neatly folded regalia of someone who was a companion of the Holy Royal Arch. On top was a note, which read:

Mr. Wheeler,

Detective Sergeant Allan Jenkins told me you were the Grand Master of the Holy Royal Arch. So I'm returning these items, as they belong to you, not my brother.

The note was signed, 'Alex Whitman.' However, in brackets afterward, Alex had written 'and on behalf of Beth Anderson, and Peter Jacobs.'

Wheeler dropped the piece of paper and sat rigid, holding the edge of the desk with both hands. It was impossible. The note was clearly intended to let him know that the police were watching him, and that Whitman had some idea of what might be going on. It was also worded to make it clear that Whitman believed Wheeler was behind the attacks on Beth Anderson and Peter Jacobs.

He stared at the piece of paper for a full two minutes before pushing the intercom button. "Carl," he yelled.

Moments later, Carl was standing in front of his desk. Wheeler wasted no time. "What is the meaning of this?" He thrust the note at him.

Carl took it and read it. After a few seconds, he said, "I am sorry to report, sir, that there have been some complications."

Chapter 25

B eth chewed at her bottom lip as she stared out of the plane's window. For the last forty minutes, there had been little to see other than a blighted desert landscape. Then, the dark green ribbon of the Nile's flood plain appeared between the desert ranges like a sinuous snake.

The river that had given birth to empires and cultures that had dominated the world, was still providing water for farmers to feed a nation. Villages composed of flat-topped houses with thick mud walls were scattered along its floodplain. Palms were dotted amongst them.

Colin was seated beside her. He had said little during the flight, or indeed, for the twenty-four hours before take-off. Bell had explained to Beth, "He's in war mode. I lose him emotionally twenty-four hours before he goes on a mission." She gave a grin. "Fortunately, he more than makes up for it when he gets home."

Beth had asked tentatively, "Bell, it's not every wife who would be happy having her husband chaperone another woman for five days. How do you feel about it? You've been so lovely to me. I couldn't bear for you to have any concerns."

Privately, Beth had looked at the beautiful woman, and thought that any man would be a fool to risk losing her.

Bell had stood for a while with both hands on the kitchen bench. "Please don't worry, Beth. Five years ago, I had cancer, which needed both chemotherapy and radiation." She lowered her head. "It was pretty grim. We didn't have sex for over a year, and it was horrible. I lost all my hair and wanted to die." She smiled. "It was his love that pulled me through. So relax; he's a one gal guy." She smiled. "And judging from what I've seen of you and Peter, I rather suspect that you are a one guy gal."

She had tried to get more information from Colin about who had engaged him to watch her back in New York. However, he'd said nothing other than to admit that he had been approached as a result of his connection with Peter. He'd then changed the subject and given her instructions on what to pack and what to wear. He went through all her items, discarding some things and suggesting others. In essence, he wanted her to pack as many different 'looks' as possible.

"Keep the luggage weight down and dress for about thirty-two degrees."

Rather more disturbing were the instructions he'd given about how they were to walk together in public, and what to do if they were attacked. He'd tested her for days on interpreting the meaning of any hand signals he might give and what to do when he gave them. Finally, he'd warned her, "I'm afraid this will not be a luxury holiday. There may be some surprises. Just keep your nerve, and do what I say."

The plane banged down onto the runway and began shuddering with its engines in reverse thrust. Beth started preparing herself mentally for what might lie ahead. The trouble was, she had no idea what to expect. She was under no illusions. Colin had told her that her enemies might be aware that her name was on the flight manifest. They could be watching for her at the airport.

She could wish for a better scenario.

Colin had grayed his hair and was walking with a limp. He'd

built up the heel of one shoe, and walked with a stick. The stick, she'd been told, was made of titanium.

The airport bus ferried them five miles to the city of Luxor. They'd got on the bus late after the rest of the people boarded. Only one passenger boarded after them.

The bus began to drop people off at different hotels. Colin elected to get off at its third stop.

Shouldering their rucksacks, they made their way down the scruffy, dusty streets. The iron-shuttered doors guarding the shops were in the process of being raised. The locals had obviously kept their shops shut during the heat of the day and were now beginning to open them again. Life certainly seemed to be lived at a leisurely pace. People walked with a languid gait and looked as if they had just stepped out of a nativity scene.

Colin stopped to purchase a heavy bladed kitchen knife, a box of tissues, and a plastic bucket. She had no idea why. He then hailed a taxi.

"Where are we going?" she asked.

"To the Fondok Sheraton. It's a hotel about two miles south of town."

The taxi took them down the main road past the luxury hotels, and on into the rural irrigation country. Before long, they turned right and began heading toward the Nile.

Beth craned her head left and right, enjoying the scenery.

Colin brought her enjoyment to an abrupt end. He tapped her arm and murmured quietly, "Beth, we're being followed by the car that pulled in behind us when we got off the bus."

"What?"

"Yeah. We've got to leave this taxi—and we'll only have a few seconds to do it if we want to avoid being seen."

Beth opened her mouth, but Colin motioned for her to keep quiet.

"We're approaching the old township of Salam. It's got lots of narrow, twisting alleyways, so it's a great place to get lost in. Grab your rucksack and get ready for a quick exit." He squeezed her arm. "You okay?"

She perjured herself, and nodded.

Colin told the driver to drop them off beyond the next bend, and then to continue on to the Sheraton where another fare would be waiting for him.

The driver took Colin's money and nodded.

When the taxi stopped, Colin hauled Beth out of the car and pulled her into a gap between two shops.

From this position, she was able to watch a white car come around the corner and follow the taxi as it headed on to the hotel.

She shivered.

Colin shouldered both rucksacks and led Beth into a maze of narrow, twisting alleyways bordered by mud walls. Wizened old men squatted amongst piles of rubble, selling vegetables from wooden boxes.

Beth followed behind Colin trying to fight down her fear. "You've been here before?"

"No."

She was shocked. "Do you know where you're going?"

"Yes. This is just one of a number of scenarios I've prepared for. Relax, we're doing fine."

Beth was soon completely disorientated by the narrow alleys and was relieved when they finally emerged at a main road. Beyond the road, Beth could see the superstructure of some cruise ships. The Nile must be quite close.

Colin led her across a road to the concourse in front of the ships.

"Where are we?" Beth's question came out almost as a sob.

Colin pointed to the road behind them. "That road is El Gazera." He glanced at her. "Rest here a moment and have a drink."

"What…what are we going to do?"

"We're going to get a boat. Wait here."

Colin made his way to a wooden jetty where five feluccas were moored and began talking with two of the boatman.

Beth rested herself against a bollard and willed her heartbeat to slow down. She had no understanding of what was happening. All she knew was that they were already being hunted. It was the worst of all starts. Anxiety gnawed away at her self-control, and she had to fight to stop herself from weeping.

Colin's conversation seemed to take forever. No one appeared to be in any rush.

Eventually, he waved to Beth and beckoned her to join him.

She got to her feet and walked over to the men.

A weather-beaten boatman and his young accomplice grinned good-naturedly at her. The older one only had three teeth left. In broken English, he told her to take off her shoes, wash her feet, and step aboard.

She did so and sat down amongst the cushions on the cockpit floor. Beth was emotionally and physically exhausted.

"Rest here," said Colin, "and don't stand up. You'll be safe if you stay out of sight. I'm going off with the young bloke to buy some food."

Too weary to protest, she simply nodded.

She lay down in the cockpit, and watched the old man work around her getting the boat ready to sail. He unlashed the top boom of the lateen sail from its upright position against the mast, and cocked it forward so that it soared up from the bow, over the top of the mast. He then squatted down and busied himself with a primus stove. Beth realized he was making tea. Sure enough, minutes later the old man handed her a glass of hot golden liquid. She tasted it tentatively. It was mint flavored and tasted wonderful. Beth nodded her thanks and felt some of her apprehensions begin to ease.

Tea—the English panacea for all trying situations. She couldn't help reflecting on the fact that she was lounging about like the Queen of Sheba on a boat, which had probably not changed in design for five thousand years. It was a broad, shallow drafted vessel about twenty-four feet long. She glanced around her. All the feluccas looked the same. They were painted white with red undersides. Each had a large cockpit covered by a canopy.

Beth could see the western bank of the Nile half a mile away. Beyond its fertile flood plain, was a distant mountain range. Somewhere out there lay the fabled Valley of the Kings.

As she took in the scene, a felucca ghosted into view on the late afternoon breeze. It was magical. The reflection of its huge triangular sail on the tranquil water seemed to epitomize all that was exotic about Egypt.

Her musings were interrupted by the return of Colin and the young Egyptian. They were carrying sacks of food and bags of ice.

After the provisions had been stowed away, the young Egyptian lifted a bicycle aboard, then crossed to the middle of the boat and eased the center-plate down.

The two boatmen poled the boat clear of the jetty, and set about unfurling the mainsail. As soon as it was released, the sail filled and heeled the boat slightly. Beth could hear the musical ripple of water at the bow as they made their way downstream. If she had not been so anxious, she would have found the experience captivating.

Colin lay down on the cushions next to Beth. He glanced up at the lateen rig. "These boats are surprisingly fast; they can even sail to windward in the right conditions."

"I'll take your word for it."

Colin smiled. "Sorry, I'm a sailor. I like boats."

"Colin," she whispered, "what exactly are we doing? Where are we going to stay?"

Colin propped himself up on one elbow. "We are going to be living on this boat—just the two of us. I've hired it for three days."

"Oh. No luxury hotel, then?"

"Not now I know we're being tailed. Sorry." He jerked his thumb at the old man at the tiller. "They think we're wanting a romantic time alone. I've asked him to sail the boat to a secluded spot on the east bank of the river, and then leave us alone for three days." He paused. "I'm sorry, but we won't be near any facilities."

Beth opened her mouth to protest, but Colin continued, "Could you change your shirt for one of another color and hide your hair under your cap? We'll be sailing past Luxor in a moment. I want you to look different."

As Colin crawled forward to retrieve her rucksack, Beth hissed, "But what about bathrooms?"

Colin did not react.

She persisted. "Toilets, showers, and things?"
"What do you think the bucket is for?"
Beth groaned in disbelief.

Once the two boatmen had berthed the felucca on the west bank of the river, they climbed up onto the bike and squeaked their way down the path toward the ferry. Both seemed happy enough to be making money from clients who didn't require their services.

The boat was tethered between two trees. However, Colin found the anchor and reorganized the mooring lines so that the vessel floated just off shore. He then let down the canvas sides of the awning so that the cockpit became enclosed like a tent.

Beth watched him with a sense of growing apprehension.

Once Colin had finished, he sat down beside her. "We need to live under this awning for a few days. We cook in here, sleep in here, and you'll wash in here. I'll use the river outside. You use the bucket. I'll go on the foredeck whenever you need privacy. No unnecessary lights. We go to bed when the sun goes down." He paused. "Survival is all about lying low and being patient." He looked at her appraisingly. "It will take strength of character to stop yourself going mad. Think you can manage?"

No.

Beth nodded.

He continued, "It will be dark in ninety minutes, so let me cook up something tasty. Good food builds good morale."

It had better be blooming marvelous, Beth thought grimly.

Rather surprisingly, it was.

Colin lifted the awning at the front of the boat to allow them to see the sun sink toward the pink cliffs of the Theban desert to the west. Around them, flocks of water birds were winging their way to their evening roosts. It would have been idyllic—if Colin had not distracted her.

He had unscrewed the handle of his walking stick and was filling the internal cavity with sand from the riverbank. Colin screwed the handle back in place, felt the weight of the stick and grunted his satisfaction.

"Is that necessary?"

"I hope not."

"Something tells me that you didn't get that walking stick from Her Majesty's armory in the Tower."

"No, from Her Majesty's armory in Hereford."

Vibrations from Beth's mobile phone forestalled further conversation. She answered the phone cautiously.

It was Peter. She gave a sob. It was overwhelming to hear his voice and hear his emotion as he asked if she was safe.

She stammered, "I don't know whether we're safe, you'd better ask Colin."

"How are you feeling?"

Beth choked back a sob. "Not very good. We're being followed...and I'm hiding with James Bond in the bilges of a boat with no toilet facilities."

"Then we'll get you home. I'm so sorry you're in this mess, Beth. Can you pass the phone to Colin?"

Beth protested, "No, I'm okay. I don't want to go through all of this and not achieve anything. I'll be all right. Colin tells me that things are still going according to plan. I...I just didn't know how tough the plan was." She choked. "Honestly, he's taking good care of me. It's just that it's all a bit scary."

"Beth, you're amazing." He paused before adding, "When you get back, I'll make it up to you. Just get back to me safe, okay?"

She said weakly, "Okay."

"Let me speak to Colin."

Colin spoke quietly with Peter for a few minutes.

When he finished, Colin handed the phone back to Beth and said, "You did well, today." He then lay down on the cushions. "Good night, Beth. Sleep well."

Beth wanted to scream.

Alex watched as Peter put down his phone. If it was five o'clock in London, Alex calculated that it would be 7pm in Egypt. "How is Beth?" he asked.

"Scared, but okay. They're lying low in a boat at the moment. Colin's confident no one knows where they are."

Peter was clenching his hands into a fist, squeezing so hard that the tendons in his neck were standing proud. Alex also noticed fresh blood beginning to seep through Peter's shirt from the bandage on the top of his arm. Peter had been dismissive of the wound, but the bullet had actually gouged a deep path across the top of his shoulder.

Alex desperately tried to think of what he could do to help. In the end, he made Peter a mug of tea and sat with him, saying nothing. He reflected on the fact that everything that had happened was the consequence of Beth and Peter choosing to help him. Both had risked their lives. Alex felt humbled by it—and very responsible.

He looked at Peter and saw his anguish. Eventually, he said, "No one can grieve much without loving much."

Peter dropped his head. "Love doesn't normally put people in harm's way."

"Have you? Didn't you make provision for Beth's safety? Didn't you give her the choice of going or not? Real love gives people choice. It doesn't suffocate, and it doesn't own. It gives people freedom."

Peter said bitterly, "I may have given her the freedom to get herself killed."

"There are worse ways of dying than losing your life."

Peter shook his head.

"If it's any consolation, I'm not feeling particularly good about this, either. A few days ago, you were shot...and now Beth is being hunted." He leaned back. "But we're doing our best to end it. That's why Beth is in Egypt. The alternative is to remain helpless victims."

Peter continued to stare out the window. "I love her, Alex."

"I have no doubt of that, Peter."

They stood in silence.

Eventually, Alex said, "Why don't you allow me to cook dinner tonight?"

Peter laid a hand on Alex's shoulder. "There's only so much courage a man can have, Alex. Let's do it together."

After the meal, Alex sat behind his computer and watched the western sun sink behind a bank of clouds. Lights had begun to prick the city's buildings. What more could he do to pull his weight? Both Peter and Beth were paying a high price to help him. It was time for him to play his part.

He switched on the computer and looked up marine traffic in the Thames estuary. Alex had made a routine of doing this every night for the last week. The ship's automatic identification systems showed the English Channel. He zoomed in and focused on the Thames estuary. Tags identifying the ships in the estuary blipped into place. Alex pushed his spectacles up his nose and studied the screen.

The ship he was looking for was called the *Grayling*, but no such name appeared on the tag of any vessel on the screen. He searched again for the boats that were stationary. Over the week, he had whittled down the number of likely boats from fifteen, to eight, and now, only two. The AIS on both of these ships showed they were positioned in the estuary on a track that could possibly have been taken by the *Beatrice*. But which one was it? Alex looked at the two small colored diamonds and placed the cursor over each in turn. Neither gave the identity of the vessel.

How could he find out which one was the research vessel?

He drummed his fingers in frustration.

Alex looked at the position of the two stationary vessels and saw that one was not far from Herne Bay on the north shore of Kent. He had a friend who owned a fishing boat there. Alex had borrowed it to do some historical investigations along the coastline. A boat would give him the opportunity to investigate the identity of at least one of the mystery ships moored a mile and a half off Birchington.

But how should he do it?

Alone, he decided. Both Beth and Peter had risked enough. It was time for him to do something.

Alex pulled out his phone and dialed a number in Kent.

Chapter 26

B eth had slept fitfully in her sleeping bag on the floor of the felucca, and was subdued as she ate her breakfast of fruit and yogurt.

"I suppose they will be waiting for me at the obelisk, won't they?"

Colin was bent over his computer. "Yes, but there are ways to deal with that."

Beth shivered. "May I borrow the computer when you're finished? I want to look at pictures on my memory stick."

Colin nodded.

She asked, "What are you looking at?"

"I'm checking the times of return flights to Gatwick and seeing how full they are. We won't buy return tickets until we're at the airport—just before we fly."

Beth reflected on their ridiculous situation. "Doesn't it seem just a bit strange to you that we are lying on cushions in the cockpit of a felucca on the Nile, sorting out air fares to London?"

"No."

"That's the trouble with you men—no imagination."

Her comment drew a smile from Colin. She pressed her advantage. "Do you think Peter has imagination?"

Colin raised an eyebrow.

She pressed on. "One moment he seems to be the key person who makes everything happen, and the next, he's content to simply be a waiter, or sit in an office. I just know he is capable of more."

Colin considered the question for a moment. "Do your instincts tell you that Peter is a loser with no imagination?"

"No."

"Then trust your instincts."

"You like him?"

"Yes." Colin pushed his computer over the floorboards toward her.

Suspecting that his comment was about as good as it got from Colin, Beth said no more.

She dragged herself back to the job in hand, inserted her memory stick, and began scrolling through her pictures of the Paris obelisk. The image she was looking for was the strange little shape half-exposed on the bottom of the obelisk—the kitchen apron with the upturned 'V' inside it.

As Beth gazed at it, the reality of what she was seeing suddenly dawned on her. It was the top half of a carved hieroglyph of the Egyptian letter 'G.' She sat back on her haunches and wondered who could have been responsible for it. It looked like a fairly recent carving, one probably done about a hundred years ago before the obelisk was protected by security. Yet, the carving was of an ancient Egyptian hieroglyph. Therefore, a person with some knowledge of Egyptology must have been responsible for it.

Who would have the audacity to graffiti a magnificent obelisk like this; and who would have access to it?

She typed in 'vandalism', 'Egyptian artifacts', and 'Egyptologist' into the search engine and examined the results. Beth ran her eyes down the list that came up, searching for names beginning with 'G.'

And there it was, on the second page: 'Giovanni Batista Belzoni.'

Of course.

Some of Giovanni Belzoni's extraordinary story started to come back to her. She typed his name into the computer to remind herself of the details.

What she read amazed her.

Belzoni was the son of a barber in Padua. Initially, he had intended to train as a monk in Rome, but the French occupation of that city caused him to move to the Netherlands. However, five years later in 1803, he had to flee to England to avoid being sent to prison. There, he married an English woman, Sara Bane, and made a living working as a 'strong man' in a traveling circus.

He left the circus and traveled to Egypt in order to sell his ideas for a new irrigation system to the Egyptian government. When it came to nothing, the British consulate in Egypt sent him to Thebes, giving him the job of removing a colossal bust of Ramses II from the temple and shipping it to the British Museum.

This began his archaeological career. He searched for ancient Egyptian artefacts and shipped them off to England. Belzoni was responsible for opening up the temple of Abu Simbel as well as the second pyramid at Giza.

One thing particularly attracted Beth's attention: Belzoni had also worked on the third pyramid in Giza—the pyramid in which Howard Vyse discovered the Menjaure sarcophagus nineteen years later. Beth raised an eyebrow as she went on to read that Belzoni was an active Freemason.

Reading on, she was reminded of Belzoni's love of deception. He claimed to have found an ancient Masonic temple in Thebes, in which a wall relief showed the Egyptian god, Osiris, being initiated into Freemasonry. The claim proved false, and the temple was discovered to be the tomb of Pharaoh Seti I.

Beth learned that Belzoni ended up dying of dysentery in 1823 during an expedition to Timbuctoo. However, despite being discredited, Belzoni had so fueled the imagination of English Freemasons that many traveled to Egypt to search for proof of an Egyptian heritage for Freemasonry. In the process, they plundered Egypt's cultural heritage.

But what did it all mean? Some threads seemed to be coming

together, but there was no coherent pattern. Beth rubbed her temples, willing herself to make sense of it all.

Her movement caused Colin to open his eyes. He was lying on his back on the floorboards. "You okay?" he asked.

"I'm fine. I'm just trying to work out a puzzle." She looked sideways at him. "Fine is a relative term. I'm actually hiding in the bottom of a boat from people who want to kill me!"

Colin did not smile.

"I hate to ask a silly question," continued Beth, "but how exactly do you intend us to cross half a mile of water to get to the Temple? I hope you're not going to ask me to sail this thing."

"We take the National Ferry." Colin pointed upstream. "It's three hundred yards that way."

"Oh," said Beth, feeling slightly foolish.

"In two days, you'll get to see your obelisk. We'll go mid-afternoon. They'll be waiting for us, but we can do something about that." Colin eased himself up into a sitting position. "So this is what we'll do."

Peter was deep in thought in an armchair, pondering how best to bring their investigations to a conclusion. What could they tell the police beyond that which they'd already been told? More particularly, what would it take to end things so that Beth and Alex could live without fear of attack? He mulled over the information they'd recently learned from the police.

"Alex, is there any significance to this guy Ernest Wheeler having two big pillars behind his desk?"

Alex was working on his computer by the window. He turned and faced Peter.

"As he's a Freemason, I suspect the two pillars symbolize Boaz and Jachin—the two pillars that were built in front of Solomon's temple."

"What's the deal with Freemasons and Solomon's temple?"

Alex sniffed. "The link with Solomon's temple is an eighteenth-century invention. It turned up suddenly in 1723 as a result of the fertile imagination of Dr. James Anderson, a minister in the Church of Scotland. He traveled to London in order to write *The Constitutions of the Freemasons: for the use of the Lodges in London and Westminster*." Alex leaned back in his chair and closed his eyes in thought.

Peter waited for him to continue.

"Anderson wanted to inject some drama into Freemasonry and give it a hero. So he borrowed the name of Hiram Abiff—a craftsman in brass and stone mentioned in the Old Testament—then constructed the story about him being a Master Mason. According to his story, three Masons tried to force Hiram to betray the secrets of a Master Mason, but Hiram wouldn't divulge them, so he was bludgeoned to death. King Solomon then captured the culprits and had them executed. The Holy Royal Arch, who claimed to have discovered a secret vault built by Hiram Abiff underneath Solomon's temple, further developed this fable. According to their story, they found the lost Ark of the Jews inside the vault. They said they opened the Ark, and discovered a book which told the secret of God's true identity." Alex shook his head. "In reality, of course, no such vault ever existed."

"But how does all this link in with Egypt?"

Alex grunted. "With such a fertile imagination at work, he made connections between Freemasons and all sorts of things. Anderson laid claim to links with medieval guilds of stonemasons, Greek philosophers, and a host of biblical characters. Later Masons expanded on this and claimed ancestry from the religions of ancient Egypt, Mithraism, Zoroastrianism, Druidism, and orders of knights such as the Knights Templar." Alex screwed up his nose. "It's bunkum of course. As soon as Anderson's historical claims were published, it was shown to contain glaring errors such as Pythagoras living in Egypt at the time King Solomon's temple was built." He snorted. "In reality, it was built hundreds of years before Pythagoras was born."

Peter shook his head. "Unbelievable. Why do people actually…"

Alex shrugged. "There's none so blind as those who want to believe."

"But given all of that, wouldn't it still be unusual to have an office built to look like a temple?"

"Yes."

"So why would he do it?"

"It would be very interesting to know the answer to that."

A tour bus returning from the Valley of the Kings disgorged its American tourists at the car park of the ferry terminal. Each paid their fare, one Egyptian pound, to cross the Nile back to Luxor. Also at the ferry terminal was a young man with a wispy mustache and glasses, wearing a baseball cap. He was escorting his grandfather, who was having some difficulty with his luggage. With generosity of spirit, the American tourists helped the old man with his luggage, and included them both into their party. They told him that a minibus would be meeting them on the other side to take them the short distance to their hotel—the Winter Palace. They could take them there if they wished.

The older man accepted gratefully.

Sure enough, a minibus met the ferry and drove the party of tourists the short distance to their hotel. Everyone got out and filed up the curving steps of the Winter Palace to the elegant white-and-gold reception area. The Victorian charm of the hotel was still much in evidence.

As the tour party began to disperse to their rooms, one of their members, an old man, hailed a porter, and asked how often the shuttle bus went to the airport.

"The minibus goes to the airport eleven times a day, sir. What time do you need to leave?"

The old man told him.

The porter then volunteered to take his luggage, and that of his young companion, to the transit room—and ensure that it was put on the right minibus.

Giving his thanks, the old man gave the porter a tip, then walked with his young friend to the front door.

Chapter 27

Beth was sweating too much. She knew it. Surely, it must betray her. She tried to follow Colin's instructions: *Swing your shoulders, not your hips. Walk like a robot from the hips down. Always walk slow.* Beth was concentrating so hard that it was a moment before she realized that the temple of Luxor, the greatest open-air theater in the world, was standing before her.

She looked around in amazement. It was incongruous that such antiquity could be nestled in the heart of a modern city. A McDonald's sat just opposite.

Colin gave her a nudge.

They made their way down the steps between the exit gate and the mosque, and bought their tickets. She'd been instructed to spend as little time as possible at the obelisk. Colin would borrow her camera and take pictures of all facets of the obelisk, whilst she attached herself to a tour group and explored the temple. If she felt in any danger, she was to call his mobile.

At the end of the tour, they were both to make their way to the temple entrance at the huge wedge-shaped northern wall. Colin would inspect the carving of Nefertari standing at the feet of a statue of Ramses, whilst Beth would examine the obelisk. Once she had finished, Colin would follow her back to the Winter Palace, just three-hundred yards away.

It felt a million miles away.

Colin limped away, leaving her feeling very vulnerable. Taking a deep breath, she made her way to what was left of the Avenue of Sphinxes. Sadly, there were only a few of the ram-headed sphinxes left of the thousand that had once flanked the causeway.

Colin was now well away from her. It was time to explore the temple.

She walked back to the two statues of Ramses II standing either side of the pylon gate. The statues, made of black granite, stood twenty-two feet tall. But it was not these she had come to see. She'd come to see the obelisk. It was just behind her. She allowed herself a fleeting glance.

And there it was, in lonely splendor. *How tragic*, she thought. There should be a pair of them. The temple now looked like the face of a dear friend with one of her front teeth missing. The other obelisk had been given to the French in 1829—in exchange for a town hall clock!

She turned and made her way into the great court of Ramses II, grateful for the shade of the ruins.

Take your time. Walk like a robot.

The twin rows of columns surrounding the court had statues of Ramses interspersed between them. It was awe-inspiring. She knew the temple's history well. Amenophis III built most of the original temple in the 14th century BC, but his son had vandalized it to curry favor with another god. Tutankhamun restored it, but it was Ramses II—the great builder—who added the great court, the entrance colonnade, and the northern pylon.

Beth wandered between the pillars of the great court toward the temple proper, which was surrounded by more pillars. Each one was multi-lobed to represent a bundle of papyrus plants. Beth recalled that Amenophis had built the temple to the great god Amun-Re and his son, Khonsu, the moon god. Whilst that was so, it seemed to Beth that it was Amenophis who took center stage in most of the wall reliefs. He obviously had a well-developed ego.

She glanced at her watch and decided she had time to continue through the temple complex, so she could see the sanctuary built by Alexander the Great.

Walk like a man.

She made her way through the vestibule into the sanctuary. There, before her, was a wall relief of Alexander dressed as an Egyptian pharaoh being honored by the Egyptian gods.

Another well-developed ego.

She turned and retraced her steps.

***

Colin was suspicious of people who wore jackets during the heat of the day. He had seen the swarthy-looking man in the lightweight suit standing outside the temple. He was doing far too little. Colin fumbled inexpertly with Beth's camera, photographing the faces of the obelisk—taking it slow—being careful not to draw attention to himself.

I am watching you, my friend.

Colin wondered how many of them there would be. He was pretty sure it would be more than one.

When he'd finished his photography, he made his way through Ramses' magnificent gate into the great court. He drifted around ostensibly inspecting the statues—waiting.

It was a relief when Beth finally appeared.

She was doing a great job of walking like a man. However, he was less pleased to see a Caucasian man in a cream jacket trailing behind her, covertly watching her movements. Colin recognized him as the man who had got onto the bus with them at the airport.

Time to move.

He limped in a direction that would cause him to intercept the man, willing Beth to keep walking through the center of the great court. Nothing much could happen to her in the middle of a public place.

But it was not to be. Beth drew aside to inspect one of the many statues standing between the pillars.

Colin snatched out his phone, scrolled down to Beth's number, and pushed the call button.

He watched Beth stop in her tracks as her phone rang.

"Yes?" she answered, timidly.

In a calm and measured voice, he said, "Beth, pretend you are talking to a much-loved friend. Smile and laugh."

Colin watched as Beth changed a look of alarm into a feigned laugh. He continued, "Don't go closer than you are to the statue. Look at it for a few seconds and then go straight to your obelisk. Do what you have to do there. When you're done, proceed to the Winter Palace. I'll see you inside the foyer."

Once Colin was out of sight behind the two rows of pillars, he moved quickly. The downside of dodging behind the pillars was that he could not maintain a line of sight on the man following Beth. Beth would be on her own for some seconds.

A lot could happen in those seconds.

The crepe soles of Colin's shoes ensured that his movements were almost silent.

He slowed his pace as he came close to the column nearest to Beth's stalker. The man began to edge toward it—presumably to seek its protection.

Not a good sign.

Colin moved up to the same column and edged round it until he could see the man from behind.

The man tugged a pistol from his jacket. It had a silencer screwed into its end.

Before he could raise it, Colin smashed the titanium walking stick down on his head. He caught the man as he fell and eased him down against the column.

The pistol had spun to the floor. Colin scooped it up and tucked it under his shirt.

Waves of anxiety washed over Beth. Why had Colin needed to ring her? What was going on? She couldn't resist glancing around her.

All she saw was a pair of legs protruding from behind a column
—probably a local having a doze. They dozed a lot. She fought her
racing thoughts to a standstill. *Get on with it, girl.*

She headed for the temple entrance and walked across to the
obelisk. It had been erected on a plinth decorated on each side with
statues of baboons. These, she remembered, were demi-gods whose
job it was to assist the sun to rise each morning.

Beth knew what she was searching for. She was looking for an
Egyptian hieroglyph, a 'G' that was disconnected from the other
hieroglyphs. However, she was not very confident of finding it.
Vandals had graffitied much of the stonework with their own crude
attempts at hieroglyphics. She couldn't help but wonder if the marks
she'd seen on the Paris obelisk were also just meaningless graffiti.

But then suddenly, there it was—the kitchen apron with the
triangle inside it. It had been carved in the same style and in the
same place as the one in Paris.

With mounting excitement, she inspected the face of the obelisk,
ignoring Ramses' hieroglyphics altogether. The surface of the
granite was textured in places. She walked from one side to the
other. Nothing made sense, except—Beth furrowed her brow. She
stepped further to the side and suddenly, when viewed at an acute
angle; the small patches of frosted granite swam into perspective
and became hieroglyphics.

She was amazed.

Barely able to contain her excitement, she read three words,
'origin,' 'Menkaure', and 'box.'

There were no other words.

The writing was small and had been ingeniously disguised, but
once you knew where to look, it was discernible. However, the significance of the words remained a total mystery. She shook her head in
frustration. Perhaps when she looked at Colin's photographs, it
would make more sense.

Beth glanced over to the bust of Ramses II that sat beside the
obelisk. It had been broken off the statue that stood nearby. She
would have dearly loved to examine it, but there was no time. Her
priority now was to get to the hotel.

Beth made her way to the exit as nonchalantly as she could. *Walk like a robot from the hips down.*

It was difficult.

Colin watched the man in the lightweight suit look at his watch. Mercifully, he was not looking at Beth as she left the temple area.

Colin followed her to the road and inspected the cars parked along the curb. There it was: the white hire car. When he drew level with it, he bent down, ostensibly to tie a shoelace, and jabbed the blade of his knife into a tire.

It collapsed with a hiss.

Moments later, he was making his way along the palm trees on the foreshore of the Nile. Cruise ships and feluccas were moored along its length. He walked out onto a jetty and began inspecting the feluccas. As he did, he slipped the gun and the knife into the water.

Beth was waiting for him in the hotel foyer. She was looking nervous. He gave her a reassuring smile and whispered, "Waiting in foyers is too conspicuous," and led her through to the 1886 Restaurant with its elegant ceiling and mustard colored walls. It was not yet time for dinner, so it was empty of patrons.

A waiter came over to ask what they wanted. Colin explained that they simply wanted a private place to talk. He sat down in one of the plush red dining chairs and ordered a pot of mint tea. *Tea soothes the nerves.*

Half an hour later, he steered Beth onto the airport minibus.

Chapter 28

Beth spent most of the flight home studying the photographs Colin had taken. The net result was a growing conviction that she finally had the answer to the riddle hidden in the carvings on the obelisk. It was simply extraordinary—almost unbelievable.

Her excitement at unraveling the mystery did much to lift her above her physical and emotional exhaustion. She could hardly wait to tell Peter and Alex.

Peter was at the airport gate. He looked grim and pallid. His dark hair was disheveled, and there was a brooding darkness about his eyes. On seeing Beth, he leaped forward, held her by the shoulders and inspected her closely.

Beth laughed. "Do I pass examination?"

Peter drew her to himself and buried his face in her hair.

Beth started to weep. In the safety of his love, she allowed the fears, anxieties, and responsibilities of the last three days to overflow. She gripped his shoulders and hung onto him.

As she did, she felt Peter wince.

Beth pulled back, but Peter gathered her back in his arms.

When some semblance of self-control had returned, Beth demanded, "What has happened to your arm?"

"Um…I got in the way of something I should have avoided. It's okay—it's healing well."

"What were you wounded with?" asked Beth suspiciously.

"It was a bullet, actually."

"What! When did this happen?"

"About two days before you left."

"Two days before I left…and you didn't think to tell me." She glared at him. "Peter Jacobs, I need to know about these things."

Peter drew her back into his arms. "And you would have, honestly. But not two days before you were going off to Egypt. You had enough demands on your emotions."

"Is that why you kept your jacket on when you saw me off at the airport?"

Peter nodded.

Colin was hovering behind them.

Peter turned to face him. For a while, he said nothing. Then he reached out his hand. "Thanks, Colin. I'll be in touch."

Colin nodded then turned to Beth. "You did well."

Beth watched him disappear in the crowd. *An extraordinary man. And still as calm as you like.*

She felt far from calm, but she was back with Peter—and that was everything.

They retrieved Beth's rucksack, and the two of them were soon driving west on the M25 around London.

Beth spent much of the journey trying to extract more information about the attack on Peter. She wasn't entirely successful. Eventually, she changed the subject. "Where are you taking me?"

"To the old pub by the Thames in Windsor. I've booked the same table we had last time."

"Peter Jacobs, I'm grimy, sweaty, and feel vile. The first thing I want is a good long shower."

"All organized. There's a bag in the boot with some clothes Bell picked out for you—and there are bathroom facilities waiting for you in one of the rooms at the pub." He glanced across at her. "But I'm still taking you back to the Tower tonight. I need to keep you safe…and I need to debrief with Colin."

She settled back into her seat contentedly and said, "I've something to tell you."

"What's that?"

"I know what the Egyptian angle is all about."

"Seriously? And it's only now you tell me! Come on, spill the beans. What's it all about?"

She closed her eyes and smiled. "Wild horses will not drag it from me until I've lingered in a hot bath, pampered myself, and changed into something clean."

Bathed and changed, Beth entered the pub's dining room and looked for Peter. The weather was cool enough for a fire to be burning in the open hearth. Light from its flames flickered on the horse brasses nailed to the ancient oak beams.

She saw Peter seated at their table by the window. He appeared to be deep in thought. Maybe it was just the candlelight highlighting his features, but he looked a little older tonight—and very handsome, she decided.

She noticed the single red rose lying across her dinner setting.

Peter got to his feet.

Beth picked up the rose. "Clichéd...but very acceptable." She kissed him on the cheek and then stood back so he could admire her. She knew she looked good. Bell had packed her a figure-hugging dress of twilight blue.

Peter helped her into her seat. She loved the way he moved... and was aware of a deep, visceral longing.

She dipped a finger in her wine, kissed it, and then reached across and placed it on his lips.

Peter kissed it and sucked the wine off the fingertip.

She laughed, cleared her throat, and said, "Peter, it was a very worthwhile trip. I'm pretty sure I know what's happening. And I also know what was put in the box on the *Beatrice*."

"So, you know what's in the box?"

"Yes, I think so."

Peter shook his head. "No, I don't think you do."

Beth looked at him with bewilderment. She was bursting to tell him what she'd discovered, but Peter was being frustratingly odd. Beth pushed herself back in her chair. "Why don't you think I know what's in the box?"

Peter fished in his pocket. He flipped open the lid of a small box…and revealed a solitaire diamond ring. "Because it is this."

Beth's mouth dropped open.

Peter continued. "Will you marry me, Beth Anderson? I couldn't bear to be separated from you ever again." He paused. "I want to share my life with you. I want to see you be all that you can be." Peter reached for her hand. "I love you."

It took a moment for shock to give way to delight. Beth was conscious of something deep within her finding a home, of something clicking into place like the lost piece of an unfinished puzzle. *At last, at last, at last.* Relief and joy danced together.

She put her hand to her mouth, unable to repress her glee, then reached across and picked the ring out of the box. Beth turned it around allowing the light from the candle to sparkle from its facets.

Peter took it from her and slid it onto her finger.

She smiled. "My darling, Peter, I won't need the box. Throw it in the fire. This will never leave my finger."

"Is that a yes?" he grinned.

Beth nodded. "It most certainly is."

Peter got up from his seat, came to her side, and kissed her. It was a long and lingering kiss. She could taste his love. It was heady, intoxicating…and dangerous.

She became aware, sadly, that she was in a public place. Reluctantly, she let Peter go so that decorum could prevail. He resumed his seat, and they held hands across the table.

"There are a thousand questions I should ask," said Beth.

"Such as?"

"How soon?"

"As soon as possible."

Beth laughed. "I agree. These last few days have taught me that life is a very uncertain thing." She paused. "I seem to have been waiting all my life for someone like you—not thinking it was possible."

Peter raised her hand and kissed her fingers. "You make me feel very special, Beth Anderson."

The waiter coming to take their order interrupted them.

Beth struggled to find an appetite in the excitement of the occasion. She recalled fleetingly that she had things to share concerning Luxor. But she wanted to savor this moment. "Let's not talk about Luxor until tomorrow."

Peter nodded. "Why don't I pick you up from the Tower tomorrow morning? Then you can share what you've learned with both Alex and me at the *Phoenix*." He smiled. "Let's be totally selfish and make this evening all about ourselves."

The top of the *Phoenix's* mast pointed up to a perfectly blue sky. Alex paused on the gangplank to look at what Lenny was doing. He was using a serving mallet to tension the twine he was wrapping around the base of a shroud.

Lenny mopped his brow. "Never thought patching up an old lady's wrinkles could be such fun."

"It's good to see you keeping the old crafts alive, Lenny."

"The old crafts are no problem. It's the new ones that get me." He nodded toward the stairwell. "Your love birds are down below."

Alex made his way down the stairs into the main cabin. Kym was sitting beside Beth in a booth. She was holding Beth's hand and admiring her ring. "Blimey, it's fantastic!" Kym looked up at Alex. "G'day, Prof. Check out this rock and see what these dumb-ass kids have done."

Alex bent over and kissed Beth on the cheek. "A very good thing."

Beth smiled shyly. "Not surprised?"

"No."

Peter came from behind the counter holding two cups of coffee. He handed one to Beth and one to Kym.

"Thanks, mate," said Kym. "But I've got work to do. She stood up, edged past Peter, then turned to face him. "Don't screw this up, Peter." Kym punched him lightly on the arm. "I don't know whether to hate you or love you. I should scorn your old-fashioned, stereotyped, class-ridden, morally straight-jacketed conventions...but I can't help but be envious."

Kym said this with a smile, but Alex suspected that her comment betrayed something of her own history.

Alex shook Peter's hand. "Congratulations, Peter. You are both wonderful people, and you will make a great couple." He searched for more words but simply added, "You give me hope."

After they'd sat down, Peter slapped the table. "Okay, Beth, spill the beans. What have you discovered?"

Beth grinned and sat herself upright. Alex could see the excitement in her eyes.

Beth began to relate her amazing story. Alex's mouth dropped open with incredulity as she related how the disgraced Italian adventurer, Giovanni Belzoni, had etched small hieroglyphics on the edge of the Luxor obelisk that could only be read when viewed from an acute angle to the side.

"He'd etched the words 'origin,' 'Menkaure,' and 'box.' By themselves, they made no sense. But when you also read them in conjunction with the hieroglyphics of Ramses II behind them, it all made sense. What Belzoni wanted us to read was: 'The origin of the power of the ultimate god is on a stele in Menkaure's box.'"

Alex massaged his forehead, trying to make sense of what he was hearing.

"Don't you see?" Beth continued. "When Belzoni was working on the third largest pyramid at Giza, he found Menkaure's sarcophagus. But he didn't tell anyone. He was still smarting at being found to be lying about his discovery of a Freemason's wall relief."

Peter furrowed his brow. "Ah...remind me: which one was that?"

"The one allegedly showing the Egyptian god Osiris being inducted as a Freemason." Beth swung back to Alex. "So he put something in Menkaure's sarcophagus to vindicate his claim.

Belzoni then sealed up the tomb and left it for Vyse to find—which he did fifteen years later."

Alex was dumbfounded.

"But why did Belzoni graffiti the obelisk?" asked Peter. "Why didn't he just tell his Freemasonry mates?"

Comprehension dawned on Alex. "Because Belzoni wanted people to think that Ramses II had put the hidden instructions on his obelisk in order to lend credibility to the find."

"Exactly," said Beth.

Alex nodded. "But wouldn't Vyse notice that the tomb had recently been opened?"

"No," said Beth. "Vyse, with his habit of blowing things up, would never notice that the tomb had been recently breached —particularly as it had already been opened centuries earlier by tomb raiders."

Beth jiggled in her seat. "Don't you see? The Freemasons don't particularly want the sarcophagus; they want Belzoni's stele inside it to vindicate their claim that Masonic spirituality is valid."

Alex felt blood drain from his face. "Oh dear."

Beth looked at him with concern. "What's the matter, Alex?"

He took his glasses off and pinched the top of his nose. "You have no idea how explosive this stele could be in the wrong hands. It could give someone huge spiritual authority...and the power to control many of the world's financial institutions."

"Oh."

Everyone was silent.

Eventually, Beth continued. "So what do we do?"

Alex looked at her with affection and took her hand. "Just let me say this: If anyone was ever going to unravel the Egyptian mystery, it was you, Beth. You've done extraordinarily well." He placed his other hand on Peter's arm. "Both of you have paid a heavy price to get this information. I'm more grateful than words can say." He paused. "But I think you've both done enough...and risked enough. So leave the rest to me. I'll write an email to Detective Sergeant Jenkins and follow it up with a letter. But before I do, there's one thing I need to check."

Chapter 29

Peter's stomach told him it was lunchtime, and he was wondering whether to join the staff in the tearoom, or sneak out with Toby to the *Phoenix* to discuss his next bid for a contract.

His phone rang.

It was Colin.

"Peter, Beth's gone missing. Bell sneaked out with Beth to do some shopping while I was on duty. She ducked into a shop for a few seconds, and when she came out, Beth was gone. She's been gone an hour. It's too early to call the police, but it doesn't look good."

A shock wave of dread washed over Peter. *No! No!* It can't be true. He took the phone from his ear, and rested it against his forehead. *No!* This couldn't be happening. He'd just discovered her; discovered life itself. She was his life. He looked up to heaven and screamed in silent anguish.

"Peter, are you there?" Colin's voice could be heard faintly from the phone.

Lord God.

"Peter!"

"What? Er..." Peter returned the phone to his ear and tried to think. "Yes, I'm here." He felt impotent.

Anger—hot burning anger—destructive anger, began to burn within him. *Don't let it get out of control. Don't.* He pinched the top of his nose, forcing himself to control it. *Harness it. Harness it. Harness it. Make the anger work for you. Think. Think. What action? I need action. What could point him in the right direction? Who?*

A moment later, he realized that Alex could. *Of course.*

"Colin, I'll get back to the flat and see if Alex knows anything. We'll take it from there."

"Understood." Colin paused, before adding, "Peter, I'm very sorry about this. Bell is distraught. Call me if I, or any of the guys here, can help."

"Thanks, Colin. I'll get back to you."

"Standing by."

Peter ran out of the office and sprinted along the dock to his block of units. He seethed with impatience as the lift made its way to the seventh floor. *Come on, come on.* He leaped out of the lift, jabbed the electronic key into the lock and burst into the apartment.

Alex wasn't there but he'd left a note on the kitchen bench.

Dear Peter,

I've gone to Herne Bay where a friend of mine has a fishing boat. He's lent it to me this afternoon so I can check on the identity of a ship moored just offshore at 1°15' East; 50°25' North. I hope to be back this evening with some answers—and this note becomes obsolete. So this is just in case!

Blessings

Alex

Peter, screwed up his eyes in anguish. *Not you too, Alex.* He tried to think what to do next. After a few minutes, he picked up the phone.

Colin answered immediately. "Any news of Beth?"

"None. You?"

"Negative."

"Colin, Alex has gone to a place called Herne Bay to check out a boat he thinks is connected with this whole Egypt thing. Beth will probably not be there, but those on the boat may well have connections with people who do know where she is."

"Are you suggesting we pay them a visit?"

"Can we?"

There was a silence from Colin for what seemed an age before he answered, "Yes. I'll bring Dicky and Jim. They're good in a tight corner. Oh, and also Gizmo. He's got some handy toys. We'll bring the Zodiac. Pick you up in an hour."

Peter was staggered at Colin's ability to think quickly under pressure. The only hint of his true feelings came at the end. "Peter, if these guys are involved, I'm not going to be very happy with them."

Peter could only guess at the significance of his comment.

A British army Land Rover, towing a trailer with an inflatable Zodiac, swung round the corner. It barely came to a stop before Peter tumbled in over the tailgate, and it drove off again.

Peter found a seat beside Gizmo, who was tapping on a computer balanced on his knee. Dicky and Jim sat opposite. Both were dressed in rubber wetsuits. Rather disturbingly, a gun case lay on the floor between them.

Dicky thrust a wetsuit at Peter. "Get into it. Put the wetsuit boots on, but leave your hood down for the moment—or you'll frighten the natives."

Peter discovered how difficult it was to strip and climb into an elastic wetsuit in the confines of a moving vehicle. Eventually, he succeeded.

The Land Rover headed out of London, through the early afternoon traffic and made its way along the A2. After crossing over the Medway Bridge, they turned left toward Herne Bay.

Alex would have normally relished the opportunity to potter about offshore in a fishing boat. There was something so elemental and free about being in a boat at sea. However, on this occasion, the stakes were too high for him to enjoy anything. The only sense of pleasure he allowed himself, was relief that he was finally doing something that might bring things to a conclusion and make things safer for Peter and Beth.

Alex stepped into the dinghy moored beside the slipway, and sculled his way across to a blue fishing boat. It was tough and business-like, with a waterline length of about twenty-two feet. Alex made the dinghy fast, and climbed on board. Then he led the dinghy forward and tied it to the mooring buoy.

Alex found the boat's keys in a side locker.

The diesel engine started with a satisfying growl.

He cast off the mooring rope and motored through the gaggle of boats moored behind Herne Bay's curving breakwater, toward the harbor entrance.

Once through the entrance, he opened the throttle, and butted his way out to sea, rolling and pitching through the short, steep waves. Alex glanced at the chart on the navigation table, calculated a rough bearing, and then set a course for Hook Spit buoy.

To the east, the bleak low-lying Kentish coastline stretched into the distance, interrupted only by wooden groins designed to keep the sand from being washed away from the beaches. It was not, Alex decided, very beautiful.

Or perhaps it was simply his mood.

Peter looked at the grim expressions of the men sitting with him. There was no banter. It was unnerving. He braced himself as Colin swung the Land Rover into the car park at the head of Herne Bay's breakwater.

Colin turned round and yelled. "Peter, you help Gizmo with his box of toys, while we launch the boat."

Peter and Gizmo climbed out and dragged the box out of the back of the Land Rover. Taking one end each, they carried it to a small beach just east of the car park.

Gizmo then opened the box and lifted out the fuselage of a radio-controlled plane.

"What's this for?" asked Peter.

"It's our 'eye in the sky,' my son." He spoke as he assembled the wings onto the fuselage. "It's my version—and I might say an infinitely superior version—of a military UAV: an unmanned aerial vehicle. It weighs twenty pounds, is six feet long, and has an eight foot wingspan." He patted the silver fuselage. "What's more, it can fly at seventy-five miles an hour and has a five-hour endurance. I've pre-programmed this baby to circle at four-hundred feet, beaming pictures to my computer."

Gizmo donned a headset microphone.

Peter glanced around with concern. Children were playing on the beach. "Isn't it dangerous launching this thing from a public beach?"

"No siree. It has a gas-powered launching rail which mounts on top of the case."

Gizmo held up his hand to forestall any more questions and listened through his earpiece. After a pause, he nodded. "Roger that." Gizmo turned to Peter. "Colin wants you back at the boat ramp, pronto."

Peter ran back up to the car park and down the slipway to the Zodiac. It was in the water, with its outboard burbling away at its stern.

"Get in and sit tight," ordered Colin. "Your job is to make up the numbers and help us look like a crowd. Nothing more."

Colin then bent his head and listened into his earpiece. "The UAV is away," he reported. "It will be on station beaming pictures in three minutes. Let's wait a moment and see what we've got."

Chapter 30

The sea was shallow, which made the waves short and spiteful. Alex braced himself as he steered the boat up Copperas Channel toward Hook Spit buoy. The wind was moderate in strength and held a hint of the coming summer warmth. However, visibility was only fair due to the light drizzle.

The boat pitched and rolled along for twenty minutes before Alex caught sight of a vessel behind the Margate Hook sandbank. He picked up the binoculars and inspected the ship. It wasn't moving. As he drew closer, Alex could see that it was some sort of salvage vessel, about ninety feet long. It had a low extended rear deck with a gantry at the end.

As he watched, a rigid inflatable peeled away from the ship's side, and began to skim across the water toward him. A few minutes later it drew abreast of Alex, throttled back, and turned in behind him. Alex came out of the wheelhouse door and stood at the side of the gunwale, ready to speak to the man at the boat's driving console.

The heavily muscled man stepped to the bow of his boat and secured it to a cleat at the rear of Alex's vessel. He then grabbed the back of the fishing boat, and heaved himself on board.

With disturbing competence, the man turned, reached into his jacket and took out an automatic pistol. "Professor Whitman, lie on your face on the floor and put your arms behind your back."

Alex realized he had badly miscalculated the sensitivities of those on the ship he had come to investigate. He also knew that whilst there was a good chance he would shortly find answers to much that had happened in the last two months, he would not live long enough to share it. He had seen into the bleak eyes of the man now slipping a plastic cable tie around his wrists.

Icy fingers of fear clutched at his heart. He forced himself to remain calm.

The big man walked into the wheelhouse and opened the throttle to maximum revs.

Alex managed to roll over onto his knees and look over the gunwale. A hundred yards away, off the starboard bow, he could see the channel buoy of Hook Spit. It was heeled away with the tide showing the seaweed on its encrusted bottom.

The launch was aiming directly for it.

Alex rolled back onto the floor and looked for something to brace himself against. Trussed up, as he was, there was nothing.

He could only wait.

The boat crashed into the buoy with a shocking, jarring crunch.

Alex was thrown forward, and his head smashed against the wheelhouse.

The boat slewed around and began to sink as water flooded in through its shattered bow.

The big man stepped out of the wheelhouse, pulled Alex on to his feet and hauled him to the back of the boat. There, he was pushed into the rigid inflatable. The man climbed in after him, unhitched the painter and took his place at the driving console.

Alex's head was bleeding profusely by the time the inflatable swung round to the diving platform at the stern of the research ship. After making the boat fast, the big man pushed Alex onto the platform.

Before he could struggle to his feet, Alex was jerked upright by the collar and propelled up the three steps leading to the ship's work deck.

The sheer physicality of it all shocked him so much, that he struggled to take in the reality of what was happening. But he knew enough to know that things were critical.

Alex forced himself to take stock of everything around him. Diving gear was stacked up beside a diesel-powered pump. In the middle of the work deck was a large oblong object wrapped in black plastic. A man stood behind it as if it were an altar. He showed no emotion as Alex was propelled toward him.

Alex was fairly sure he knew who he was. He decided to take the initiative. "Ernest Wheeler, I presume."

"Professor Whitman." The man inspected him balefully. "You have been an inconvenience to me. But your arrival is extraordinarily propitious and well timed. I have something to show you."

"You have found Belzoni's stone, then."

Wheeler was silent for a moment. "You mean the Pharaoh's stone?"

"No, I mean the fake stone left by Belzoni for Vyse to find. The one with the false claim of Osiris being inducted as a Freemason." Alex shrugged. "I know all about it, as do a number of others. The police were sent an email with the details yesterday, so it's all over, Wheeler. So far, no one's been hurt, so why don't you hand yourself over to the police while you still can."

"Aah, the email you sent to Detective Sergeant Jenkins. I've employed a rather clever accomplice to intercept his emails. Nothing reaches him unless I allow it." He shook his head slowly. "I assure you, your email to him will be waiting for me to read and edit when I get back to the office."

Alex was shocked, but pressed on. "The police are not the only ones who know. You must know that."

"Your assistant, Miss Anderson?"

Alex nodded. "Amongst others."

Wheeler appeared unperturbed.

Something was wrong.

Wheeler turned to the man who had brought Alex on board, and said, "Carl, bring her."

Carl opened a steel door behind Wheeler. A few moments later, he emerged, pushing Beth out in front of him.

Beth twisted away from her captor, trying to shake off his manhandling. Her hands were tied behind her back.

When she saw Alex, she lunged toward him. Carl jerked her back and cuffed her across the side of her head.

"What have you done to him? Leave Alex alone," Beth screamed. "He's a good man. He's done nothing wrong. He doesn't know what I know."

"You should have thought about the implications of your meddling a lot earlier, young lady," said Wheeler.

Alex was appalled at the sight of Beth.

He called out, "Wheeler, let her go. It's useless. She's not the only one who knows. It's over. See sense. Don't make it worse for yourself."

"I don't kill for pleasure, Professor, but a few things are going to happen very quickly." He nodded toward Carl. "Carl will go back to London and kill Mr. Jacobs tonight."

Beth immediately started to scream hysterically and pull away from Carl.

Carl cuffed her savagely until she fell on her knees, whimpering.

Wheeler continued to speak. "Your arrival here is very fortuitous. Your death by drowning, along with Miss Anderson, will be the lamentable result of poor navigation in your recently sunk fishing boat." He gestured around him. "There being only a skeleton staff on board at present, we didn't see your small boat sink. The crew had been ferried ashore two hours earlier to celebrate the conclusion of a successful salvage operation."

Wheeler stepped forward and lifted the corner of the plastic sheeting in front of him.

Alex could see the mud-stained cornice of a stone sarcophagus.

Wheeler had a look of triumph in his eyes. "You are looking at Menkaure's sarcophagus." He smiled. "Guess what will be found inside it?"

"As I've said, the fake stele put there by Belzoni."

"No. The world will learn that we found the stone put there by

Ramses II to tell future generations what the true spiritual power was behind his kingdom." He beckoned. "Come over here. You might as well see the Pharaoh's stone."

Carl drew the pistol from his jacket and trained it on Alex. Wheeler led Alex over to a workbench bolted alongside the gunwale. A wooden box, about three feet long, sat on top of it.

Wheeler lifted up the lid of the box and folded back the protective bubble wrap.

There, before Alex, was Belzoni's stele—the Pharaoh's stone.

The carving on it showed Osiris, dressed in a Mason's apron, being inducted as a Mason by the Egyptian god Huh, the god of eternity. Other Egyptian gods had also been etched around the central figures.

Alex inspected the stone closely.

A moment later, he started to laugh.

"Why do you laugh? You are looking at one of the greatest archaeological finds in history."

"Poppycock, Wheeler. Look at the bottom of the stele. Belzoni, in his arrogance, couldn't resist putting his signature on the bottom. See the small hieroglyph there. That's 'G' for Giovanni."

Wheeler pushed in front of Alex and stared at the offending hieroglyph. Then he turned and walked over to a toolbox. He flipped open the lid, rummaged inside, and returned with a hammer and a cold chisel. Without bothering to take the stone out of the box, Wheeler placed the chisel at the bottom of the stele and gave it a sharp tap. The offending hieroglyph split off.

Wheeler picked up the chip of stone and threw it overboard.

Alex was aghast. "Wheeler, are you seriously going to lie to the world in order to promote your spiritual claims?" He shook his head in disbelief. "It is just lies."

"We live in a postmodern world, Whitman. Truth is whatever works for you."

Wheeler's eyes were bleak as he continued. "Your Johnny-cum-lately Christ has had his day. We've been waiting long enough."

"By 'we,' I assume you mean your form of Freemasonry—the one given its particularly ungodly gloss by Golden Dawn."

Wheeler nodded. "I see you understand." His face was expressionless. "It may appear that we have been in decline for some decades, but the reality is we have been the power behind the civilized world for a long time. You have no idea of the power we have...nor of the power we will have." He sniffed derisively. "The West has become weak and pathetic. It's ready for our leadership."

"A leadership founded on murder and lies?" Alex shook his head. "I don't think so."

"Hah!" scoffed Wheeler. "Your church has lied and killed since its inception."

"There is a difference. When you lie and kill, you are obeying your god. But when the church does it, it is disobeying God."

Whilst part of Alex's mind was engaging with Wheeler, much of it was trying to work out what he should do. He was buying time to think. However, there was one question he did want an answer to.

"What did my brother do to deserve death?"

Wheeler said nothing.

Alex persisted. "What did he do?"

"He became a threat when he started to be troubled by the scruples of your God."

Alex closed his eyes with relief, grateful beyond words to hear evidence of his brother's integrity.

Wheeler continued without expression. "He suffered a consequence—one that you will shortly share." He paused. "For surely you have heard what happens...*where the tide regularly ebbs and flows.*"

Chapter 31

Gizmo had dismantled the UAV's launch ramp and now had his computer perched on top of the box. He chewed on a piece of gum as he tapped in the instructions for a wide-angled shot from the plane's camera.

A visual image of the sea surface swam into focus on his screen. There, just to the right, was the outline of a small ship. "Bingo," he murmured to himself. "Now let's have a closer look at you, my darling."

Gizmo zoomed in on the target and hit the 'acquire' button. He then called for eighty-percent magnification—and studied what he saw.

Four people could be seen on the aft deck. One had auburn hair. He zoomed in further. "Bloody hell," he exclaimed.

He spoke into the microphone. "Boss, Beth is on the aft deck of the research vessel with three men. One of them looks as if he has his hands tied."

"How many? What armaments?"

"Wait. Out."

Colin gave the start-up signal. "Go, go. Don't worry about speed restrictions in the harbor. Flat out."

Dicky immediately unleashed the power of the big Mercury, and they began skimming across the water. The Zodiac scythed out of the harbor entrance and headed out to sea.

Colin yelled, "ETA, eight minutes. Get ready."

Dicky and Jim gave Colin a thumbs up and pulled their rubber hoods over their heads. Jim reached across to a bag containing the diving gear, pulled out four deflated life vests, and handed one to each person. He then reached down, picked up the gun case, and lashed it into place on the floor alongside the buoyancy chamber.

Colin's earphone came to life. "Colin. Negative armaments seen. Two men on the bridge, and the four on the aft deck. Zero others seen."

"Copy that. Call police assistance."

"Wilco."

"Monitor and stand by."

"Monitor and stand by. Out."

Colin beckoned to Peter, then leaned across to shout above the howling engine. "Beth is on board. Looks unharmed." He deemed it unhelpful to say anything more. Peter must already be way out of his comfort zone. Colin scrutinized him briefly. His face looked pale and grim, but he was holding it together. "You okay?"

He watched Peter grip the safety rope along the buoyancy chamber and twist it in his fist. "Let's just get her."

Colin nodded. Peter was ready for a fight. He hoped it wouldn't come to that. Colin turned and spoke into his microphone. "Gizmo, describe the vessel."

"Eighty feet long. Modern. Metal. Possibly aluminum. Not painted. Twin hulled. It has a main deck housing with a bridge on top. Low working deck aft. She has a rigid inflatable, a RIB, parked off the stern quarter."

"Copy that. Out."

Thirty seconds later, Gizmo was speaking again. "You've been seen. One man from the bridge has climbed down to the work deck. He's pointing toward you. Wait. Out."

A few moments later Gizmo was back. "One gun. Repeat, one gun seen. Handgun. One man taking Beth to the dive platform."

People were coming. It was disturbing. He would need to act quickly. Wheeler cocked his head and thought he could detect the distant whine of an outboard motor.

Carl was pushing Beth down the steps to the dive platform.

"Finish it quickly," Wheeler yelled. "We've only got a few minutes."

Carl had fitted weighted dive belts to both Alex and Beth. Rather than use the buckles, he had fastened them tight with multiple strands of blue suture thread. It would dissolve in three weeks and release their bodies. If discovered, they would be found to have head wounds consistent with a collision at sea.

A three-inch steel pipe lay within reach of Carl on the work deck. The prisoners would have no chance to pull off their weight belts.

Beth was partly hysterical, partly in shock, and partly defiant. She would do anything to save Peter and Alex. Dazed and in pain from the beatings she had suffered, she forced herself to think. *What can I do? What? What?* But she could think of nothing.

She reeled sideways as Carl slapped her, forcing her down to the dive platform.

Carl's savagery helped clear her mind. If she was ever going to do something, it had to be now.

She recalled hearing Wheeler say that they only had a few minutes. Time was not just running out for her, it was also running out for her captors.

Carl reached behind him for the metal pipe.

This was it.

No! She wouldn't allow it. She would buy as much time as she could before she died.

Beth jumped off the dive platform.

As soon as she was in the water, she began to kick frantically to prevent herself from being dragged under by the weight belt. The effort required was horrendous. She fought herself to the surface and gasped for breath.

To her horror, Carl reached out, grabbed her hair, and pushed her back under the water.

Colin yelled at Dicky above the noise of the engine, "All the action is at the back of the boat. I need to get there quickly. Drive under her bows between the hulls. Drop Peter and me over and come out fast. Disable their RIB, then stand away and watch."

Dicky nodded.

Colin tapped Jim on the arm and pointed to the gun case strapped alongside the buoyancy chamber. Jim unfastened the end, and pulled out a shotgun.

Colin glanced again at Peter. The boy was wound tight like a coiled spring. He needed to do something. Colin tapped him on the leg and shouted into his ear, "Can you swim well?"

Peter nodded.

"Are you okay swimming with mask, fins, and snorkel?"

Peter yelled back, "Did it a lot in Australia."

"You and I are going over the side under their boat. Hold your mask into position with one hand and fall backward into the water when I give the word." He paused. "Are you up for this?"

Peter nodded.

Colin turned back and inspected the ship. The vessel that had sat on the horizon for so long was now beginning to loom up quickly. It was as Gizmo had described: a twin-hulled research ship.

Dicky headed straight for its bows, killing the engine just yards in front of it so that they slid under the sloping floor between the two metal hulls. Once inside, Dicky put the engine in reverse. The water boiled, and the inflatable came to a stop.

Colin yelled, "Go."

He and Peter tumbled over the side.

Colin rose to the surface and checked on Peter. He then put a fist over his head to signal to Dicky that all was well.

Dicky edged the inflatable backward, and turned it around by bouncing it off the metal hulls. He then gunned the throttle, and sped out from underneath the boat.

Colin turned back to Peter and signaled that he should follow him.

Peter found it eerily quiet after the roar of the inflatable's engine had died away. The only sound was the wavelets slapping the sides of the twin hulls—and some splashing just ahead of them.

He kicked along with his flippers, swimming just behind Colin.

He'd only swum ten yards when Peter saw a body ahead, writhing in the water under the surface. He recognized the streaming auburn hair instantly.

Beth.

Two hands were on top of her head, pushing her under the surface.

Beth's movements appeared to be growing weaker by the second.

Colin spat out his snorkel and hissed to Peter. "I'll take the attacker. You get Beth." With that, Colin duck-dived under the water.

As Peter swam up to Beth, Colin erupted from the water like a killer whale—a knife in his hand.

As Colin swung the knife, Peter grabbed at the hand pushing Beth under the water and pulled. He'd reasoned that if the killer were in the water, he wouldn't be much of a threat to anyone.

A big man fell over the top of him and splashed into the water next to Colin.

Peter immediately reached for Beth and began tugging her under the protection of the boat's hull. However, he was appalled to discover she was so heavy. They were sinking.

With his lungs screaming for air he remembered his buoyancy vest. He pulled the inflation toggle.

The vest puffed up around his neck.

Peter and Beth floated to the surface.

Beth's head lolled on his shoulder. She appeared completely lifeless. Peter bent her head back, covered her nose, and began administering mouth-to-mouth resuscitation.

Nothing. Nothing. No sign. No life. *Keep going. Keep going.* With rising desperation, he breathed into her mouth.

Suddenly, Beth coughed and gurgled. Peter tilted her head as she retched and gasped for air. Beth's eyes opened—wild with panic. She gasped and retched again.

He held her close and crooned into her ear, "It's all right, Beth. I've got you. I've got you. You're safe. I won't let you go."

Two yards away, the sea turned pink. The killer's body stopped moving and lay still, just under the surface.

Peter was not surprised. Few would have proved a match for Colin's particular skills.

Chapter 32

G izmo watched the drama on his computer screen. Although he was six miles away, he was living every bit of the action.

He watched as the Zodiac came flying out from under the bows of the research vessel like a spat watermelon seed.

Just two in the boat, he noted.

Once the Zodiac was free of the research vessel, it swung around and hurtled back toward the ship at high speed.

Gizmo saw Jim pull the shotgun across his lap and hold it ready.

Things are going to get interesting.

The inflatable came surging to a halt as it drew level with the RIB moored off the back of the ship. Gizmo watched as Jim blasted away at the boat's buoyancy chambers.

The side of the RIB collapsed.

The inflatable then sped away from the ship until it was eighty yards away, where it throttled back and began to circle slowly…waiting.

Wheeler ran to the gunwale and stared across at the men in the inflatable who had rendered his RIB useless.

Recognizing that the people in the inflatable could not see the dive platform, he turned round to look for Carl. He should have done what he had to do by now.

But Carl was nowhere to be seen. *Where is he, damn him!*

There was no time to waste. He needed to dispatch Whitman himself—immediately.

Picking up a knife from the toolbox, he bent over Whitman, and cut the threads of plastic suture from the dive belt. He then refastened the weight-belt around Whitman using the buckle. He would simply shoot Whitman and trust that no one would find his weighted body.

And no one would hear his silenced gun.

Gizmo chewed on his gum and smiled appreciatively at the work of his colleagues. The disabled RIB was now leaning to one side like a drunken sailor.

"Crazy bastards."

However, what he saw next caused a frisson of alarm.

"Oh, shit!"

Gizmo saw that the man with the gun was pushing a person with his hands tied toward the back of the ship. The man being pushed was walking unsteadily. He was being forced down the steps onto the diving platform, where he was brought to his knees.

Dammit. He was going to be shot!

Gizmo sighed.

He locked the camera's target frame onto the man with the gun and tapped 'acquire.' Then he watched the screen as the UAV began its thirty-five degree dive.

Alex knew he was going to die...just as Beth had died. He felt intensely sad. So much potential, so much hope—now dashed.

And now he would die.

He was curiously at peace.

Wheeler pointed the gun at his head.

Alex turned to face him. The gun muzzle was inches from his forehead. "Death is the final gamble, isn't it? It's where you find out who is right."

Wheeler said nothing.

"Tell me, Wheeler: if the situation was reversed, and you risked the possibility of meeting God, would you be frightened?"

"Curse you, Whitman..." but he got no further.

An object came screaming out of the sky at an impossible speed.

Wheeler paused and lifted his head.

An instant later, the flying object smashed into Wheeler's back, throwing him over the edge of the dive platform.

The sudden brutality of it all was bewildering.

Everything went quiet.

Water gurgled and lapped against the boat hulls.

Gradually, the shock of what had just happened began to dissipate. Alex stared at Wheeler's shattered body drifting behind the ship amongst the wreckage of what looked to be a miniature airplane wing. He then struggled to his feet and made his way up the stairs from the dive platform. Once on deck, Alex limped across the deck toward a member of Wheeler's crew.

The man looked at him sullenly.

"It's over. Please cut this cable tie from my wrists."

The shuddering clatter of a helicopter could be heard in the distance.

The man looked up to the sky, took a knife from his boot, cut Alex free, and threw the knife overboard.

Alex nodded his thanks and made his way unsteadily to the wooden box that held the Pharaoh's stone. He lifted the lid and stared inside at the stele. The wretched thing had been the cause of unspeakable grief, and would have been used to perpetrate a monstrous evil.

Alex picked up the hammer lying beside the box and smashed it down on the stele. He didn't know what had happened to the big man called Carl, but he knew that Beth was dead. With savage passion, he pounded at the stone again and again, giving vent to his grief and despair—turning the stele into dust and rubble.

"Alex, are you all right?"

A soft voice. A woman's voice.

Alex swung around.

Beth was standing between two men dressed in wetsuits. She was dripping wet, pale and shivering—but very much alive.

Epilogue

D ust motes danced in the shafts of sunlight streaming from the windows of St. John's chapel. A woman wrapped in a cloak was seated in the front pew with Hamish O'Brien, Chaplain to the Tower of London. Both had spoken the words they needed to say and they were now enjoying silence.

After some time, Hamish coughed politely. "Ma'am, may I ask a permission of you?"

"What do you wish to ask?"

"May I use this chapel for a wedding?"

The woman thought for a while. "Are the couple deserving of this privilege?"

"Yes, ma'am, I believe they are. Both were instrumental in preventing a great evil being perpetrated in your city."

"Will you be conducting the wedding?"

"Yes, ma'am."

The woman nodded. "Then yes. Give them my best wishes for their future."

"Thank you, Your Majesty."

Peter leaned on the counter in *Phoenix's* main cabin. "Lenny, I've got a problem."

Lenny paused in his act of polishing a wineglass. "What's that, my boy?"

"I would like to have my wedding reception on the *Phoenix* if it's possible, but I want to invite you guys as guests." Peter shrugged. "So who can we get to do the catering?"

Lenny turned around and yelled, "Hey, Kym, got a moment?"

Kym came out of the kitchen, wearing a frown. She had a smudge of flour on one side of her nose. "Geeze, can't a girl get on, without her hearing the call of a helpless male?"

Lenny jerked his thumb at Peter. "Peter wants to invite us to his wedding reception here on the *Phoenix*, but he can't work out who can cater for us."

Kym stepped across to Peter, pulled his head down and gave him a kiss on the mouth. She then turned and walked back into the kitchen, saying over her shoulder, "Then you'd better tell Peter that if he thinks I'm letting any other 'pillock' use my kitchen, he's got another think coming. I'm ambidextrous. I can cook and party at the same time!"

Beth spent four days in hospital recovering from hypothermia. Although Peter and Colin had found blankets in the ship's cabin to warm her, she had been badly chilled and was still very weak.

Peter watched her, savoring her nearness. Her auburn hair was spilling over the pillow. He longed to climb into bed, wrap his arms around her, and...

He settled for holding her hand and stroking it.

Beth opened her eyes. "I love you, Peter Jacobs."

Peter squeezed her hand. "I know."

Beth continued. "I've made a decision."

"And what's that?"

"I'm organizing the honeymoon. I'm taking you to Paris."

"Hmm. You'd better ask my parole officer about that."

"Do you think she'd mind?"

"Probably not."

"Well?"

Peter smiled. "I'll ask."

"Good," she said, closing her eyes again.

"There is one small proviso."

"What's that?" she said sleepily.

"That I organize our wedding night here in London."

"Where?"

"Well, that would normally be a secret, but I'll break with tradition and tell you—just to whet your appetite. It's a luxury penthouse suite next to St. Katharine's Dock—with spectacular views over the city."

Beth opened her eyes wide. "How on earth did you manage that? It sounds divine."

"Well, as it happens, it belongs to the bloke who has been sponsoring our investigations over the last few months. He recently bought it from the company I work for."

"That's wonderful." Beth closed her eyes again. "I'd love to invite him to the wedding. Do you suppose he would come if Alex invited him?"

"Oh, I think he'll be there."

London 'Cockney' terms used in prison

- Black dog = depression
- Bovva (Bother) = trouble
- Care Bear = social worker
- China = friend
- Minding = body guard work
- Pie = pie is slang for 'prison chaplain.' The Cockney worker's lunch was pie and liquor = liquor = Cockney rhyming for 'vicar.'
- The Manor = London
- The Scrubs = Wormwood Scrubs is a category B men's prison in Hammersmith, London.

Historical Notes

The historical details concerning the life of Richard Vyse and Giovanni Belzoni detailed in this novel are correct according to information publicly available. The only literary fiction concerns Belzoni carving his own marks on Egyptian obelisks—and placing a stele inside the sarcophagus that Vyse discovered. It must also be said that Edward Burles, personal clerk to Richard Vyse, is a fictional character.

With these provisos, it can be fairly said that the archaeological activities of the Freemasons in the eighteenth century were as they have been described in the book, and make for extraordinary reading.

Freemasonry

Membership of the Freemasons

Membership of the Freemasons begins by entry to the Blue
Lodge. A man becomes a fully accepted Blue Lodge Mason after he
has worked his way through the first three degrees, known respec-
tively as 'Entered Apprentice,' 'Fellow Craft' and 'Master Mason.'
Technically, there is no higher degree than that of Master Mason
(the Third Degree), but if a man wishes to explore the secrets and
symbolism of Freemasonry further, he can join the Scottish Rite
and/or the York Rite. From there, a man can progress through
successive levels of Freemasonry, and have the deeper meanings of
the craft revealed to him. The highest level in the Scottish Rite is
that of the Thirty-third Degree.

Hiram Abiff and Solomon's temple

The link with Solomon's temple is an eighteenth-century invention. It turned up suddenly in 1723 as a result of the fertile imagination of Dr. James Anderson, a minister in the Church of Scotland.
He travelled to London in order to write *The Constitutions of the
Freemasons: for the use of the Lodges in London and Westminster*. Anderson
wanted to inject some drama into Freemasonry, and give it a hero;

so he borrowed the name of Hiram Abiff, a craftsman in brass and stone mentioned in the Old Testament (1 Kings 7:13-14 and 2 Chronicles 2:13-14).

His fictional story alleged that three fellow Masons tried to force Hiram to betray the secrets of a Master Mason, but he wouldn't divulge them. He was therefore bludgeoned to death. King Solomon captured the culprits, and had them executed.

This event is now celebrated in the Third Degree Masonic ritual in which the bare-chested candidate is struck down (with symbolic gestures only), and laid in a grave next to a skeleton (or placed in a coffin).

Anderson's fiction was reprinted in America in 1734 by Benjamin Franklin, who became Grand Master of the Masons of Pennsylvania.

Jahbulon

All members (Companions) of the Royal Arch are required to listen to the 'Mystical Lecture' in which they are taught that the JAH in their term for God 'JAHBULON' is a Chaldee name for God signifying 'His essence and majesty.' They are not taught that BUL is a term for Baal—the anti-Jewish God.

Aleister Crowley

Aleister Crowley (1875-1947) was a renowned poet, occultist, sexual libertine, poet, mountaineer and (probably) spy. He was inducted into The Golden Dawn rite of Freemasonry at the Isis-Urania Temple in London's Mark Masons Hall in 1898. Later, he became head of Ordo Templi Orientis (Order of the Temple of the East). This was a body of people who believed they had amassed most of history's available secret wisdom concerning spiritual things.

Crowley went on to found the Thelemite order of spiritualists. His unorthodox lifestyle resulted in him being denounced in the popular press as 'the wickedest man in the world.'

Golden Dawn

The Hermetic Order of the Golden Dawn was an occultist

organization that flourished in the late 19th and early 20th century. Golden Dawn was given its formal structure by William Wescott, Samuel Mathers, and William Woodman. All of them were Freemasons, and they modeled the structure of Golden Dawn on Freemasonry. The Order contained different levels to which people were successively initiated. Both men and women were allowed to join.

The first temple (the Isis-Urania Temple) was founded in London in 1888.

Shriners

The Ancient Arabic Order of the Nobles of the Mystic Shrine (commonly known as 'Shriners') was first established in 1872 in New York. It is an organization associated with Freemasonry. No one is allowed to be a Shriner unless they have first become a Third Degree Freemason.

At the time of writing, a Youtube video exists which features an alleged Shriner speaking outside their Southeastern Convention in Chattanooga, Tennessee in July, 2007. It records him speaking of Lucifer as 'pure, virtuous, wholesome and innocent.'

Roberto Calvi

The story of Roberto Calvi, as recorded in the novel, is essentially true. Calvi was found hanging from Blackfriars Bridge in 1982 (see: BBC News 19th June, 1982). Calvi's death was first thought to be suicide, but was later investigated as a possible murder. One of the lines of enquiry the police explored was Calvi's connection with Italian Freemasonry.

Archaeology

Richard Vyse

Richard William Howard Vyse lived from 1784 – 1853. He was
the only son of a General, from whom he inherited no less than
three estates. After an undemanding military career in the Dragoons
and Life Guards, Vyse turned to politics. However, as a dedicated
Freemason, his real love was archaeology.

Vyse teamed up with a largely uneducated sailor from Genoa
called, Giovanni Cavigula, who had been employed by some
European collectors of Egyptian artifacts. Cavigula taught Vyse how
to blast his way into pyramids using dynamite. Despite these
destructive techniques—or perhaps because of them, Vyse managed
to find four hidden chambers in the Great Pyramid of Giza.

He also explored the third largest of Giza's pyramids—within
which he discovered the remains of an old wooden coffin in 1837.
This can now be viewed in the British Museum. In the same pyramid, he discovered an ornate sarcophagus made of polished blue
basalt. This was the sarcophagus of Menkaure, one of Egypt's
greatest Pharaohs. Vyse loaded the sarcophagus onto the sailing
ship, *Beatrice*. Sadly, the ship sank without trace before it reached its
destination in London.

Giovanni Belzoni

Giovanni Belzoni was one of fourteen children born to a barber in Padua. When Giovanni was sixteen, he studied hydraulics in Rome, and intended to train as a monk. However, the French occupation of Rome caused him to move to the Netherlands, where he worked as a barber. Something then went badly wrong, as he had to flee to England in 1803 to avoid being sent to prison. There, he married an English woman, Sara Bane, and made a living working as a 'strong man' in a travelling circus. Evidently, he was a big man who stood just over two meters tall.

Giovanni's entrepreneurial spirit caused him to leave the circus and travel to Egypt in order to sell his ideas for a hydraulic irrigation system to the Egyptian government. Sadly, it came to nothing. However, the British consulate in Egypt must have recognized his entrepreneurial skills, because it sent him to Thebes, with the exacting task of removing a seven-ton bust of Ramses II from the temple, and shipping it to the British Museum.

This launched his career as an archeologist. He was responsible for opening up the temple of Abu Simbel, as well as the second pyramid at Giza. Belzoni also worked on the third pyramid in Giza —the pyramid in which Howard Vyse discovered the Menkaure sarcophagus nineteen years later.

Belzoni was an active Freemason. He began his Masonic career in Cairo where he joined, appropriately enough, the Lodge of the Pyramids. He later joined lodges in Cambridge and Norwich in the UK.

The Rosetta stone

The Rosetta Stone is an ancient Egyptian stone, dating from 196 BC, which bears a decree from Ptolemy V written in three languages. The stone had originally been placed in a temple, but was later removed, and used as a building stone in the construction of Fort Julien, located near Rosetta (also known as el-Rashid)—a town on the coast of the Nile Delta.

A French soldier, Pierre-Francois Bouchard, discovered the stone in 1799 when Napoleon's Egyptian expeditionary force occupied the fort.

The stone came into British possession when they defeated the French two years later. It was transported to London and put on display in the British Museum.

Ptolemy's decree had been written in Egyptian hieroglyphs, classical Greek, and another Demotic language. Because each text said the same thing, it provided the key to understanding how Egyptian hieroglyphics should be read.

Mary Rose

The *Mary Rose* was the flagship of King Henry VIII's navy. It sank in the Solent in 1545 after an engagement with the French fleet. The ship was raised from the seabed of the Solent in 1982, and is now on display in Portsmouth, UK.

Note from the author

Thank you for reading *The Pharaoh's Stone*. I hope you enjoyed it. If you did, please consider leaving a review on Amazon to encourage other readers.

Some of what you read was based on my personal experience of living on a boat in St. Katharine's Dock under the shadow of the Tower of London... and learning the secrets of 'The City.'

I'm pleased to be able to report that the "Stone Collection" has grown to include:

The Celtic Stone
The Martyr's Stone
The Peacock Stone
The Fire Stone
The Dragon Stone
The Syrian Stone
The Atlantis Stone
The Viking Stone
The Scorpion Stone

I invite you to keep up to date on new releases, by signing up to my mailing list at www.author-nick.com. New subscribers will receive a free novelette, *The Mystic Stone*.

About the Author

Nick Hawkes has lived in several countries of the world, and collected many an adventure. Along the way, he has earned degrees in both science and theology—and has written books on both. Since then, he has turned his hand to novels, writing romantic thrillers that feed the heart, mind, and soul.

His nine novels are known as, 'The Stone Collection.'

His first novel, *The Celtic Stone*, won the Australian Caleb Award in 2014.

Also by Nick Hawkes

The Atlantis Stone

Benjamin is part Aborigine, but nightmares from the past cause him to disown his heritage. Unfortunately, he feels no more at home in the Western world and so struggles to know his identity. Benjamin seeks to hide from both worlds in his workshop where he ekes out a living as a wood-turner. However, an attempt on his life propels him into a mysterious affair surrounding the fabled "mahogany ship" sighted by early white settlers near Warrnambool in Australia.

Felicity, a historian, is seeking to rebuild her life in the nearby town of Port Fairy after a messy divorce. The discovery of the "Atlantis stone" whilst scuba diving results in her joining Benjamin in an adventure that takes them overseas to the ancient city of Cagliari in Sardinia.

An anthropologist dying of cancer and an ex-SAS soldier with post-traumatic stress, join Benjamin and Felicity in an adventure that centres on a medieval treaty, a hunger for gold… and, of course, the Atlantis stone.

More details at www.author-nick.com

(See next page for more)

Also by Nick Hawkes

The Celtic Stone

Chris Norman's dreams of being a commercial pilot are shattered when he crashes his light plane in central Australia and is badly wounded. His life hangs in the balance—a balance that is swayed by the intervention of an Aboriginal bushman bent on his own murderous mission. The bushman leaves Chris with a mysterious and incongruous legacy, a Celtic cross made of stone.

Partly blinded and in deep grief at no longer being able to fly, Chris finds his way to the inhospitable Hebridean islands off the west coast of Scotland where he seeks to unravel the secrets of the Celtic stone.

A blind Hebridean woman, shunned by many in her local community, becomes Chris's reluctant ally, along with a seven-year-old boy who is as wild as the storm-tossed seas surrounding the islands.

It becomes apparent that the violence of the island's history has carried on into the present. Chris needs to recover from his grief, discover his identity… and avoid being murdered.

More details at www.author-nick.com

Made in United States
Troutdale, OR
10/01/2023

13329541R00186